Harry

Harry

by
Robert Wales

Franklin Watts   New York   1986

First published in England in 1985 by Robert Royce Ltd.
First published in the United States in 1986 by Franklin Watts, Inc.,
387 Park Avenue South, New York, NY 10016
ISBN 0-531-15017-8
Printed in Great Britain

One

As usual, Harry Walford woke around four and scratched at a few flea bites. Several times he had tried refilling his sacking mattress with fresh, dried grass, but it hadn't made any difference. His friend, the Irishman, Bluey McGuirk, asleep in the bunk closest to him, never seemed to get bitten at all. For some unknown reason they preferred Harry and migrated to him. There was no point in complaining about it. There were more important things to think about. He rose quietly so as not to wake the others and felt for his clothes piled on the earthen floor. With his shirt and trousers on he reached for his 'Alberts', strips of old flannel that wrapped round the feet to serve as socks. These wound on, he pulled his boots on over them then, picking up his hat, he made his way noiselessly out through the open door that hung askew on leather hinges.

The stars were still bright, the air soft and warm, but the faintest glimmer of the coming dawn was already showing over the low, undulating hills to the east. As soon as the sun shot up here on Central Queensland, it would start to turn hot again. By noon, a man could sweat heavily sitting in the shade doing nothing.

Harry dipped his strong, cupped hands into a bucket

of creek water he placed there for the purpose every evening and splashed it over his yellow mop of hair, face, and wild yellow beard. 'I hope you remember to wash your hands before you milk, Harry,' the Manager's wife would sometimes caution him, kindly but as if to a child. 'I never forgets, Mrs McKenzie,' Harry would return with a smile and that would please her.

Harry didn't mind Mrs McKenzie. She was a woman and there were few enough of them around on Albert Downs cattle station. Although he was twenty-eight years of age, he had never had the opportunity of having much to do with them. And he knew that Mrs McKenzie's intentions were well enough meant. What he didn't like was being reminded that he milked at all, but he never said so. His father who had come from England and worked as a shepherd in New South Wales had raised him to believe that it was a woman's job and no work for a man. It was why Harry was the first thing to move in the morning around the homestead, even before the flies. Although everyone knew it was his first chore of the day, he didn't want other men to see him actually at it, afraid it might give them something else to laugh at.

He had come here in 1876 from another menial job further south, cheerfully hoping that fresh territory would give him the chance of making a new start and becoming a real cattleman. It hadn't happened. Six years later he was still the homestead rouseabout, the wood and water joey, the lowest paid hand on this English-owned Company's books. Only the blacks who sometimes came through and worked a couple of days for a handful of flour, tea and sugar, got less. It had gone on far too long. He had worked hard, shown willing, and never complained but it hadn't been enough. Water dripping from his beard, he plucked his hat from the ground to put it on. He would see McKenzie again and put it to him straight this time.

There was enough light to see by as he headed in the direction of the small buttery, an enclosed lean-to attached to the main house, to get the milk buckets, but as he passed the blacksmith shed he stopped to have a pee. Even cold, the shed smelt of burnt iron. Harry worked there, too, pouring sweat as he pumped at the big leather bellows whenever the blacksmith, Jimmy Case, needed him. Harry disliked the man. Although Jimmy Case had never said anything in front of him, he knew well enough that he was the first to remind every newcomer that the rouseabout was not all there. Certainly, there was evidence for a weakness in Harry. As when two years before his old dog had died. It was Jimmy Case who had spied Harry at night carrying the dead dog off the homestead in his arms and followed him at a distance to see what he was up to, especially as he was also carrying a post-hole shovel. He had followed him unseen for two miles to a small gully and watched with amazement in the moonlight as Harry had dug a grave, buried the carcass, made a cross from two pieces of wood he had concealed down his trouser legs and knelt there. Even from a distance he could hear Harry weeping and by the time Harry had returned, there wasn't a soul around the homestead who hadn't heard about it. Some even refused to believe it and trekked out the following morning to look for themselves. As men were accustomed to simply tossing dogs far enough away where the stink wouldn't bother them when they died, this Christian and emotional burial had been a source of amusement at the homestead for an entire year.

Harry did up his buttons and walked on past the store and book-keeper's office. All the heavy sacks and barrels that went in and out of there were usually carried on Harry's back. He liked old Charley, the book-keeper, a quiet man who kept very much to himself.

That he was as educated as Harry considered himself ignorant, made him seem a sad figure to Harry. A man who could have had better things in life but who chose to turn his back on them. He also liked to drink with the flies and people said he tickled the books so that his grog came extra with his wages.

'Is yer happy here, Charley?' a concerned Harry had once asked him while he was shifting stores for him and they were alone. Old Charley had looked at him for a moment with his faded eyes. 'Happiness isn't an achievement, Harry,' he had replied, 'but there comes a time in everyone's life when they find themself alone on earth. It's then they must find a new direction and no one is going to help them. They have to find it on their own. If they don't they're lost forever.' At the time, Harry didn't know what he meant and didn't want to show his stupidity by having to ask but he had thought of it a lot since and believed he was beginning to understand.

He opened the small garden gate of the fence that surrounded the main house, closed it quietly behind him and went towards the small buttery. This time he would tell McKenzie that if he didn't get a better job, he was clearing out. It was totally dark inside but he knew where everything was, the hanging bits of muslin, the quart butter churn, the bowls, and the buckets upside down on a board. He took the two buckets, went out and headed for the horse paddock. It was the only fenced enclosure on the whole ten thousand square miles of the property. In it were the bullocks used for hauling the wagon, the horses in use and the few milkers that supplied milk for the main house.

The two cows in milk Harry found lying in a patch of wild sorghum. 'Mornin', ladies,' he greeted them and, without further bidding, they rose and started to walk towards the small milking yard back in the direction of the homestead, udders swaying as they went, Harry following behind.

The cow's head locked in the bail, Harry sat milking with his cheek pressed against its flank. There was an intimate comfort in it that he did not want to admit. He would ask to see McKenzie this very day.

The first real glow of dawn began as he returned the cows to the paddock and walked back towards the buttery with both buckets brimming. It would be easier if McKenzie wasn't such a hard man to talk to. He never seemed to listen to what you were trying to bloody say. There was enough light to see by as he poured the milk into three large, wide bowls that he covered over with muslin to keep off the flies. There was nothing to stop him taking a drink of it but he never had. Harry Walford had never stolen anything from anybody in his life. To remove any temptation, Mrs McKenzie had told him not long after he had first arrived, 'If you want a cup, you can have it but not before the cream's settled and skimmed off, mind. We need all we can get of that for butter.' It sounded better than it was because later in the day he found there was never any left. What didn't go into cooking and making cheese, McKenzie drank like water before it went sour.

Dawn swept the entire sky as Harry picked up two kerosene tins with the tops cut off and wire handles added to head for the waterhole. What if he said no? Where could he clear out to? If he landed on another cattle station the first thing they would ask him was what experience he'd had. It had been a mistake to tell them the truth when he had come here. If he had lied, maybe he could have got away with it. The flies were up and settling on his sweat-stained hat and back as he filled the tins and started back towards the main house.

The Manager's meat safe was the same as the one for the hands, a raised, wooden frame covered in layers of sacking and made fly-proof. Above it was a small tank with tiny holes in its bottom through which water dripped and kept the sacking damp. Constant evaporation on the outside kept the inside cool. Harry stood on a log, lifted up one of the tins and filled the tank. He would just have to convince McKenzie he would make as good a cattleman as anybody.

The sun burst up over the Tropic of Capricorn, striking first at the tops of trees that lined the creek bed before sweeping over the grasslands that were sunburnt in every direction to the horizon. And as it streamed into the bedroom, Dora McKenzie woke and lay trying to plan her day. It wasn't easy. With no guests staying, there was only Don who lay asleep beside her to plan for. But it was necessary to keep busy. Not only were idle hands sinful ones, but keeping occupied helped her from going mad. Only when all ideas of finding more to do were utterly exhausted did she resort to her needlework. Suddenly she became aware of her nakedness and glanced anxiously at Don in case he woke, then carefully reached for her nightdress that she had taken off to please him the night before. She did not feel like pleasing him again so soon. Nightdress in hand, she got out of bed to hurriedly put it on. When God made Adam, he should have put limits on his apple eating. The nightdress, severe and voluminous, covered her from chin to wrists to toes. She went to the dressing-table at the window to brush her auburn hair and put it up. As she considered it the best part of her, she liked to take good care of it. As she sat, she saw someone move outside, some way beyond, and parted the lace curtains a little to look. It was Harry, his beard glowing gold in the risen sun, busy watering her little vegetable garden which was such a struggle. She silently thanked him for that. By midday the soft leaves would look as if they were wilting to death but somehow Harry managed to keep them alive. She returned happily to her mirror and hair.

It was reassuring to see Harry always around. On this tiny island surrounded by a sea of endless downs and black soil plain where men landed looking for work and others went away, only Harry outside her own, even tinier world, remained a constant. As far as she was concerned he was a godsend. A treasure. It was rather a pity about him. In a way, he was even quite handsome.

The other station hands were already up and about when Harry shook Bluey McGuirk awake. It startled Bluey and he opened his eyes to look up at the grinning face, unhappy about being back in the world of reality.

'Begod, an' I was havin' a fine dream,' he complained. 'That Lilly.'

'Well, if yer don't get up off yer jack, they'll be askin' yer ter go an' do yer dreamin' somewhere's else, mate,' Harry told him and Bluey sat up, brushing away flies from his face, to start pulling on his clothes. Harry stood for a moment, no longer smiling. 'I's askin' ter see McKenzie terday,' he said, and Bluey stopped for a moment to glance up at him. He didn't have to ask what about. Several times in the eighteen months since he had been here, Harry had confided his deep unhappiness, an unhappiness not at all apparent on the surface.

'T'en ye's better take a post-hole shovel wit' yer ter dig t'e bloody wax out of his ears first,' he suggested.

'This time I'll make 'im listen,' Harry said, but Bluey detected a certain lack of confidence in his words and watched him as he made his way out to go to another rough shed where he was already preparing the men's breakfast. He worried for him a little.

When Bluey had first arrived, it had been Harry who had gone to the trouble of making him familiar with how the station was run and the two had quickly struck up a close friendship. It only came to him later that there was an added advantage in that. Dark haired, a year younger, clean shaven when he got around to it, he was much smaller and of lighter build than his bearded friend who was obviously very strong. Physically, anyway. Mentally, there seemed to be some doubt and Jimmy Case was quite sure about it but he, Bluey, hadn't seen any signs of it for himself. In any case, he was only too pleased to have Harry around while he was back on the homestead. A few bottles of rum going down and there was always someone spoiling for a fight. Although no one had yet picked on him, he was sure that Harry would come to his aid if they tried. He was a loyal man, a kind man, a good mate. What did it matter here in these god-forsaken Colonies that his friend was a Protestant? If he was even that, bejasus. He strapped on his spurs, completely unaware of where this day was going to lead him, and headed for his meal.

The other half dozen hands at present on the main station were already seated on benches at a rough table, waving away the buzzing flies as they waited, ready to attack their breakfast with pocket knives. At the fire with its stone base and sheet-iron chimney, Harry threw a handful of tea into a big, black billy and followed with a handful of dark sugar, then stirred it with a stick. He put it on the table and returned for the steaks that were sizzling and smoking in spluttering fat in two iron pans. These went on the table, too, and Purdy and Spence who always sat together were first to stab with their blades for the biggest. At the fire, Harry kicked the hot camp oven over with his boot, dislodging the lid and spilling hot wood coals and ash from the top of the damper, a bread made simply from flour and water. He prised out the round, flat loaf, brushed more ash off it with his hand, tossed it on the table and breakfast was served. He had just taken his own place beside Bluey when Frank Murray came in and stood there. Only Harry recognised his presence. 'Mornin',' he greeted him.

Murray, at twenty-three years of age, did his best to look older but his whiskers still were not thick enough to help very much. No one liked him. Although educated at a college in Brisbane, he wrongly believed that by talking as roughly to the men as they talked themselves, it would make him appear as tough, and give him the authority he needed in his job as second Overseer.

'I hope you got your crowbar sharpened up, Harry,' he said, directing himself to the easiest first. 'The shit hole at the main house is fillin' up. As soon as you've finished here, get started diggin' a new pit.'

Harry nodded and waited for him to finish with the rest of his instructions.

'McGuirk,' Murray went on, 'you and Rudd'll go out and see how things are holding at Bodman's Creek. Purdy and Spence, maintenance on the yards. The others will be riding out with either Mr Hill or myself. Any bloody questions, then?'

There were no questions. No one but Harry offered him as much as a glance. Instead, they stuffed bits of meat and fat into their mouths with their fingers, broke off bits of damper and sipped at their tin mugs of sweet, black tea. 'Right,' ended Murray and strode out.

'Chuck the bastard inter the old fly bog before yer covers it in, Harry,' muttered Purdy as a suggestion with Murray hardly gone, but Harry wasn't listening and quietly rose to go after him. 'Mr Murray,' he called when far enough away for a conversation to be out of earshot of the others. Murray stopped and turned, waiting for Harry to reach him.

'I wants ter see Mr McKenzie terday,' Harry told him.

'What for?'

'It's between me an' him,' Harry said a little boldly.

Murray looked directly into his grey-blue eyes. Was this simple man, always so compliant and respectful suddenly trying to give him cheek. Harry smiled disarmingly. That was better. No harm there after all. Although he still wondered what it might be about, he didn't press it. It was better to make little allowances for Harry.

'All right, I'll tell him,' he eventually replied, 'but don't blame me if he's too busy to see you. You understand?'

'I won't blame yer,' Harry returned, 'I just wants ter see 'im.'

Murray walked away, his moleskin trousers gleaming white even in the sharp, morning shadow of the storehouse.

Don McKenzie, his dark hair side whiskered and moustached, liked to read the Brisbane newspaper at breakfast and this morning was no different. Dora had put it by his place at the polished dining table. Although the papers arrived in big bundles, the most recent always several weeks old, McKenzie always kept them in strict, chronological order, reading the oldest first and never dipping into another day before its turn, no matter what fascination there might be in some continuing story. This simple act might have indicated that he was a man of great self-discipline but in every other direction he was highly impatient. He sat down and opened it.

'Curse this damned heat,' he complained. 'If it keeps up, every waterhole in the place will be dry.'

'Don't be so pessimistic,' Dora said and pushed a rack of toast and dish of melting butter towards him. Don knew he was lucky to have her. Not every woman would have been content to live in such a remote station and tolerate such hot conditions. She was a good wife and made his life as comfortable as possible. Even if she was a little stubborn and argumentative at times, he could put up with that. Generally, she was most supportive.

Lilly Boyd, the housemaid, came in with a tray on which was his plate of bacon and eggs and put it in front of him.

'Thank you,' he muttered. Lilly was in no hurry to go. Seventeen, dressed in a shapeless, dark cotton frock that covered her to her feet, she liked to admire people sitting at meals like this amidst silver, drinking tea from fine, china cups. Raised in an orphanage from the age of six, she had experienced little in her short life, going into service at the age of thirteen on another property, then coming here.

'That will be all, Lilly,' Dora said, dismissing her, and Lilly went. McKenzie started into his bacon and eggs. As Manager of Albert Downs he had a lot to contend with. Good reliable men were hard to come by and even harder to keep. They got restless for women and here there weren't any. Dora was right to hold an eagle eye on Lilly and keep her a virtual prisoner in the house. The girl wouldn't have been safe even from his Overseers. For lack of anything else, the more desperate chased like animals after lubras, aborigine girls. Damn them for that. Only three years before the blacks had speared one of his best station-hands to death for taking one against her will and the murderers hadn't been caught. At other times mobs of cattle had been killed in revenge. Paying men more money was only self-defeating because the quicker they could save some, the sooner they left to head for a town to spend it. And as it was, the Company in London constantly questioned the level of wages that he did his best to keep to a minimum. Despite all his reports to them, they understood only a fraction of his problems. All the same, he liked his job and enjoyed both his status and authority. If it wasn't for all this damned heat.

'What's that noise?' Dora asked.

McKenzie raised his head and listened for a moment.

From somewhere outside, the sound of a thudding in a regular rhythm reached in.

'It's only Harry,' he concluded, 'I asked for him to dig a new pit,' and returned to his breakfast, paper and thoughts.

Harry raised the heavy crowbar and drove it down into the hard earth where it shuddered with the shock. Quickly, he prised it back and forth then raised it to drive down yet again. Already, he was down a few inches but it was going to take him all day to finish it. Once that was done it only needed a horse or bullock to haul the entire structure of the outside lavatory over the top of it in one piece and the old hole could be filled in. He drove the crowbar down again. Further down in this particular spot it would be harder still, almost like rock. Sweat ran down his face from the brim of his hat but he paid no attention to either that or the flies that tried to pester him. If McKenzie didn't see him today, he would wait a week. No more. It wasn't work he minded, just his job. He would have to make that clear to him once and for all. As the figure on horseback caught his eye, he stopped and looked up. It was Jim Hill with his big bushy moustache riding at a walk towards him. Hill pulled up ten yards from him.

'They want muscle over at the yards,' he called across to Harry, and turned his horse to walk away. He never said any more than he had to did Jim Hill. Harry put down his crowbar beside the post-hole shovel and followed.

At the yards, Purdy and Spence were standing by a new corner post that Harry had cut himself a mile up the creek bed and hauled back on a sled with two bullocks. It was a twisted trunk of tree but as straight as he could find. Purdy and Spence were claiming it was too heavy to lift up to drop in the post-hole Harry had dug himself two days before. Hill sat astride his horse and watched as Harry bent his back to it, Purdy and Spence helping him. They heaved it off the ground, Harry doing most of it. Once he got it on to his shoulder, his veins bulging with the effort, he walked into it and the great post slipped into the ground, only having to be pushed upright before the earth was rammed in around it.

'All right, now you can get back to work,' Hill told him, unaware of the irony, and Harry started to walk back in the direction of the homestead complex and the main house while Hill turned his horse to go and join a small group of mounted hands waiting for him. Left alone, Purdy and Spence sat to take a spell and a drink of water. In the six months they had been there, they had stuck so close together that Jimmy Case had nick-named them the Siamese Twins.

Harry was down almost a foot in his four foot square pit when he heard Dora McKenzie call his name from the back door and turned. 'Wood!' she shouted and Harry waved back to show he had understood. He put down his crowbar and headed for the wood-pile. Good, solid, dead wood for the big, hungry kitchen range was getting harder to find nearby. This last lot he had hauled in and axed up from two miles away. He filled his arms.

Shortly afterwards he was standing at the kitchen's flyscreen door and Dora saw him. 'You can come in, Harry,' she said and he backed into the kitchen with his load. Lilly Boyd was mixing flour and milk in a bowl and stirring under Dora's direction.

'Mornin', Mrs McKenzie, mornin' Miss Boyd,' said Harry. Dora had insisted on all the men calling her housemaid that. It made it more difficult for them to be familiar with the girl. Not that she thought Harry would ever have tried to touch her, but she couldn't make him an exception.

'We's makin' pancakes,' Lilly said in a tone that

clearly suggested it was an event and Harry put down the wood to turn and go.

'I'll give you some later, Harry,' Dora said to him, 'you'd like that, wouldn't you?'

'Very much, Mrs McKenzie,' he smiled, and went.

It was mid-morning as Don McKenzie sat in his tiny study, writing in fine, copperplate hand. At the head of the letter he had put 'Albert Downs, via Bari, Queensland' and dated it 'The 24th of February, 1882' then, beneath, 'The Drysdale Cattle Company, 18 Fetters Lane, London.' He invariably took time in composing exactly what he would say but, for once, he was going to be able to give them a good report. He would also tell them that although the bull they had taken so much trouble to procure was not yet here, its imminent arrival was eagerly awaited. That would be a lie. The bull had been worrying him ever since they had written about it. Without consulting him, they had bought it for the enormous cost of five hundred guineas and shipped it out from England to him for the purpose of improving the quality of their stock. They didn't seem to understand that animals as well as men had to be tough out here. For all he knew, the beast was as likely to take one sniff of the scorching conditions and wilt to death like Dora's vegetables. And he, Don McKenzie, would be blamed for it. Damn them for that.

Old Charley appeared standing in the open doorway loaded down with three heavy ledgers. His voice was educated and soft. 'Excuse me for interrupting, Mr McKenzie, but I brought over the latest figures you asked for.'

McKenzie nodded towards the corner of his desk for Charley to put them there and Charley did so. With his head closer, McKenzie picked up a whiff of his breath. It smelt like a distillery. Several times he had warned him he drank too much and too often but it hadn't made any difference. He thanked him curtly and Charley turned to go, almost bumping into Dora who was arriving with two hot pancakes on a plate. 'I do beg your pardon, M'am,' he apologised, and went. Dora could never decide whether the man used to be a butler or a gentleman. She held out the plate to her husband. 'Taste them.'

McKenzie did so and nodded his approval, 'Very good, but without a cup of tea, another one would stick in my throat.'

'I'll get Lilly to bring you some. By the way, I hear Harry's asking to see you. What's all that about?'

'God knows. Probably the same as last year. Wanting a better job.'

'Can't you give him one?'

'For heaven's sake, woman, give him what?' McKenzie said irritably. 'What kind of man behaves like he does? Harry isn't a man, he's a child. And real men die out there if they get lost or run out of water, even experienced ones. Apart from that, I'm thinking of you.'

'How?'

'He's the best rouseabout you've ever had, isn't he?'

'Yes, he is,' Dora agreed.

'Then why turn him into an inferior stockrider who might be in danger of losing his life and replace him with an inferior wood and water joey? That would be sheer bad management.'

Dora was forced to see the sense in his argument but she was not entirely satisfied. 'Then at least be kind to him.'

'I'm not going to whip him, Dora.'

'And patient with him. Invite him into the house.'

'Into the house?'

'Please, Don. For me. It'll make him feel more important.' And before McKenzie could protest further, she was hurriedly gone. He took out his handkerchief and mopped the sweat from his face.

The sun was overhead and Harry was down over two feet. His shirt was soaked and covered in flies and his face was smeared where the sweat ran over the dust. He would have been down further if Jimmy Case hadn't come for him twice to help lift the heavy bullock wagon wheels he was putting new iron tyres on. He was shovelling out when he became aware of the authoritative looking figure of McKenzie standing above him.

'I believe you want to see me, Harry,' he said. Harry laid the shovel aside and stepped out of his hole. 'Mr McKenzie,' he began, 'I just wants ter...' But McKenzie cut him short.

'It's too hot to stand talking here,' he said, 'come into the house.' And he turned away, not seeing the irony in that, either.

Harry stood for a moment, taken aback. McKenzie had never asked him into the house before and he didn't know whether to take it as a good sign or a bad one. Hurriedly, he tried to dust himself down and wipe his dirty hands on his shirt, then followed.

Dora had made a mistake for suggesting such a thing. The moment Harry entered McKenzie's study he felt at a great disadvantage. It would have been much easier for him on his own territory or on the neutral ground of the open. He was not prepared for this. The shelf of books, the papers on the desk. It was an alien and unfriendly place of which he was not part. He felt nervous.

'Sit down, Harry.'

The upholstered chair. He would dirty that and leave a stain on it. He sat uncomfortably on the edge of it as McKenzie sat down behind his desk.

'Now, Harry, what is it you want to talk about?'

'A better job, Mr McKenzie.'

'It's money we're discussing then, is it, Harry?'

Harry had known exactly what he had wanted to say beforehand but suddenly planted in McKenzie's private surroundings, he became confused. And smaller.

'No, Mr McKenzie, a better job.'

Didn't the fool realise that a better job was the same thing as better money? For Dora's sake, McKenzie kept his patience.

'What do you mean a better job?'

'A proper station-hand's job.'

'What do you know about cattle, Harry? You were a sheep man.'

'I got eyes ter see an' ears ter listen, Mr McKenzie.'

Coming from Harry that sounded almost profound to McKenzie and he smiled. He reached for one of the ledgers still on the desk, opened it and swung it around for Harry to look at.

'What can you make of that?' he asked. He knew perfectly well that Harry had never been taught to read and write. He wasn't meaning to be cruel but felt it might be a way of getting the man to realise his limitations. Harry stared long and hard at the pages of writing and columns of figures. They were meaningless. They might as well have been written in Chinese. He was defeated.

'I'd be willin' ter learn if somebody would teach us,' was all he could find to say. 'But I can ride as well as any man. I can even break 'em in.'

McKenzie sat back and looked at him. How was it possible to explain to him? Well, he would try.

'Harry, we all have our different jobs here and we are both employees of the Company, you and I. Someone has to do your work and someone has to do mine. Without us both the place couldn't function. You do yours well, I have no complaint, and I only hope I do mine well, too. Do you understand?'

Harry felt all his determined intentions slipping away from him. 'I does know cattle an' if yer gives us the chance I'll show yer.'

It sounded like an accusation. McKenzie felt his

impatience rising but held it in control. The man had found his right place in life. Why was he trying to be so damn difficult? Maybe a little treat for him would see him over his present hump. He rose and came round from his desk, indicating that the discussion was at a close. Harry, anxious, rose too.

'You know we're expecting the new bull to arrive at the railhead any day,' McKenzie said, 'well, I'd like you to come with us and drive the bullock wagon to pick it up. You'd like that, wouldn't you?'

'Yeah, but . . .' Harry got out when McKenzie put a hand on his shoulder. It was intended to be friendly and fatherly but came over as being patronising. All the same, as McKenzie always stayed very remote from his men and had never done anything like this before, Harry was thrown by it.

'I believe Mrs McKenzie has some pancakes for you,' McKenzie said, ending his gesture and the entire interview at the same time. Harry made his final effort at the door.

'All I's askin' is for a proper station-hand's job, Mr McKenzie.'

'We'll see, Harry, we'll see.'

Harry went, knowing full well McKenzie's words were as empty as Black Dog Creek in a drought.

McKenzie felt proud of himself. He had done everything Dora had asked of him. Not once had he raised his voice. He had no idea that he was to remember this little talk with Harry for the rest of his life and wouldn't have believed it if Harry had told him himself.

It was dark when Bluey and Rudd arrived back at the tack room, unhitched their water bags, unsaddled, took their bridles off and released their horses into the horse paddock. All the noise on the homestead was coming from the eating shed and they went there to look in. A game had been got up. Men were throwing their sixpences into a hat on the middle of the table and rolling a dice for the pool. Rum was also going down.

'You puttin' in?' someone asked on seeing them.

'Not me, I's flyblown,' said Bluey making the excuse of having no money, because Harry wasn't there and he sensed his mate's day hadn't gone well for him. Rudd stayed and Bluey walked over to the sleeping shed. The faint light of the lantern was shining out through the open door. Inside, he found Harry sitting alone with a bottle. Although he sat quite still, not even turning to see who had come in, Bluey could feel the anger in him even at a distance. He was going to have to cheer him up. Quietly, he went and sat by him.

'Ye saw 'im, then.'

Harry just passed him the bottle and Bluey took a swig from it. For some time, a mad notion that had been flitting about in the back of Harry's mind had now crystalised. It was something he had mentioned to no one, not even Bluey.

'I's clearin' out,' he said, and Bluey knew he meant it. That was worrying for him. He didn't want to lose his friend.

'Comes ter t'at, t'ere's not'in here for me, either. We could go down to the gold fields in N.S.W. How about t'at?'

'There's gold out there, mate.'

'Where? Where is t'ere gold?' asked Bluey in some surprise.

Harry took another swig and passed the bottle again.

'They ain't never goin' ter give us a bloody chance. It's my own fault. For six years I've smiled an' crawled an' worked my guts out an' it's come to nothin'. I gotter make my own chances now. I think that was what old Charley was tryin' ter tell us.'

Bluey was thoroughly confused. He knew Harry was a man slow to anger and could never hold it long. And if he'd found gold he wouldn't be angry at all. He wasn't making sense.

'What's old Charley got to do wit' it and where's t'e gold, Harry, where's t'e gold?'

Harry raised his head and grinned at him. Bluey smiled back. That was better. He was cheering him up already.

'There's sixty thousand head out there,' Harry said. 'They wouldn't miss a thousand of them.'

Bluey stared at him for a moment. He knew exactly what he was talking about and took a swift, anxious glance back towards the doorway in case anyone might be listening and get his friend into trouble. Then he looked into Harry's face, speaking quietly but urgently. 'Holy Mot'er of Jasus, has yer got bush fever? T'ey'd have yer swingin' from t'end of a rope before you'd gone a mile.'

'Not if we did it right,' said Harry and Bluey felt the shockwave hit him, looking around quickly again.

'And who in the hell does yer mean by *we*?'

Ten minutes before he had only been thinking of food and a good drink and rest and now he was being dragged in as an accomplice in what had to be the biggest cattle theft of all time. Maybe his friend was out of his yellow bearded head as they all tried to make out. There was no doubt he was being perfectly serious.

'Listen,' Harry explained, 'they don't even know how many they have. What's on their books is only a guess. And it'll be another two years before they have another bang-tail muster. Even then, they wouldn't know how many ter expect. All I need is ter find a gully some-where's ter the west I can cut off an' use as a holdin' paddock. We could work at nights bringing in some from here an' there an' be back here during ther days. Nobody would know. An' when we had them tergether, we could head out. Nobody would miss us, either. They'd just think we went lookin' for work somewhere's else. I'm tellin' yer, we could be clear an' gone an' none of 'em would ever know.'

20

He made it sound as easy as plucking off ripe plums.

'Two men couldn't handle a mob that big,' Bluey heard himself object. Bejasus, what was he saying? He was an honest man.

'I know,' Harry replied, 'the two best bets are Purdy and Spence. I know yer doesn't like 'em but yer doesn't have to. With them I got my reasons. I bin watchin' 'em an' can tell the signs. They's about to clear out anyhow, an' I reckon they'd be in it. An' I know if they tried ter give us any trouble we could handle 'em.'

It was only then that Bluey's eye caught sight of something bundled in cloth beside Harry and glanced at it as if it might be about to explode. 'What's t'at?' Harry picked it up and handed it to him. 'Pancakes. They're for you, mate.'

'Steal t'em, did yer?' Bluey said unhappily, yet even before he had wrapped himself around a few more rums for comfort he knew in his heart that either he had to put his trust in Harry or he would never have another friend in the world again worth knowing.

Two

Harry, who had never had to organise anything in his life before, found his head spinning with a thousand problems but there was no turning back for him. The following morning he saw his chance of approaching Jack Purdy and Dan Spence as they headed for the tack room on their own. He directed Bluey to play cockatoo and keep an eye open for Hill and Murray while he went after them.

He knew the risk he was taking because although he did not think for a moment that the two men would turn dog on him if they refused to go in on his scheme, there was always the chance they might babble to other hands in drink, and that would be the end of him.

Inside the tack room, Purdy and Spence were picking up their saddles when Harry walked in on them.

'I wants ter talk to yer,' he said, and Purdy and Spence looked at him in curiosity. There was an urgency and seriousness about the rouseabout they weren't used to.

'What's the matter, Harry?' Purdy asked him. He quite liked the man if for no other reason than he presented no threat, no danger to him. Come to that, no danger to anyone.

Harry had already decided that a direct approach would be the better course with them. He came right out with it and told them of his plan to take a thousand head, that Bluey was with him but that he needed another two men. At first, Purdy and Spence looked astonished. This was Harry talking to them but, fool or not, he had certainly made the scheme sound convincing, and workable. As Harry waited anxiously for their answer, Purdy and Spence kept glancing at each other with no need to communicate by words. A thousand head! Greed shone from their eyes. Finally, Purdy nodded and turned to Spence for final confirmation. Spence nodded, too.

'We're in,' Purdy said and Harry's bearded face lit up.

'There's only one other thing,' Harry said, 'I'm boss drover and we goes where I says, an' no splittin' up till we get rid of the whole mob.'

Again, Purdy and Spence exchanged their silent thoughts, and again both nodded.

An apprehensive Bluey knew from the look on Harry's face the moment he emerged that he had his other recruits. He had been half hoping that Harry wouldn't be able to get anyone else and that since he was insisting on taking a thousand head and no less, he would have to drop the idea. It would have been impossible just with the two of them. Despite all the rum he had drunk the night before it had been a very restless sleep, interrupted with visions of the gallows. And Harry had tossed and turned all night, too.

It wasn't until Purdy and Spence were left alone that they talked. The money could make them rich and would be well worth the risk but the idea of Harry being a boss drover amused them. They had other plans.

'We let him do all the bloody work,' Purdy said, 'an' let 'im think he's boss until we's all settled down, then we can take over when we feels like it.'

'What about the Irishman?'

But Purdy was quite confident about Bluey too. 'He'll come in with us once he sees his mate don't know nothin'.'

Harry walked towards the blacksmith shed where Jimmy Case was calling for him. He knew without telling that Case wanted him to light up his forge fire. The blacksmith could just as easily have done it himself but liked to misuse Harry when he got the chance. Harry went towards him, trying to appear normal. He didn't feel it, flushed as he was with his success in getting Purdy and Spence. Case watched him come closer. The idiot was grinning. What the hell was there to grin about? It was too bloody hot already and the day had hardly started.

'Lick the bloody cream off Mrs McKenzie's milk this mornin', did yer?' he said when Harry reached him, but Harry didn't reply and walked past him into the shed to set about the job. He wouldn't have to put up with the bastard much longer. He thought about the part of his plan he had deliberately failed to mention to the others. He knew well enough that if he did, even Bluey would have taken him to be out of his wits, and his whole idea would have been scuttled there and then. That was his secret and he was going to have to keep it until the time came. He was eager to get on with it and there were a lot of things to think about, including keeping Jimmy Case's small, rat-like nose from sniffing out his purpose. To get caught out by this man would be worse than putting the rope around his neck by himself.

Delay appeared in the shape of a messenger who rode in shortly afterwards from the railhead with the news that the bull had arrived and was waiting there in the charge of the groom who had cared for it all the way from England. Harry had forgotten about it, but he was the only one. There was a sudden excitement at the news with Frank Murray striding about trying to look important and even old Charley emerging from his book-hole to try and overhear all that was being said. No bull had ever been sent here directly from England before and everyone was curious to know more about it and see it. All except the wood and water joey. Once, he was, but no longer. He had set a different course now, and it had nothing to do with their new bull. Or so he very mistakenly thought.

The call 'Harry!' rang out across the heat and dust of the homestead earth yet again and he reluctantly presented himself to McKenzie, Hill and Murray who had gathered at the gate to the main house with the messenger. McKenzie rarely gave instructions to hands directly and did not do so now.

'Four bullocks and a shaft horse,' Hill told him in his laconic fashion, and Harry went off to fetch a rope before making for the horse paddock. He felt frustrated. It would take three days to get to the railhead and the same to get back. A whole week.

Murray, with nothing to do, felt obliged to at least be heard in the exciting proceedings. Harry heard him shout, 'Hey, Paddy! Go and give him a bloody hand, we don't want to take all day!' He sometimes used the name 'Paddy' for Bluey when he couldn't immediately remember the name of McGuirk, and Harry was pleased that his mate was being sent to help him. It gave him a chance of having another word with him before he left.

'Listen,' he said when Bluey caught up, 'there's no point in wastin' time. With them all away yer can do what yer likes. Spend all yer time findin' that gully. It's got ter be big enough with good feed an' water. Twenty miles or so out should be fair enough. Get Purdy an' Spence to help yer, but keep a look out for Jimmy Case. Then as soon as I'm back we'll set up ter start. An' don't worry.'

Bluey worried, but nodded before quickly turning

away to find a bullock, feeling that accusing eyes were already being fixed on him.

In just over an hour, the team was hitched up and ready to go. McKenzie, Hill and Murray climbed into the buggy that had a hood to give them shade. With Hill driving, they started out on the track that led to the south-east, Dora watching her husband go and giving a wave. McKenzie wished she wouldn't do that in front of others. Displays of affection in public embarrassed him. He had told her before but the damned woman would do it, and he did not wave back. Dora didn't expect him to.

Behind them, Harry urged the bullocks to get moving, walking by the side of the leader, guiding it, flies intent on eating both of them. The hauled wagon trundled away, its high frame sides constructed of saplings wired together swaying drunkenly.

Annoyance stuck out from the stubbled face of Jimmy Case as he watched them go. 'Can't be much of a bloody bull, trustin' a loppy bastard like that ter drive it,' he grumbled across to old Charley, but the book-keeper wasn't to be drawn and turned away to go back into his shade. He was pleased Harry had been given this job for a change. Perhaps the responsibility of it would give him a little more confidence in himself. It was a pity that the only tears welcomed in this hard dry land came from the sky and not the eyes of men.

With Don away for six days, Dora was harder pushed than ever to keep occupied but, for the moment, she was to be saved. As if sensing that the Chiefs of Albert Downs had departed from what was once their waterhole, a small group of aborigines wandered in, three men, two women and a girl, apart from their few decorations and bark dillybags, all as naked as the day they were born. None of the station-hands tried to chase them away because of the exciting possibility of being able to bed the girl. It was Rudd who first felt obliged to warn Mrs McKenzie they were there and Dora immediately sprang into action, rummaging through every drawer and cupboard in the house for rags with which to cover them. There weren't enough for dresses and Lilly watched in anger and horror as her mistress stripped the curtains from her tiny room. Lilly liked those. 'You can't do that, Mrs McKenzie, they's mine!' she objected. They were not hers but she liked to think so. Dora was in far too much of a hurry to listen. There was stitching to be done.

It was at times like these that Lilly was forcibly reminded of her position in life and she didn't like it. Mrs McKenzie could have taken the clothes off her back and she would have been unable to do anything about it. Serving meals at a pretty setting and working with her mistress in the kitchen she often felt herself to be part of the family, and she resented having it brought home to her that in reality she was little more than a slave.

The aborigines squatted outside the eating shed in the shade, quite unaware that preparations were under way to cover their shameless sin, while Bluey knew that Purdy and Spence would not be helping him that day, not so long as that pair of protruding bare breasts and dark, rounded hips were there to tease their lascivious eyes. At the same time, it gave him the opportunity of slipping away without attracting much attention. He filled his water bag, saddled up, and rode out alone, heading north-east in case anyone was watching him, then, once out of sight, swinging round to go west.

Fifteen miles out along the track leading to the railhead, the country began to flatten out, the track itself running dead straight all the way to the shimmering horizon. Although it was called black soil here, the earth between the patches of Mitchell grass and other shrubby bits of vegetation was a dusty, light grey and it rose from the hoofs and wheels to hang for a while in the hot air before very slowly settling back.

'Keep up,' Harry coaxed the bullocks, sweat stinging his eyes and blinding him as he walked alongside, the flies following around his head. Bullock drivers normally used other words of encouragement with their whips and Harry had heard a lot of them as they hauled their loads of dumped wool bales back in New South Wales. 'You lop-eared, wall-eyed, knock-kneed, scab-ridden, pigeon-toed, dag-jacked, motherless bunch of bastards!' they would curse at the top of their voices at their beasts, making up long lengths of fresh insults between breaths, but Harry's team was moving along well without it.

And he was still busy making plans. Half a dozen good horses and a strong pack horse to carry the supplies. There were hundreds of horses on Albert Downs. They didn't even know how many of those they had either, grazing out in the open country in herds and only rounded up for the big musters. A lot of flour, sugar and tea. Salted beef to start with. An axe, shovel and gun. What else? Lots of things. Double up on water bags. Spare stirrup leathers. It was important he didn't forget anything.

A long way up ahead, Jim Hill pulled the buggy to a halt, waiting for Harry to catch up while McKenzie wiped his sweat away and worried about the bull. Murray stuck his head out into the roasting sun. 'Hurry up! Come on!' he yelled back along the track although Harry was still out of earshot.

When it was dark, Murray directed him step by step as if the rouseabout didn't know what he was doing, tethering the bullocks separately amongst patches of feed and hobbling the horse to let it hop around and graze where it liked. Harry felt better when the irritating Overseer left him alone to light a fire and cook their meal. McKenzie, Hill and Murray then took advantage of the tray of the wagon which had been thickly laid with dried grass before they left, and bedded down on it for the night.

Some way off, Harry scooped a hip-hole out of the earth with his hands and settled on the ground. It wasn't going to be easy finding cattle at night and mustering them in without frightening them. Once he had his first lot in he would quieten them down, let them get used to him, then use them as coachers, driving the same ones out again every night as decoys to assure others.

He looked at the stars for a few moments. They were friends he had come to know as a child and, without ever having to think about it or know all their names, he was familiar with many of them. Born on the earth under the shelter of a dray, he had never known a home and had grown up with the sky above him. The Southern Cross had already turned. He closed his eyes and was overcome by sleep.

Three days after they left, they reached the railhead, the tall, stick-like figure of Eddie Giraldi shaded under the brim of his hat, coming out to meet them.

'I would er let yer know yer bull was comin' sooner, Mr McKenzie,' he drawled, 'but the telegraph down the line wasn't workin' an' it took a few days ter find where it was broke. First thing I knew, a train come up an' it was here.'

'Where is it?' McKenzie asked, seeing nothing in the yards, and Giraldi who ran the place nodded towards the storage shed, 'Over there with its hand.'

The open-sided storage shed and set of cattle yards with their loading ramps was most of it here where the single line ended. Otherwise there was only the water tank and a couple of small houses.

The pint-sized English groom emerged from the shed looking distressed from the heat and wiping sweat from his face with a big, red kerchief, but very relieved to see them. 'Thank God,' he muttered to himself. He had been sitting there waiting for six days in this hell-hole at the ends of the earth and it had brought on his final decision. Originally, it had been his intention to stay in the Colony and find a better job than he could have got in England. His doubts began when he disembarked with the bull at Brisbane in heat and high humidity but that had been nothing. Now, he felt that he had been roasted in his own juices almost beyond recovery and was intent on getting back home as quickly as possible.

The bull had no say in the matter.

McKenzie and his Overseers inspected it while Harry unhitched the bullocks and buggy horse to feed and water them. Then, as all the others went to Giraldi's house for a drink and for the papers to be handed over and signed, he walked over to the shed and into its shade to have a look for himself.

There, amongst barrels, boxes and sacks waiting to be picked up, stood a big, white, magnificent bull, tied to a heavy post both by the lead of its rope halter and by a ring on its nose. Although he had heard of it, Harry had never seen a bull with a ring in its nose before, but it wasn't that. It was the most wonderful looking animal he had ever set eyes on, and it emanated strength, dignity and pride. It fixed Harry with a bold, red-rimmed eye and Harry felt an enormous sense of pleasure in that.

'G'day, mate,' he grinned, 'I'm Harry.'

No one could have got that close on foot to any other bull on Albert Downs without their life being in danger but this one was different. It was used to being handled and having people around it. Yet, it gave the strong impression that it could have snapped its ropes like rotten threads if it had wanted to and torn down the entire shed with its great white horns. Why didn't it? It clearly had all the spirit and power in the world.

Then Harry noticed that its ropes were tied too high

to allow it to lie down in comfort if it wanted to. There could have been a reason for that he didn't know about but, after searching his memory amongst all the tales he had ever heard about bulls, he couldn't find one. All the same, if he interfered, they might want to rip his bloody ears off. What did it matter now he was clearing out? Let them.

He loosened the ropes and slid them down the post, then sat back on a few sacks of grain to continue looking at it with admiration. After a few moments, the big white bull lowered itself to lie. It still kept an eye fixed on him, its sides heaving with its hot breath, but it began to chew its cud.

Harry felt even more pleasure that this wonderful animal trusted him and when he leaned forward to touch its coat, it didn't flinch. He sat there for well over an hour before Hill and Murray appeared back out of the house and Harry stood for Hill to give him his instructions.

'Some of that's ours,' he said, nodding at the supplies there, and turned to point at a loading ramp. 'We load over there.'

Harry had been hoping McKenzie wouldn't decide to stay the night. The sooner he could get back and get started the better. As he fetched the bullocks out of a yard, he saw McKenzie, Giraldi and the groom appear. He hurried to hitch up and Murray, keen to show his capabilities off to the little Englishman, helped him by shoving, cursing and shouting to get the wagon backed into the ramp. But he only directed from the side as Harry rolled across a couple of heavy barrels of salt to heave them on and get them upright. 'Right up the front there,' he ordered, and repeated himself as Harry carried the first of half a dozen sacks of flour. Then the sweating little groom led on the big white bull to tie it up. McKenzie had hoped that the man might come to work on Albert Downs and keep on being responsible for the animal but he was to be disappointed.

'You sure you won't change your mind?' he said, and the groom wiped himself with his soaked kerchief yet again.

'I wouldn't change my mind for nothing, sir.'

It was bad enough for him that he was going to have to wait there another five days for a train to come and take him away. If it wasn't his cooked remains they took.

Eddie Giraldi rode out several miles with them to see them off. He liked to talk and there were never enough people around to talk to. He drawled out weeks of news of people away down the line who neither McKenzie, Murray or Hill had ever heard of as he rode alongside their buggy.

'Well, I'd better be gettin' back,' he said finally, 'in case the telegraph is chatterin'. I'm a martyr to it. For days there might be nothin' at all, then it talks. But I gotter stay around, Mr McKenzie. Gotter stay around,' and he turned his horse, only giving a wave of recognition to Harry as he passed him. Had he had the slightest inkling of what was going on under Harry's hat, there is no doubt that he would have turned his horse again and ridden all the way to Albert Downs beside him, talking non-stop, and made himself famous with the memory.

At every brief stop, McKenzie hopped down to hurry back to the wagon to study the bull closely for signs of collapse. That he couldn't see any made no difference. He continued to worry. He drank from his water bag and looked at the animal again. Damn them. The beast might have been all right in the cool, green fields of England but not damn well here. Good God, look at it. It was soft. Stupid looking. All you had to do was paint it yellow, get it to cry and you could have called it Harry. He ordered Hill and Murray to feed and water it again then returned to sit in the shade of the buggy hood.

The sun had been up two hours on the third day back as Harry trudged on alongside the bullocks. Since he had left the homestead he had walked for over a hundred and fifty miles. Flies drank from his sweat and his feet felt sore and raw from the edges of his Alberts curling and rubbing. 'Up!' he encouraged as the lead bullock started to drag its hoofs, and the animal obeyed. He wanted to slow himself to ease the pain and even tried to will McKenzie to call another halt, but it didn't work. Away up ahead, he saw Murray's head poke out to look back at him yet again. He had been doing it every few minutes ever since they left the homestead. Harry knew they'd be expecting him to show some weakness, but he was not going to give them the satisfaction. If blood ran down from his boots and left a trail in the dust behind him, he was going to keep up. He made his footsteps solid, did his best to look happy and even grinned, although he doubted if Murray would be able to see it at that distance. Murray did, and pulled his head back in.

'He won't be bothering you for a long time to come, Don,' he said to McKenzie. 'Like a babe in a lolly shop. He'll be talking about it for years.'

There was less than twenty miles to go and the buggy quarter of a mile ahead when it happened. The first noise was like a gun shot and the bullocks were suddenly being jolted to a stop. Harry turned to see the rear wheel smash against the side of the wagon then part from it as the tray dipped precariously in the same direction. As he started to run back, the big white bull struggling to keep its feet and tipping it more, one of the heavy barrels fell over and rolled right past it to smash its way through the rear to thud on the earth then, unbroken, roll a few more feet. Harry jumped right on to the wagon through the broken rails to get at the bull.

The others heard the noise, too. 'In the name of God, what was that!' McKenzie exploded, and Hill was swinging the horse around, whipping it into a canter in a cloud of dust.

By the time they got there, Harry had undone the rear frame, untied the bull, coaxed it to jump down and was standing holding it. That he was smiling both from the relief of the big white bull being uninjured and from the pleasure he felt at holding a bull for the first time in his life, didn't make it easier for him. McKenzie looked black with anger. 'What in the hell did you do?' he shouted, forcing Harry to cover his feelings.

'I didn't do nothin', Mr McKenzie,' he returned, stern faced, 'the axle broke.'

Murray quickly grabbed the bull away from him while McKenzie examined it. Hill, confident the animal was all right, inspected the wagon instead. 'Broken's right,' he muttered, and took a plug of black tobacco from his pocket to bite off a bit and start chewing it. It helped to keep him calm when Don was worked up.

'That barrel could have damn well killed it!' McKenzie swore.

Murray knew the accusation was meant for himself since it was he who had overseen the loading but as he was about to protest, McKenzie threw him a threatening glance that stopped him.

Finally satisfied that the big white bull had suffered no damage, McKenzie's anger began to subside and he turned his attention to the state of the transport. There was nothing to be done. It would take two days for Case and a couple of men to get out, make repairs and get it back.

'Let the bullocks go, we can pick them up later,' he directed Hill, 'and cover over the flour in case we get a flash storm. The bull will have to be led back.'

Harry released the bullocks and it dawned on both Hill and Murray that they might be in for a twenty mile walk. Neither of them relished that at all and they were both pleased indeed when Murray handed the bull leads back to Harry and McKenzie made no objection.

'You think you can do it without breaking one of its damned legs?' was all he said.

Shortly afterwards, McKenzie, Hill and Murray clambered back on to the buggy and into the shade to set off again, Harry following behind leading the big white bull and grinning with delight. It was a new experience for him. For a while, the raw sores on his feet were forgotten as he shared the closeness of the animal, but he waited until the buggy was far enough ahead before he spoke.

'My father an' mother came from England, too,' he said quietly to his charge, 'but they didn't come as convicts. Unfettered ter do what they liked. Worked as shepherds. I dunno where they is right now. After I had ter leave 'em in New South Wales ter find work for meself we got outer touch. It's the way things has ter be. But don't worry, mate, yer'll get used ter it. An' you gotter lot er ladies waitin' for yer. Bloody thousands of 'em.'

An hour later, he realised it was getting thirsty but he didn't wait for Hill or Murray to come back and attend to it. Instead, he took off his hat, emptied his water bag into it and held it out. The bull drank and they went on.

'Water's what yer gotter keep a look out for,' he told it. 'Don't go too far from a permanent water-hole and you'll be all right. I won't be able to do that myself where I's goin' but then I gotter take the risk.'

The westering sun was low as they approached the homestead and it was then that Murray jumped down from the moving buggy and waited for Harry to reach him. 'All right, I'll take it now,' he said, reaching for the ropes. Looking important, he led the bull into the homestead as people ran from everywhere to look at it in wonderment. Dora and Lilly stood looking from the little gate, old Charley at the door of the storeroom, Jimmy Case outside his shed and every station-hand on the place looking on. The group of aborigines, now dressed in a ragged assortment of coverings and a hurriedly stitched together frock, rose to their feet in awe and fear. It was an animal god, a huge, white beast unlike any other with what looked like a great gold ring growing out of its pink nose. No one noticed the yellow bearded figure of Harry as he trudged in behind on his own.

Dora McKenzie was more pleased to see her husband back than anything else. 'Now you've seen it, go and make some tea,' she said to her housemaid and Lilly returned reluctantly into the house. Dora waited patiently for her husband to approach her, eager to show her pleasure at his return. When Don was away, the loneliness was almost more than she could bear. McKenzie didn't give her a glance. For the time being she had to be content to watch him attend to things as he talked to Jim Hill.

As Murray led the big white bull towards the horse paddock, giving a few rough jerks on its nosering to show his audience that he was its undisputed master, opinions on it began to flow freely amongst the hands.

Old Charley simply gazed with tired-looking eyes and said nothing. No one could have guessed his strength of admiration for it. Without knowing much about cattle, it was clear that this was an animal of quality, of breeding, of distinction. But it was doubtful if any of them would know an aristocrat if they saw one.

'I'll give it two weeks,' he heard Rudd remark, 'an' yer can go out an' pick up the bloody bones.' Then he heard Jimmy Case give a coarse laugh of derision, 'Call that a bull? Look at it. Wouldn't go two rounds with a one-legged bloody cockerel.'

Old Charley returned indoors to his retreat and his rum.

McKenzie was annoyed on his arrival to see the family of aborigines on the homestead and rightly suspected that he was looking at a pair of his own trousers on one of them. Trousers that still had some good wear in them. It had been his instruction that no blacks were to be allowed near the place whenever he was absent. Dora knew it, too. He would show her he was not to be disobeyed and wasted no time in correcting the matter. He ordered Hill to see that they were driven out immediately, and in the direction of the Christian Mission that lay two hundred and fifty miles to the east. 'And if I find out that anyone has been fornicating with their women,' he added, 'I'll have them driven there as well – with a whip across their cursed backs.'

It was not until everything was done – the bull safely settled, the blacksmith briefed on the damaged wagon, the buggy parked, the horse unharnessed and the blacks run over the downs by a horseman towards the dimming horizon – that McKenzie finally turned towards his house and his waiting wife. He had made his point to her. There would be no need for him to say any more about it. She would want to know every detail of his trip, about his opinion on the bull, on how Harry had enjoyed being a man of importance – everything. That would have to wait, too. What was needed first was a tub of cool water, a change of clothes and a cup of tea. Dora greeted him with a happy smile. She knew full well that he had driven off the blacks in order to teach her a lesson, but she had no intention of mentioning the subject either. Inside, alone, they would kiss, and all would be back to normal.

Harry appeared not to hurry either although he was itching to get to Bluey as quickly as possible to find out how he had managed. After he had deliberately taken his time to hang up the harness neatly in the tack room, he strolled casually over to the sleeping shed and went in. He found Bluey there alone, looking as tense as a cornered rabbit and was immediately apprehensive.

'What's the matter?'

'I been havin' nightmares, t'at's what's t'e matter.'

That was a relief and Harry laughed. 'You ain't done nothin' yet, mate. An' there's nothin' ter worry about, I'm tellin' yer. I've thought of everythin'. Did yer find a gully?'

'I did, I did. It's just what ye asked for an' won't take much fencin' at all,' Bluey replied to the ground in a low whisper, although there was no one else around to hear.

After Harry had left for the railhead, Bluey's nerves had deteriorated further. There had been no question of his backing out but with Purdy and Spence constantly occupied in getting the aborigine girl off the homestead and putting her back to the ground, he had been bereft of companionship. And with no one else to talk to about their plans, he had been bombarded by doubts. But now, with Harry back and seated beside him, happily grinning and laughing at his fears, reassuring him all over again that the dangers were more imagined than real, he started to feel better.

Bluey watched his friend as he pulled off his boots and unwound his Alberts to reveal his broken-blistered feet. Harry reached for some Stockholm tar that was used for cracks in horses hoofs and which he had taken from the tack room. He smeared it on his wounds. 'I's only sorry in a way they *ain't* ever goin' ter find out,' he said, "specially Frank Murray. I dunno how McKenzie bloody stands 'im.' And he started to wrap himself up again. Harry swore by the tar as a cure for all ailments external and had already added it to the list of everything else in his head.

'All right,' he said, pulling his boots back on, 'we start fencin' it off ternight.'

'Tonight?'

'We'll need two axes, a post-hole shovel, a pair of pliers and a bit of wire.' He got to his feet. 'I'll go an' get Jack and Dan before they start gettin' themselves rotten.'

Bluey looked surprised because in a land where one day was much the same as the next and tomorrow preferable to today, such urgency was unusual unless directed to be so by one of the bosses.

'What's yer hurry?' he asked.

'The moon's startin' up an' we'll need all we can get of it in the next week, mate.' And with that, Harry left to find Purdy and Spence, leaving Bluey looking a little bewildered. He had no idea that Harry knew how the moon behaved and had never even thought about it himself. It was either there or it wasn't. Begod, how did Harry know that? He'd never mentioned he knew anything about the bloody moon before. There were mysteries to the man he'd been keeping under that yellow mop of hair.

Less than two hours after sundown, the four men were riding out with all they needed. Bluey led the way, Harry by his side while Purdy and Spence followed a little way behind. There was little conversation amongst them but they were all beginning to feel the excitement in their different ways at making a sudden start. In truth, Harry's decision to move quickly was not only the moon. He was afraid that because of Bluey's nervousness, his mate might try to make excuses for delay and that Jack Purdy and Dan Spence might lose faith in him. Once he had got it all under way, they would be forced to go on and get it over with. For that reason, too, he made them all hurry.

It was well before midnight when Bluey pulled up his horse at the edge of a steep drop. 'T'is is it,' he said, and Harry rode around the lip of the gully to its western end, delighted with what he could see.

The gully had been formed over many years by erosion during flood times, cutting out an area of more than fifty acres which had eventually become grassed and leaving only a narrow exit. And there were enough

trees and bushes around with which to build a temporary hedge in the way of a fence with a set of slip rails
in the middle.

Harry, who had never given an order to any other
man in his life, did not try to do so now. He knew full
well that both Purdy and Spence would resent him for
that and even try to start an argument to put him down.
He would have to keep his mouth shut and do it by
example. Taking the post-hole shovel he began to drive
it hard and fast into the ground where he would put up
the posts for the slip rails and felt pleased when he saw
Purdy and Spence follow Bluey with axes to start
cutting.

It was only then that Harry began to feel something
else, a heaviness he had never known before, and he
knew what it was. Although he had made out to them
that there was no chance of them getting caught, he
knew well enough that nothing in life was fool-proof.
While it still had been only an idea in his mind, that
and the planning had been enough to think about. Now,
there was a lot more. He wasn't only risking his own
neck on the gallows but those of the others. They were
putting their faith in him that it was going to work just
as he had said. He could be causing the deaths of three
other men, the best friend he had ever known amongst
them.

Bluey dragged in the first lot of bushes to begin making the fence and Harry looked at him solemn-faced
under the quarter moon. 'You'll just have ter trust us,
mate,' he said.

'An' what else, Bejasus, does ye t'ink I'm doin'?'

For a moment, he watched Bluey as he went for
more. He mustn't say things like that again. The only
way was to show them he had enough faith for all of
them. Show confidence in himself. Smile and laugh
when they expected it. Say cheerful things. Doubt could
be a disease that might see them all under.

The posts were in, the rails ready to hook up and the rough fence almost completed when Harry noted the moon. 'I gotter get back quick ter start ther day,' he told the others and made for his horse. It was absolutely essential that he stuck to his normal times if he was to avoid raising suspicion. He swung himself into the saddle but paused long enough to sit grinning down at them. 'It's all poppin' up sweet, mates. Termorrer night we'll have our first mob in an' tucked up safe as babes in a basket.' Then he dug in his heels and took off towards the east at a fast canter.

As soon as Harry had gone, Spence thought he would sound out Bluey's strength of loyalty to him and asked him to be honest about it.

'Is it right he's a bit loose in the bloody nanny?' he said to him. 'What d'yer reckon? Straight wire.'

Bluey knew what they were after and thought for a moment to find the right way of putting it. 'Well, look at it like t'is. If t'ere wasn't more in his head t'an t'ere is in the t'ree of ours put toget'er, t'en tell us t'is – what in t'e name of all t'e Saints is we all doin' here?'

There seemed to be no reasonable, quick answer to that and Purdy and Spence exchanged glances. The Irishman wasn't ready to come over on their side. It didn't matter. There was plenty of time. They would just keep on doing what Harry wanted as long as it suited them.

In the nights that followed it was hard work but they went exactly as Harry had planned and in each ride out they brought supplies and made a cache. Even his idea of using coachers worked well and he marked each one on the horns so he could easily identify them in the dark to cut them out each time. To hurry the process, they worked in pairs, making their casts further and further out from the gully.

Don McKenzie, smelling of soap, whiskers neatly

groomed and feeling a little physical relief from the relative cool of the evening, sat down with Dora for his meal. But there was not the same relief in his mind, for the new bull still occupied most of it. That day, they had taken it from the horse paddock and put it out with a selected herd of good cows around Cuff's Waterhole seven miles to the north. He'd had no alternative.

Many months before when they had first told him of the animal, he had written back to London and asked them if they wanted him to set up a proper stud, pointing out the investment that would be needed – new sheds, more fenced paddocks, yards, hand feeding, a steam engine and pump to bring water from the creek, and extra hands. They had still not replied on the issue. Not a single damned word. If their bull died of heat exhaustion or ended in the bellies of a tribe of blacks it wasn't going to be his fault. He had done everything he could. Hill and Murray could back him up on that. So could every man of any intelligence in Central Queensland. All he could do now was damned well pray that somehow the stupid beast might survive. And his job with it.

Lilly came in with the food, still smarting from having her curtains taken away. She had loved those curtains. Never had she had curtains of her own before. It had given her pleasure to wake up every morning and see them. Now she only had an empty window. It had made her realise who she was. Not Lilly Boyd as she liked to think but housemaid to the Manager's wife on Albert Downs. There was a world of difference between the two. And it was why she wore such a stiff expression on her face.

'Now, don't be silly,' Dora said to her quietly, 'I told you I'd get you new ones, didn't I?'

It was just like Don to hear something he wasn't supposed to. 'New what?' he asked.

'Boots. Lilly needs new boots.'

Lilly returned to the kitchen and Dora avoided the subject of her excursions into charity which Don firmly believed not only began at home but ended there as well. Besides, she had a question of her own.

'What are you doing to Harry?' she said, and Don's fork stopped halfway to his mouth.

'Not damned Harry again.'

'And please don't swear at me. I simply wanted to know if you're overworking him.'

'Of course I'm not overworking him. He's doing the same things he always does. What's he saying now?'

'He's not saying anything and seems perfectly happy, but he looks rather tired.'

'We're all tired, woman. It's the heat.'

It was another small conversation that McKenzie was going to remember, but, at the time, he only wished that his wife would leave the running of the station to him and stick to worrying about Lilly's boots and the running of the house.

After ten days of working day and night, only sheer determination, his responsibility for the other men's lives and the stimulation of what he was doing, kept Harry awake. Unlike Bluey, Purdy and Spence who had been able to sneak off on jobs and catch a few hours under a tree, around the homestead Harry had found very little opportunity. The odd half hour now and again left him red-eyed and weakening. He got together with Bluey, Purdy and Spence in the hut when no one else was around.

'We gotter have enough,' he said, and turned to Purdy. 'How many has you put in?'

Purdy glanced at Spence and Spence just shrugged. Purdy returned his gaze to Harry. 'We ain't rightly sure,' he said.

'Didn't yer keep a tally?'

It was then that it became clear to Bluey that neither

of the two men could count.

'Ye can't bloody add up, can yez?' he said, but Purdy was quick to poke a thumb at Harry, 'Neither can he.'

'Maybe I can't count normal,' Harry defended himself, 'but I can tell the number in a mob just by looking at 'em.'

'You tell us, then,' Purdy challenged.

'I gotter see 'em in daylight.'

It was true what Harry said. Although his arithmetic was not of the ordinary kind, he had learned as a child with the sheep how to add up to ten and with a flock rushing past him transfer a pebble or a bit of stick from one hand to the other every time the number went by. He had also learned how to tell the number in a flock to the nearest ten just by glancing at them, whether they were spread out or herded tightly together. No one on Albert Downs had ever come to know he had this bit of expertise and he had never had any cause to tell them. It was something he just knew and took for granted.

'Anyhow, we gotter have a thousand near enough. Is we ready ter go?'

They nodded, and agreed that they would leave for the gully to get there by Piccaninny dawn and get the drove under way. Not even Jimmy Case had the slightest suspicion of anything untoward going on under his little nose. And for the first time in ten days, Harry lay down on his bunk, not even removing his boots, closed his stinging eyes and fell immediately asleep.

Despite that, he was the first awake and quietly shook the others in the dark, Bluey jumping nervously as if he'd been struck. Rudd or someone else would have to milk the cows like they had when he had gone to the railhead. He would be rid of that forever. He would be a proper cattleman now, what he had always wanted.

And into the darkness under the final sliver of the moon, they rode out west from Albert Downs homestead for the very last time.

Three

As they reached the eastern end of the steep sided gully at first light, Harry pulled his horse up on the rim and looked down. 'My Gawd,' he said in astonishment, 'we got fifteen hundred of 'em.'

Bluey nearly fell out of his saddle with the announcement. 'Holy Mot'er of God, t'ey'll hang us twice.'

Purdy and Spence, on the other hand, were pleased. It simply meant more money, a big bonus for them. But there was yet another surprise to come and this time it was to be a disturbing one. As they rounded the top edge of the fence and began to push on down, they saw the big white bull standing large as life right outside the slip rails.

'How the hell did that get there?' Purdy exclaimed. 'They put it out at Cuff's Hole only two bloody days ago!'

As the four of them approached the animal, shouting at it, expecting it to clear off at a trot, it made no difference. The big white bull stayed where it was and even seemed to want to follow Harry around like a dog.

'What is we goin' to do?' a nervous Bluey asked.

'It's nothing ter worry about,' Harry assured them,

'I'll drive it back east while you get the pack saddle loaded up an' everythin' ready.' He cracked the air with his stockwhip and started to get the bull moving. The bull, unused to the sound, was apprehensive about it and decided that a trot might be safer until it realised it was coming to no harm and slowed to a walk again. Harry, reluctant to teach it that a whip could cut its hide, put up with that.

He pushed it along at a good walk for an hour then stopped. 'Now, you keep on goin', mate. Yer hear us?' he said roughly, then swung his horse around to head back towards the gully at a canter. Looking over his shoulder as he went he was relieved to see the big white bull at least stay where it was, putting its head down to start grazing.

The sun burst up and, at the slip rails, all was ready. The pack horse was loaded up, the spare mounts haltered and held by leads. 'All right, let's go,' said Harry, briefly dismounting to take down the slip rails and throw them aside, leaving the open gap. Purdy and Spence rode in, whips cracking, to begin driving the cattle out while Harry and Bluey stayed outside to head the leaders south-west.

Eager to be released, the lowing set up by the big mob was almost deafening as they crowded at the gap, shoulders and horns pushing and shoving. They rushed out like a great dam that had burst its banks and was turning into a river in flood. Dust rose to the sky.

'Easy! Easy!' Harry tried to yell at Purdy and Spence inside, knowing that the cloud they were making could be seen for miles. Heels dug in, he took off anxiously towards the head to try and slow them down. In no time, the huge mob had spread out half a mile wide, many of them breaking off from the main stream to try and take off in another direction. There was no time to think of anything else but trying to keep the mob together as the four men rode hard to contain one break after the other, hoofs thudding the earth and whips cracking across the noses of beasts like pistol shots.

Lilly came back in from the buttery empty handed. 'There isn't no milk *there*, Mrs McKenzie.'

Dora looked at her a little anxiously for a moment then hurried out to look for herself. The buckets were still upside down on their board. Nothing had been touched. She knew it. The poor fellow was ill and no one had done anything about it. Probably lying in his bunk with fever. Totally incapacitated. And no one paying the slightest attention. Men could be incredibly unsympathetic when it came to others' sickness. Cruel, even. She would tell Don that when he got up.

As she came out of the buttery she caught sight of old Charley returning to his book-hole with a bucket of water and went to the fence to call him. Old Charley put down his load and came to her.

'M'am,' he said.

'I think Harry must be ill. Could you see for me, please, and come back and tell me what you think he needs. And could you get Mr Hill or Mr Murray to arrange for someone to milk.'

'Yes, of course, m'am. I'm very sorry if he's ill.'

'Thank you, it's most kind of you.'

Dora always felt obliged to say that to old Charley whenever she had to make a request of him. There was something about the man that forced it on her. She returned indoors, angry about men. Well, most of them.

'I hope that if you ever marry, Lilly, you choose very, very carefully.'

Lilly, lighting the stove, her face in smoke, didn't reply. What was she talking about marriage for? If anybody had asked her to marry them, she wouldn't have been there being a housemaid. She would have been in a place of her own. Hanging up her curtains. Even if it was only a tiny, one room hut with an ant-bed floor.

'He must be able to support you emotionally as well as financially,' she heard her mistress say, 'in sickness and in health equally.'

She was getting in a really funny mood this morning, she was. All because Harry hadn't milked. Served her right.

The big black range had heated up and the kettle was boiling to make McKenzie's morning cup of tea when old Charley appeared at the door. Dora turned to him.

'I'm afraid, m'am, that Harry has gone,' he said.

At first, Dora didn't understand. He couldn't mean dead because he looked almost pleased about it. The faintest hint of a smile on his as yet unshaven face. Anyway, that was unthinkable.

'Gone where? No one told me he was going anywhere.'

'I mean left the station, m'am. Permanently by the looks of it as he has taken all his things with him. Gone on the track as they say.'

Dora looked dumbstruck. Harry would never go. Other men walked off without a word at times. There was nothing unusual in that. But not Harry. Something was very wrong. It was as if old Charley knew what she was looking for.

'Unless it is by a very strange coincidence, he did not go alone,' he told her. 'His Irish friend has gone, too, as well as two other men, one called Purdy, the other Spence. I believe it would be safe to assume that they have all gone on the track together in search of work elsewhere.'

Dora ran with her vexation to the bedroom where McKenzie had just come awake and was rubbing the sleep from his face before raising his head from the pillow. 'Now, look what you've done!' she shouted at him.

To be suddenly accused of something undefined when barely conscious confounded him and he stared at

Dora standing at the bottom of the bed, almost trembling. But as he opened his mouth to ask in all innocence what he was supposed to have done, Dora was at him again.

'He's come under a bad influence and they've somehow seduced him away. God knows what trouble they might lead him into. You'll have to go after them and bring him back. They can't have gone far.'

McKenzie swung himself out of bed to stand in his night-shirt, annoyance coming over his face. There was only one 'he' on Albert Downs who could have got her into such a state and the name sprung quickly to his mind, God-damned Harry again.

'If you hurry you can catch him,' Dora urged.

Such was her flutter, it took him several minutes to get the full story from her. There was no shock or any great surprise in it which was what he suspected. Men had walked off without notice many times before, just as suddenly as they often rode in, usually when work was over for the day so that they could tuck in and fill their bellies without having done a stroke for it. Purdy and Spence were no loss. He had observed them. They were permanent discontents, lead swingers, untrustworthy. It was a pity about the Irishman, he had shown promise. As for Harry, there was no doubt that he would be missed. And in some ways he had even come to like him. It was only a wonder that he hadn't come under someone's influence before considering his weaknesses. Anyone could take advantage of his genial nature if they so chose. It had been too much to hope, perhaps, that for his wife's sake, he might stay forever.

'You must hurry, Don,' Dora said, 'they could only have gone either east or on the track to the railhead.'

At first, McKenzie was at a loss as to what to say to her. Life wasn't easy for her here and Harry had provided some outlet to her innate sense of charity. More. Childless as they were, he had also given some little comfort to her motherly instincts. But he couldn't say those things. She would either fail to understand or refuse to believe him and it would make her more distressed than she already was.

'I'm sorry, Dora, but there's nothing I can do,' he said.

'What do you mean, there's nothing you can do? You can go after him and bring him back.'

'He is a free man, Dora, not a pet dog.'

Dora continued to plead for the impossible while McKenzie, doing his best, alternated between annoyance and sympathy. It was going to take time for her to see it and accept it. She argued for half an hour.

'I'll write to the Agents in Bari and get a good replacement,' McKenzie said. 'A boy.'

He knew that no replacement would satisfy her easily. The best that he could hope for was that the boy might be a smiling, genial half-wit.

In the kitchen as she waited, Lilly felt a little excitement at the news of the four men going on the track, especially that Harry was one of them. It gave her a curious sense of joy in knowing that someone as lowly could turn his back on his conditions and simply walk away without so much as bothering to raise his fingers to his nose. Not that he was likely to be any better off wherever he was going. He would still be only a rouseabout. But it was the idea of it. A gesture against subservience. Men were lucky. Women couldn't just pick up their bag and go if they felt like it. Women were different. They had nowhere to go. All the same, it was good to glow in the reflection of men who could. It was only a little sad that the homestead wasn't going to be quite the same without Harry's grinning face coming into the kitchen with the wood.

She heard a door slam, footsteps, and Dora swept in with anger and unhappiness. 'Have I not always been kind to him, Lilly?' she asked, 'Have I not?'

For a moment, Lilly was not quite sure which man she was talking about but since it was highly unlikely her mistress would ever have brought up Mr McKenzie in such a way to her, she decided it had to be Harry.

'You has, Mrs McKenzie.'

'I could kill those people. Kill them. God knows how he'll end in their company.'

But for all that was said by everyone on Albert Downs on that day, Harry had judged their reactions correctly. Not one had the slightest suspicion that the greatest cattle theft the Colony had ever known was under way only twenty odd miles to the west.

Not only Purdy and Spence but Bluey, too, were surprised by Harry on that first day out from the secret gully. To them, it didn't matter if some cattle got away. What was a hundred? Two hundred? There were enough. More than enough. Another half dozen hands would not have been too many to hold the great mob together. But Harry was having none of it. So desperate was he not to lose as much as one single head that what they saw was a man obsessed. Three times he had quickly changed his foaming horses, himself soaked in sweat that turned to trickling mud with dust as he continued to ride like a demon to contain attempted breaks.

Once, as he turned a big yearling at full gallop, forcing its head round, leaning hard, a horn ripped his trouser leg from ankle to knee, leaving a long, raw weal on his flesh. Several times, Bluey thought he was going to kill himself. But no instructions or cries for help had once passed Harry's lips.

In truth, Harry was a very anxious man. Having taken his new direction in life, he was aware of how easily he could have allowed himself to slip into failure. It was his sole responsibility to make it all work and see their necks safe. Above all, he had to prove to himself that he could do it. He also sensed that if he eased for a moment, the others might start to give up and half the mob would have been lost. As it was, Purdy and Spence were going about it half-heartedly but in the brief moments when he careered past them he said nothing. He was determined that, by nightfall, he was going to have every beast he started out with. And every moment he got a chance clear of the cloud of dust, he glanced towards the east with his other anxiety. But there was no McKenzie, Hill or Murray or anyone else riding across the open country to come and arrest them.

There were to be no smiles or cheerful encouragement from Harry on that day, simply a temporary feeling of relief when the sun finally sank over the horizon and the big mob began to settle for the night, every single head still with them. But relief did not mean rest.

'I'll take first turn,' he told them and stayed in the saddle while Bluey began to scratch around for enough to make a fire. Purdy and Spence unsaddled their mounts, hobbled them, then sat on the ground to do nothing.

'I bet they bloody jump on 'im,' Purdy predicted pessimistically as he watched Harry ride off to start ringing the great mob, talking loudly to make a noise as he went.

'He's gone outer his bloody cobra,' Spence said.

Harry had heard all about caring for a mob at night and was well aware of the dangers. Anything could give them a fright and make them jump, even a bird, particularly while they were still fresh. If they jumped, they would scatter in all directions into the night in terror and it might take another week to find them and muster them all together again. Riding round them continuously throughout the night, shouting, making noises or singing, let them know there was still someone there. And riding round meant all the way round and not just part of the way to turn back. If the rider left a gap in his circle, there were cattle who would quickly wake up to it and start to make their way out through it.

On his second time around, Bluey walked out to him with a quart-pot of sweet, black tea and handed it up. Harry sipped at it gratefully and sensed the nervousness in his friend.

'It'll be a lot easier termorrer, mate,' he said. That was true, too. The first day was always the worst. After a week, the mob would settle to go wherever they were pushed. After two weeks, nights would be easier, too.

After Harry had ringed for just over three hours, he shook Bluey awake to take his turn, then took the opportunity of getting some food, putting tar on his wounded leg and roughly stitching up his torn trouser leg in the fire light. Finally, he lay down. But exhausted as he was, sleep would not come and he listened to Bluey sing an Irish song he had never heard him sing before. It sounded sad. He turned his head and looked at Purdy and Spence who were out dead to it. They had disappointed him but he couldn't complain. He had chosen them. There were better men but it would have been far too much of a risk to have approached them. He wondered what they might be saying at Albert Downs and worried that he might have raised any suspicion. After six years of being his home, he had felt a little wrench at having to leave it. She was a good woman at heart, Mrs McKenzie. He would miss her in a way. The only thing he felt good about was that neither Purdy nor Spence nor even Bluey had raised the subject of where they might be going. It had been enough for them to think about in getting the mob together and trying to get clear. They were far from clear yet. One step at a time. He would just have to handle it as best he could when it eventually came into their minds.

He looked at his stars, and began to feel a strange remoteness, everything far away. Like a dream. Watching himself lying there from somewhere else. Who was he? Where was he? Why was he? The answers were unreachable. For a while he drifted, his only contact with the reality of the world the faint sound of Bluey's voice. Then he slept.

Darkness still surrounded them as they saddled up, ready to try and take control of the great herd as it moved off at first light.

'We keep 'em goin' as far west as we can,' Harry said, and no one questioned him because it made sense at that point. It meant keeping clear of any out-station that might have been set up on any other cattle run further south, thereby avoiding any risk of being sighted.

The second day was a bit less difficult than the first as Harry had hoped and, at the end of it, the great herd was still intact. And there was still no sign of anyone coming after them. But a jump in the night was still an enormous worry. It didn't happen. A shock came only with another dawn.

Bluey mounted, turned his horse, looked towards the mob, stopped and stared. To anyone else it may simply have looked like a small, indistinguishable blob of lightness.

'Holy Mot'er of Jasus!' he exclaimed, 'it's a ghost!' And, a superstitious man, he at first fully believed it. Harry, Purdy and Spence rose in their stirrups to follow his frightened gaze. The blob was unmistakable. There, amongst the great herd of spread out cattle stood the big white bull. For a full minute of disbelief, no one said a word. It was Purdy who first found his voice.

'That ain't no bloody ghost but the bastard's goin' ter give us away.' And he pushed his horse forward as he pulled his rifle out of his sheath.

'Shoot it an' I'll kill yez,' Harry said quietly without moving. But such was the strength and sharpness behind his words that they sounded like no idle threat and Purdy pulled up to turn and face him. Spence glanced anxiously towards his mate to see what he was going to do. Purdy had to say something. He did.

'You talkin' ter me, Harry?' he said with the advantage of the rifle in his hand. Bluey felt the tension gripping at his throat, tried to swallow and couldn't. He sat perfectly still, afraid that if he moved a muscle it could be disastrous. It only needed Harry to take up the challenge and he might end with a bullet in him.

For the first time in two days, Harry grinned. His voice, too, was friendly and relaxed.

'It ain't no big problem, Jack. I'll spend ther day drivin' it back if you reckon yer can hold the mob tergether.'

Purdy and Spence exchanged quick glances and silently agreed it was far too soon to put the rouseabout back in his rightful place. Apart from that, they were both becoming a little worried about Harry. He wasn't quite the simpleton they had taken him for and seemed to know a bit more about handling cattle thanhe had ever let on. There was a streak in him that needed a bit more careful measuring up.

'Me an' Dan can hold any mob tergether we bloody want,' Purdy boasted, and the dangerous moment had passed.

Harry cut out the big white bull from the herd without any trouble and, with only a water bag in the way of provisions, started to push the bull back towards the north-east.

Bluey, Purdy and Spence knew that giving the big herd room to graze and contain them like that without trying to push them on was as much as they were going to be able to do. And Purdy, put in a position where his boast was going to be a great embarrassment to him if he lost any, worked a lot harder.

The westering sun lowered without any signs of Harry's return and their apprehension rose with the coming of dark.

'He's gone an' bloody lost i'self,' Purdy said, but

Spence had a much more serious suggestion.

'Or got i'self bloody caught.'

That raised another disturbance in Purdy and he turned angrily on Bluey. 'If he's caught, the bastard'll turn bloody dog on us. You know he ain't got no guts.'

'Harry wouldn't turn dog on nobody,' Bluey said, 'an' if he got caught or got lost or speared by blacks I'd know about it. I'd feel it in me bones.' If it was an unholy lie, he could only hope on hope that it might turn out to be the truth. Saints Patrick and Christopher, help us.

A nervous and worried Bluey started off on the first night watch. After each time around the mob, he rode in close to the fire, praying for the sight of a yellow beard but Harry wasn't there.

Two hours later, he rode to the fire yet again and this time dismounted to talk in the hope of getting some comfort. But before he could say anything, Purdy and Spence were suddenly getting to their feet and looking behind them. Hearing someone coming, they grabbed the reins of their mounts, ready to take off on them, then stopped in relief as a tired looking Harry rode into the firelight. The sheepish looking expression on his face didn't mean anything to them. Bluey smiled almost ear to ear at the sight of him.

'Everyt'in all right, t'en, Harry?' he said, trying to sound casual but hardly able to conceal his overwhelming joy.

'Didn't sight a single soul all day,' Harry said, swinging himself to the ground. It was then that it walked into the light behind him and Bluey nearly jumped right out of his skin. Purdy and Spence stared open mouthed. The big white bull, its nose ring gleaming red and shiny in the reflected light just stopped and stood there. Harry knew perfectly well it was behind him without having to look.

'I decided ter keep it,' he said.

It wasn't quite the truth. He had tried very hard to

get rid of it. But every time he had stopped to turn round and leave it, the big white bull had turned and come after him. It had been a battle of wills from dawn to dusk with only a truce around midday when they had shared the spotted shade of a tree for an hour's rest. But the bull had proved stronger than man and horse and had shown an indomitable spirit in refusing to surrender. The only solution in the end was to join forces. Purdy and Spence were still speechless and it was Bluey who first dragged his shattered composure together to find words.

'It's not human, Harry!'

'Course it ain't human, mate. It's a bloody bull, ain't it?'

Then Spence found voice. 'Stupid bloody animal!'

'The animal's got a name,' Harry said. 'I heard 'em say it at the railhead. It's called Lord Wallah Wallah Banjo. An' if nobody's ringin', I better do it.'

Half stunned they watched him as he drained a quart-pot of luke-warm tea to quench his thirst, remounted, and rode out towards the herd, the big white bull following.

He was pleased to get away from them so quickly. They'd be over the shock a bit by the time he had to get in to all the arguments. He could hear Bluey's already. 'It's bad luck, Harry, I's tellin' ye.' He would have to convince them that the bull wasn't the danger they thought it was. He had worked all that out. If McKenzie wasn't ever going to find the big mob, they were never going to find the bull either. As simple as that. And McKenzie was expecting it to die anyway. He could tell that by the looks on him. They wouldn't bother looking for the hide.

What Harry didn't know was that the bull was still insured under the policy taken out by the owners in London when they bought it and that even the hide, by way of evidence of its demise, might be needed to make the claim. A part of the dead beast was therefore just as financially valuable to the Drysdale Cattle Company as the whole, live one. No one had ever bothered to explain the strange logics of such an exotic trade as Insurance to Harry. The word itself was not included in a station-hand's vocabulary. But even if it had been explained to him, it would still have made no difference. The bull was determined to stay with them and Harry was just as determined that it was staying alive.

Rudd dismounted at the gate of the main house, unbuckled the mail bag from his saddle and handed it to Frank Murray. Since it was rare for any station-hand to ever receive a letter, none of them ever expected any. That didn't stop them taking an interest in it and anyone sent to the railhead to pick it up always took a look at them so he could tell the others who they were for. They were either for the McKenzies, Hill or Murray and sometimes the hands would take bets on how many there were for each. Whenever he got the chance, Jimmy Case always inspected the envelopes for himself, for no other reason than to satisfy himself that he had actually set eyes on other people's personal property.

'What's going on down the line, then?' Murray asked.

Rudd, a pleasant enough but rather dull man in most respects, didn't quite have the capacity for creating gossip out of nothing like many could, even after listening to Eddie Giraldi.

'Nothin',' he said, and at least it was the truth. All he was hoping was that a few bets might be on because there was a letter in the bag they would never guess in a dozen years. He glanced across the homestead. It looked empty. 'Where is everybody, Mr Murray?'

Murray had opened the bag and was going through the contents to see what was for himself. He was usually disappointed in what he got. Although he wrote regularly to his old college friends back in Brisbane about his difficulties in running a ten thousand square mile cattle run which was all of their substance, he wrote five to their one. There were only two for him, one from his parents and one from his sister.

'Mr Hill took most of them out to check up on the new bull,' he said dejectedly and looked at the last envelope with raised eyebrows. It was addressed to Miss Lillian Boyd.

Shortly afterwards in his tiny oven of an office, McKenzie, mopping sweat from his face, was looking at it with some surprise, too. The girl had never received a letter since she had been there and it was highly unusual for anyone to write to someone of her class. Not only someone, but the hand of an educated man: neater copperplate than his own. Initially it had been addressed to 'Galgeela Station' in Southern Queensland where she had previously been in service and forwarded. No doubt he would hear in time through his wife what the curiosity contained.

He had been avoiding Dora as much as possible of late during the day. Although he had Jim Hill put a station-hand to fill Harry's place until a replacement could be found, the woman had been full of complaint. The milkers were going off. The wood wasn't there. The tank on the meat safe hadn't been filled. What little cream there was refused to churn to butter. The tins for watering her dying vegetables were empty. And a dozen other things. As he suspected, when he checked up on the complaints for himself, most of them were entirely unjustified. Although she had not spoken his name again since the day after he left, 'HARRY. R.I.P.' might as well have been written all over the damned and cursed walls. Time would heal as it always did. He would just have to be patient. A few weeks and she would start to forget all about her idiot of a pet goat.

Lilly came in with tea for him and put it down on his desk. 'Mrs McKenzie says to tell yer, sir, she would er made scones but there's too many weevils in the flour an' it's got ter to be put out in the sun for a while first ter get rid of them.'

McKenzie decided to make no comment on the message. He simply held out the letter to her. Lilly just looked at it but made no attempt to take it. Stupid damned girl. What did she think he was offering her? Someone else's mail?

'It's for you, girl,' he said impatiently, almost poking her in the face with it, 'for you.'

Lilly took it and looked at it. It was even more of a mystery to her than it had been to Rudd, Murray and McKenzie. She hurried back to the kitchen, full of excitement.

'I got a letter, Mrs McKenzie,' she said. 'Look.'

'A letter? Who from?'

'I dunno. I dunno who would want ter write ter me. I don't know anybody.' And she stood there just holding it, looking at it as if half expecting that snakes might jump out of it if she did any more.

'Well, open it, girl, open it,' Dora said. Lilly opened it and read, Dora watching her, as curious as everyone else. Lilly started to turn pale at first and Dora thought for a moment the girl was going to faint.

'What is it, then? What is it?'

Lilly raised stunned eyes to her then collapsed on to the kitchen chair behind her without a word. Aunt Aggie? The name came to mind from away out of the past but there was no face to go with it. For years and years she had had private fantasies that something like this might happen to her but she had never truly believed that it ever would. They had been girlish daydreams. Now, suddenly, without any warning, she was holding them in her hand. Was this the kitchen? Was she really here? Was this really to her?

It was too much for Dora to stand there in front of the stupid girl and be left in ignorance. 'Can I see it?'

she said, which was more of a direction than a request, and Lilly held the letter out. Dora took it quickly before the girl had a chance to change her mind, but even as she touched it, she felt a sense of foreboding. She started to read. It was dated the 5th of January 1882, over two months before and was from Huggert and Huggert, a firm of Adelaide solicitors in the Colony of South Australia. Although written in the usual pompous, legal tone, Lilly had clearly understood it. So did Dora. In essence, it informed Miss Lillian Boyd that she had been named as a beneficiary in the Last Will and Testament of the late Mrs Agnes Thompson and requested her to contact them at the earliest opportunity so that the matter could be concluded to their mutual satisfaction. They also advised that it would be most desirable for her to provide proof of her identity.

Although she knew she shouldn't have been, Dora felt extremely annoyed on finishing it. It wasn't the impertinence or the sudden assault on the relationship of their status but the feeling of people being plucked away from her by outside forces that were beyond her control. At least this time she had been given a warning and she was going to fight. Appearances could be deceptive.

'Who was this woman?' she said, making woman sound like a harlot. 'You've never mentioned any Mrs Thompson before. I don't know if that was deliberate but I think I have the right to know.'

The initial shock in Lilly was beginning to be overtaken by excitement again and her words tumbled over each other as they tried to get out.

'I can hardly remember 'er. She said she was an aunt. Me Aunt Aggie. I'd never seen 'er before. I didn't know 'er. She came ter see us once in the Home when I was little. Maybe I was eight. Maybe before. She brought us a bag of lollies an' Miss Carey shared 'em out an' I only got one. An' she wrote to us sayin' how I had ter be a good girl an' say me prayers every night an' thank God for all 'is mercies. I remember that. But Miss Carey read it out ter us an' wouldn't let us keep the letter but took it away an' I forgot about it. I'd nearly forgot all about 'er. I haven't thought about 'er in years. I didn't even know 'er. I wanted ter have an aunt – anybody – back then, but I couldn't talk about 'er because people would want ter know about 'er an' there was nothin' I could tell 'em, not even where she lived an' it would make us look stupid or I was lyin'. A lot of the girls did that all the time, makin' people up, an' we would laugh at 'em.'

Dora had never heard Lilly come out with so many words before at the one time. And the charitable soul in her felt a little touched. That was quickly overcome. It was no time for sentimentality.

'I will not see you do anything foolish, Lilly,' she said, 'you will consider all this very, very carefully and I'll help you.'

There was no time to take the discussion further. A sudden commotion had broken out in the direction of the front door with McKenzie's voice shouting in anger. Dora hurried there but as she reached the hall, McKenzie swept past her as if she weren't there, on his way to fetch his spurs. Jim Hill stood there, sweaty and dusty, smelling strongly of horse, chewing over-fast on his quid of tobacco. Frank Murray stood behind him frowning.

'What's happened?' Dora asked, and Jim Hill stopped chewing just long enough to say it.

'The new bull.'

'What's the matter with it?'

This time, Frank Murray got in first. 'It isn't where they left it,' he said, 'and they can't find it.'

Hill threw him back a brief but hostile glance. Murray had made it sound as if it was all his fault and he didn't like it. Before Dora could ask any more, McKenzie reappeared, spurs in hand.

'You must all be damned well blind!' he shouted and headed straight past them out through the door, Hill and Murray after him. Dora followed to the gate, her head reeling from all that had happened so quickly. McKenzie stopped just long enough to say to her what he had to, 'Don't expect me back until at least two hours after dark.'

Torn between concern for her husband and the situation with Lilly and her astonishing letter, Dora stood and watched until the men finally rode off towards the north, then hurried back into the house.

Lilly was not in the kitchen and she called her but there was no answer. Neither was she in her little room. The only other place she could have been was outside in the dunny and Dora went halfway to it and called again. Sure enough, Lilly answered from inside it and there was nothing else Dora could do but to return to the house and wait.

It had been the only place Lilly could have gone to be undisturbed and she sat there fully clad reading the letter over and over again with joy, heedless of flies, of what the commotion had been about, and of time. Again, she heard an impatient Mrs McKenzie call from outside in pretence of wanting to know if she was all right, and again she answered. But she was secure there, locked in with the wooden bolt that slid across. What would she look like all dressed up in fine clothes? Nobody would know her. She would get soft, shiny shoes. A hat too. A big one with ribbons on it. People would look at her and wonder who she was. Miss Lillian Boyd, a woman of importance and means, that's who. It was all there beautifully written down.

Dora continued to spy out of the kitchen window. There was no reason for the silly girl to want to hide from her. How long was she going to be in there for heaven's sake? She should have tried to tell Don, even if he was so distressed. The bull would turn up. He wouldn't have listened. She would just have to wait until he got back. People were more important than animals. Was she going to stay in there all day? If only there were someone else she could talk to. The girl was in there making up her own mind, that's what she was doing. Making stupid, ill-considered decisions.

It was a long time before the dunny door opened and Lilly finally emerged. Dora came away from the window and made herself look busy. Lilly came in, looking happy Dora smiled at her.

'I have an idea,' she said. 'Clearly, your very good fortune would make it impossible for you to continue as housemaid but there is absolutely no reason why you shouldn't be my companion. And I would be quite prepared to do my share of the housework. I've had to go down on my knees before, you know, and am perfectly capable. It may even be that Mr McKenzie would be agreeable to employing another girl who could serve us both. In any case, you must stay safely here and not leap suddenly into a world you know little about. You're young, you have time. When you've found out exactly what your true situation is and had time to consider sensibly, then we can work out what is best for your future.'

Once, such a speech coming from Mrs McKenzie would have astounded Lilly, but she wasn't totally surprised by it. As she had already noted, the woman had been funny since Harry left. She'd said all that as if she were talking to a daughter but although Lilly had been starting to feel sorry for her, she didn't for a moment regard her mistress as any kind of foster mother. Or companion either. She had already decided what she was going to do. Leave as soon as possible, get to Adelaide and collect the inheritance before it dissolved into the hot air like all the rest of her dreams.

'Mrs McKenzie,' she began, but Dora was quick to stop her.

'I don't want you to say anything now, Lilly. Just sleep on it and we can talk about it tomorrow.' And she turned towards the cupboard, 'Now, what was it I was thinking of for dinner? It will be late tonight. That silly bull has wandered off somewhere and they're looking for it.'

As darkness fell around Cuff's Water-hole miles to the north, the searchers began to appear from different directions in pairs. A worried McKenzie and an unusually silent Frank Murray were the last to come in and McKenzie rode straight to Jim Hill who was standing waiting by his horse. There was hardly any need for him to ask. The Overseer's cud-chewing was answer enough. Although the cast had covered every likely grazing location within an area of almost three hundred square miles since Hill had first gone out with several hands early that morning, there had been no sign of the bull. McKenzie was in no mood to waste any more time by having fools going on searching day after day and telling him they couldn't find it. He was the one who was going to look the fool if he had to tell them in London. They might even sack him.

'Do you know a good tracker?' he said, and Hill nodded.

'I know somebody who . . .' Murray started to say.

'Shut up,' McKenzie said and turned to Hill again, 'Get him. And quick.'

'That might not be so easy, Don.'

'Don't tell me the obstacles! Just get him and bring him back! Promise him the damned moon if you like!'

The blacktracker Hill was thinking of he had never met but he had a reputation even amongst the blacks. Nicknamed 'Wooly', he belonged to a tribe that often camped near a water-hole just over a hundred miles to the north. But it would be luck if they happened to be around when he got there. And even if Wooly was with them, he might refuse to co-operate. Hill knew the police had used him once for a job and had wanted to keep him but Wooly hadn't liked them and deserted. There was no point in him trying to explain all that to the anxious McKenzie. It would have been a waste of breath.

Hill collected up the few supplies the hands had carried between them, selected one of them, then headed north into the dark while McKenzie, Murray and the others returned south towards the homestead.

Jimmy Case, greatly irritated at having no one to knock around since Harry's departure was delighted to hear that the bull was missing. 'I told yer, didn't I? I told yer. Dead in a bloody week. All bloody useless, the lot of 'em. Wouldn't know how ter tell the difference between a bull an' a bloody old cow if they didn't bloody turn it over.'

In the house, Dora listened to her husband's anxieties with sympathy and did her best to give comfort and provide the support he needed, patiently delaying any mention of the problems of her own. 'You're worrying far too much. With all that country out there, I really don't know how you expect to find one small animal in a single day. It will turn up. Perfectly safe and sound.'

It wasn't until they sat down for their very late dinner that Dora felt she could have his ear on any other subject.

'Lilly's been left money in a Will,' she said casually, and McKenzie looked surprised. 'It was in that letter. Some silly aunt she doesn't even remember.'

McKenzie had forgotten all about the strange letter, but if it had been of interest earlier on in the day, it had been overtaken by much more serious events.

'I wouldn't have believed she knew anyone with any money,' he said. 'I suppose she'll be going, then.'

The reaction he did not expect. Dora sprang to her feet in sudden anger. 'That's right, that's right!' she shouted at him, 'why don't you go, too. Just go, go on, why don't you leave me here all on my Godless own!' And she ran from the dining-room leaving McKenzie sitting there agape. His wife had been angry many times before but he had always been given warning. This explosive outburst had come as a complete shock to him. It was unlike her to lose her self control so easily. He had done nothing, said nothing to provoke it. Despite the worry clawing at his stomach over the bull, he had been patiently listening to what she had to say, been perfectly pleasant. He rose and took his wounded dignity to the bedroom where Dora was wiping her eyes by the lamplight in front of her mirror. It was a rare sight and he was moved by it. He loved her.

'What did I do to warrant that?' he said, 'I think at least you owe me an explanation.'

Dora pulled herself together and turned to face him.

'I don't want her to leave. It would be stupid for her to go.'

Lilly. He hadn't realised she had such a strong affection for the girl. He'd been mistaken. Or perhaps he hadn't. Perhaps it was Harry that was still troubling her. Loneliness was at the heart of it.

'If it's what the girl wants to do, I don't see how I can stop her.'

'You could at least look at the letter and talk to her. Put some sense into her head.'

'All right, I'll talk to her in the morning before I go. We'll have to keep on looking for the bull until Jim gets back with the blacktracker.'

Peace and dignities restored, they left the rest of their meal, put out the lamp, undressed, and got into bed where McKenzie started to make love to her.

In the morning, Lilly was surprised when he walked into the kitchen and she rose from lighting the stove. It was one part of the house where he never went. And he was up unusually early, too.

'I believe you've had news of good fortune, Lilly,' he

said. 'Can I see it?'

Lilly hesitated, wondering why, but then saw no harm in it. It should be natural that even Mr McKenzie was interested in such great luck. Everybody on the homestead was talking about it in amazement and, within a week, half of Central Queensland would know. The bush telegraph which consisted of no more than mouths and horses' hoofs to carry them, thrived on such goings on. She turned away, took the letter from inside her clothing and handed it to him, smiling. It was limp from being next to her skin and refolded so many times it already looked aged.

Just outside the doorway, unseen, Dora waited in hope, able to hear clearly every word that would be said.

McKenzie read. He was no stranger to legal documents and it often irked him that solicitors' communications were always couched in vagueness and ambiguity as if in terror that someone might sue them for clarity. As he suspected, there was no indication as to the extent of the legacy. Not as much as a hint.

'How wealthy was this woman?' he asked.

'I dunno, sir, but she must er had somethin', otherwise she wouldn't er made a Will, would she?'

McKenzie threw her a brief glance. That was clever of her. Poor people didn't make them. But another question came to his mind.

'If she saw fit to remember you like this and had the means, why didn't she adopt you?'

Lilly had no answer to that and hadn't thought about it, but it made her feel uneasy. What was Mr McKenzie trying to do to her? Tell her it wasn't true? Destroy her dreams? She resented him. Think. Quickly. Tell him something to restore it all. Anything.

'She said she would er done, but that her husband didn't like children,' she said, and the sense of being back in the orphanage flooded over her. There, she had often been forced to come out with such lies, either to survive or avoid punishment. But because she hadn't had to do it since, she blushed, and heard McKenzie speak again.

'You realise it doesn't say how much.'

Although the words were straightforward enough, Lilly thought there was an inference in them. Did he think she was an idiot? Of course she knew it didn't say how much. She'd read it a thousand times.

'I don't care,' she said.

'Well, you'd better find out. The thing to do is write back. I know how to put it to them. I'll help you compose it if you like.'

Fear as well as anger rose in Lilly. 'No, sir, I'll not be writin', I'll be goin'.'

Her stubborn stance and impudent attitude was something McKenzie wouldn't tolerate even in his Overseers, never mind a servant girl and his voice rose in authority.

'It might be as little as a hundred pounds, you stupid girl!'

But Lilly wasn't going to be trapped. They were only trying to keep her down and in her place without a penny and she knew it.

'A hundred pounds? With a hundred pounds I could buy a hat shop.'

Dora, unable to contain herself a moment longer, swept in through the doorway. 'What do you know about making hats, Lilly?'

Lilly, angrier than ever, overflowing, surrounded, turned on her.

'You just don't want me ter be a lady like yerself, do yer?' she shouted, then pushed past her to run to her little room.

McKenzie and Dora stood for a few moments in silence and failure, not looking at each other.

'You'll have to let her go,' McKenzie said finally and,

without another word, Dora turned and walked out.

McKenzie stood despairing of cursed, damned women. There he was, three hands and a rouseabout short, a five hundred guinea English bull missing or dead, his reputation as a good Manager and perhaps even his job at stake, a hard day's riding ahead of him in insufferable heat with filthy flies crawling all over his face and whiskers, and it looked like he wasn't even going to get his breakfast. Damn them all to bloody hell!

Four

In clear, bright, hot air under a cloudless, blue sky, the big white bull scrambled up over one of an endless landscape of ridges that ran a tortured but roughly parallel course towards the west. Within a day of joining Harry and his great mob of cattle, it had taken over as their unchallenged leader. And after a week, the huge herd had settled down. No longer did any of them try to break away and the droving began to become much easier. Whichever way the big white bull was pointed, the spread out river of beasts that were pushed along followed. Only at night in fear of a jump did the tension for Harry run as high and when he wasn't ringing himself, his sleep was light.

He sat astride his horse on another ridge alone, his stock-whip coiled over his arm, hat well down over his eyes, scanning the horizon towards the east and north for the slightest movement. There was nothing and he grinned to himself with satisfaction. They were getting clear. In the past two days, Bluey hadn't mentioned the looped rope dangling over their heads once. He tried to visualise the reaction at Albert Downs when they went to check up on the bull which he knew they would do. He felt a little sorry and sad as he saw them searching fruitlessly under every Gidgee and Coolibah tree over hundreds of square miles for what was left of its carcass. It would have been good to let them know it was still alive and as game as a pebble but he couldn't. It wasn't his fault. The bull had chosen for itself where it wanted to be and he hadn't believed Bluey either when he'd said: 'T'e devil's walkin' back to England, t'at's what it's doin', an' begod, will it not be walkin' right across t'e ocean an' makin' a mockery of t'e Holy Mot'er's own son.'

But despite the Irishman's superstition, Harry knew that, secretly, his mate was starting to admire it, bad luck or not. Jack Purdy and Dan Spence were another matter. They had hardly spoken to him since the night he had come back with it and were keeping very much to themselves. Because it was hard to know what they were thinking, he kept a close, surreptitious eye on them. He turned his horse and pushed it on down the ridge to catch up again, eventually coming up alongside Bluey on the left flank of the great mob, cracking his whip.

'Let 'em take it easy, mate,' he said, 'the feed's gettin' thinner.'

Bluey stopped his whip and coiled it. He'd been aware of the gradual change taking place in his friend. There was a growing confidence in him and as he relaxed more and more, an added glow of happiness coming from him. He was also starting to act more like boss drover, with the occasional suggestion starting to sound more like the occasional instruction. He didn't mind that at all and was even beginning to appreciate Harry's concern for the welfare of the mob and keeping them in good condition, but he knew Purdy and Spence didn't like it. Harry was only a rouseabout. The Siamese Twins were supposed to be experienced drovers. And they weren't the only ones who were getting worried about going further and further west.

'I'd like te know where we is, Harry,' Bluey said.

'West and well clear of Albert Downs, mate, an' safe as drunks in Mary Brady's deadhouse.'

Harry had heard someone say that once and liked it. He knew what a deadhouse was, the straw covered room kept by some publicans into which the drunks were thrown to sleep it off for the night, but he didn't know where Mary Brady's was. Bluey still worried.

'You ever heard of t'is country, t'en?'

'I heard it mentioned, but I didn't know it gets in flood. It must look like a sea with thousands er islands.'

'An' what makes ye t'ink it gets in flood?'

'I can see it does, mate. Every few years or so, I reckon, except in bad drought times.'

Bluey looked around. There were patches of grasses and low, hard shrubs on the higher ground and certainly, up until then, they'd been lucky in coming across surface water lying in pools in some of the channels but that was all. He took off his hat to wipe the sweat running from his brow, puzzled as to what Harry could see that he couldn't, but before he could ask for an explanation, Harry swung his horse to go back towards the stragglers to start pushing them gently up into the main herd. Bluey watched him from a distance. There was something his friend was hiding but he didn't know what and he didn't know why. There seemed to be no reason in keeping anything from him.

Away across on the other flank of the herd, Jack Purdy and Dan Spence were in a quandary. Although they had a rough idea of how far they had gone from Albert Downs homestead and in which direction, for all intents and purposes they were lost. They had never heard of this strange country before and were feeling very uneasy about keeping going further west. Worse, Harry was starting to take over and no bloody wood and water joey was going to tell *them* what to do. The problem was that the big mob needed all of them to keep it moving.

Spence rode back to Purdy to talk to him for a few minutes.

'It's a bloody long roundabout way of gettin' ter New South Wales, isn't it, Jack?' he said.

'Yeah, but it ain't time yet. If you can put up with the giggle-headed bastard a bit longer, so can I.'

The destination of New South Wales had been a perfectly reasonable assumption from the beginning. So much so, there had been no need to even mention it. It was either that or Southern Queensland. There was nowhere else except the Colony of Victoria and neither Purdy nor Spence saw any need to go that far. New South Wales would be safe enough. No one was likely to know the Albert Downs brand away down there. Only the big white bull would raise suspicion and there would be plenty of opportunity to put a bullet between its eyes long before.

'Not too much bloody longer,' Spence said, and rode back towards the head where the big white bull, right out in front, scrambled up another ridge.

Left with no alternative but to accept Lilly's decision, Dora became determined that at least the girl would never have any reason to speak ill of her and might even return. She lent her thirty shillings in case she should run short on her long journey and with Rudd driving the buggy, even accompanied her all the way to the railhead and saw her safely on the train.

'Remember, I'd still like you to become my companion, Lilly,' were her last words. Lilly had simply nodded and smiled her thanks and the carriage had pulled away to leave her standing alone in the heat.

It was an unhappy Dora who returned to Albert Downs homestead and even before Rudd pulled up to let her alight, she saw the black squatted on his haunches outside her gate. He was naked but for a pair of ragged, tartan trousers and held a spear and a throwing stick. His dark, half-matted hair turned to a golden brown at its ends. He was perfectly still, didn't look up at the arrivals and made no attempt at brushing away the few flies that crawled over his wide nose and cheeks. As Dora got down, McKenzie, Hill and Murray came out of the house. McKenzie was very relieved and pleased to see his wife back safely but it was as well she knew it because he gave little indication of it. He went to her and stopped long enough to say, 'Old Charley's agreed to help out for a while. He's inside. He'll make you a cup of tea and fetch water for a bath.'

Old Charley? She had no intention of asking any such thing of the mysterious book-keeper. She would make her own tea and carry her own water, thank you very much. Tired, solemn faced, she made her way into the house with her travelling bag.

McKenzie, Hill and Murray stood over the squatted Wooly.

'Boss McKenzie, Albert Downs,' Hill said to him, and Wooly glanced up at the whiskered white chief before rising to his feet.

'Me pella call 'im Wooly, boss,' he said, and McKenzie looked him over. He wasn't quite sure whether it was a hint of intelligence in the blacktracker's eyes, or whether it was a touch of impudence. That didn't matter for the moment, he needed him.

'Mr Hill's told you I want to find a big white bull,' he said, 'and if you find it I'll give you plenty flour, plenty tea, plenty sugar.'

'Pella Wooly findim pella bull, boss.'

Wooly was led first to a bare corner of the horse paddock where the big white bull had been fond of standing while it had been there. With no rain or dust storm in the interim, Wooly squatted by the tangle of marks that had been left there and looked around, picking them out from others, reading an ancient language that few men could master.

The sun was lowering and Jim Hill was tired, dirty and hungry. 'I'll take him out in the morning, Don,' he said, but his hope lasted only a second as McKenzie flared up.

'You'll take him out as soon as you've had something to eat so he'll be ready to start at first light.'

'I'll do it,' Murray said, but McKenzie completely ignored him and turned away to walk back towards the house.

Hill had his meal and Wooly was fed, too, before they both headed out into the darkness, Hill mounted, Wooly, spear and stick in hand, trotting behind him.

In the house, McKenzie and Dora sat down to a meal that was almost inedible. She could have cooked it herself but decided that a little suffering might help to make a point and let old Charley do it. As she chewed her way through it she kept glancing at Don, waiting for angry complaints but as he knew that was just the opening she wanted, he dared make no comment. There was no milk, either. The milkers had gone right off and weren't producing half a bucket between them. They chewed in silence, and to help it down, McKenzie drank a glass of warm water that had been put by his place.

The bull was an overwhelming worry to him. If he wrote to London, it might be premature. If he left it too long he might be accused of deliberate delay. And as the insurance coverage only lasted another two months, it could all be very awkward. It seemed that whatever he did he was in trouble.

Hill woke in the dawn at Cuff's Water-hole and saw the blacktracker squatted under a tree some good distance off. The Gidgee wood he had used to make a fire the night before was still red hot and he rose to stir it up for making tea. He was lucky to have found the black at all and luckier still that he had shown willing. He'd been stupid to admit he knew of one in the first place. A man could bring trouble down on his head by just opening his mouth. Even just bloody nodding. He gave Wooly sweet, black tea and flour cakes fried in fat.

'Pella Wooly tinkum good tucker, boss,' Wooly said and Hill walked back to the fire to have his own without saying anything at all.

As the sun burst over the east, Wooly began circling out, his eyes never leaving the ground while Hill rode behind him watching. Every now and then, the black-tracker would stop, squat, rise again and go on.

The heat was scorching and it was near midday when on a cast about five miles to the west of the Water-hole, Wooly, down on one of his squats, turned his head to grin back up at Hill.

'Bull, boss,' he said, and Hill dismounted to come and look. He could just make out parts of tracks on a patch of hard, red clay but they could have been anything.

'Are you sure?' he said.

'Big bull, boss.'

Wooly rose, eyes on the ground, and walked on towards the west while Hill remounted to follow.

It was three o'clock in the morning when both McKenzie and Dora awoke with the pounding on the door. McKenzie rose, lit a lamp, hurried with it in his nightshirt and opened it. Jim Hill was standing there in his big bushy moustache, chewing fast. He put his quid to his cheek to speak but hesitated. He had already decided the best way of putting it but now he wasn't so sure. Best to leave the bull to the last.

'Cattle duffers, Don,' he said, and saw the lamp-lighted shock on McKenzie's face.

'How? Where?'

'A gully about twenty miles west they fenced off as a holding paddock.'

My God! As if things weren't bad enough already!

'How many?'

'Hard to tell. The blacktracker can only say "plurry plurry plenty" but there's got to be a few hundred.'

In all his experience as Overseer and Manager on Queensland cattle runs, McKenzie had never had cattle stolen from him before. Dora, a dressing-gown over, appeared behind but he didn't see her. Only his mind spun, and the thought suddenly struck him.

'What were you doing twenty miles west?'

'Tracking the bull.'

'Did you find it?'

Again Hill hesitated. Holy Christ. Don would blow up like a Chinaman's New Year. But it had to be.

'The blacktracker reckons it went with them.'

Instead of blowing up, McKenzie just froze and went pale between his whiskers. For a few moments, the only sound was that of a mosquito and Hill chewing. Then he burst.

'In the name of God! Am I surrounded by bloody idiots! Get a hand ready to ride to the railhead with a message for the police!' And he turned, almost pushing Dora out of the way as he hurried to his little office to get pen to paper, Dora after him.

'How dare you swear like that in my presence,' she said, but the chastisement went well over his head and he put the lamp down to start writing, addressing it to 'The Officer in Charge, Police Station, Bari.'

As Hill had already done, it was simple to put two and two together. The men who had supposedly left their jobs to go on the track were the only ones who could have been responsible. McKenzie muttered to himself in anger as he scratched out his message.

'Gully rakers. Blackguards. Cursed, damned thieves. What the hell were their names? Purdy. Spence. McGuirk. And God-damned Harry. Walford.'

Dora, her ears assaulted yet again with swearing,

could only stare at him in astonishment for another reason.

'Harry? Harry is with them?'

'Of course he's with them, woman. And, by God, they'll pay for this when we catch them.'

Dora felt a sudden chill of horror come over her. She knew Harry. He was a pure and honest man. He would never have allowed himself to become involved with thieves unless it had been against his will. Under threat of death. Other men were suspected of having been shot by companions in the back-blocks of the Colonies but, in the great vastness, their bodies were rarely found. There was absolutely no doubt in her mind that Harry was an innocent. A child that the men had taken advantage of simply to use. When his use was over, they would kill him, his body left to wild dogs and meat ants.

'You must find them quickly,' she said, 'Harry had nothing to do with it.'

There was no need to shout on Albert Downs homestead for news to get around quickly. Within half an hour, everyone there, in various states of undress, stood around in the dark outside the huts watching Rudd ride out towards the railhead and Eddie Giraldi's Telegraph Office.

Jimmy Case was annoyed that he'd been the last to know. 'It couldn't er been them,' he said, 'couldn't er been. If it'd been them, I'd er bloody known about it.' But others were prepared to argue with him.

'If it wasn't them, who bloody was it, then?' a hand said. 'An' Murray's looked in the tack room an' says there's a bloody pack saddle missin'.'

Carrying a lantern, Frank Murray went in and out of huts looking for any evidence he could find, angry that it had been Jim Hill and the black who had made the important discovery and not himself. Eager to add something to it and have his name involved, he became frustrated in not being able to find anything more and swore that with only two lead swingers, an Irishman and an idiot involved, there had to be a wider conspiracy. He glared at every hand he passed on his search as a suspect.

Old Charley stood in his bare feet, trousers and unbuttoned shirt outside his book-hole, holding a lantern. He could hardly believe that Harry had been drawn into such a bold plan and felt a tinge of pleasure. It couldn't have been an easy decision for him to have made, throwing in his hand with cattle duffers. Outrageous as it was, it still took courage. He had suspected all along that there was a suppressed spirit in the man and, although he feared for him, he believed that if he were to be caught, he would face his punishment without complaint, seeing it as fair. He may have wept over other things but never over justice. What mattered most was that, for good or for evil, for better or for worse, influenced by others or not, Harry had at last come out from under his shelter of humbling servility and lifted his head to his destiny.

No one asked the book-keeper for his thoughts and even had they done so, he would not have given them. They would not have understood. While the heated arguments continued around the huts, he retired inside with his lantern to have a drink.

For McKenzie, Hill and Murray, the night was over, but it was a distressed Dora who lit the stove and made them tea. Harry was in great danger and no one but herself seemed to realise it. They didn't even want to listen to her. As far as they were concerned, four men had turned cattle thieves, had stolen their silly, precious white bull, and Harry was one of them. It was ridiculous. Madness to believe such a thing of him. Don's anger had blinded him to the truth. Made him deaf. Well, she would force him to see. He simply had to be brought to his senses.

In the lamplit dining-room, McKenzie paced, Hill

and Murray sitting watching him. What in the hell was he going to say to them in London now? He would have to put it off in the hope that they would be caught quickly and the bull and cattle retrieved.

'You must have been walking around with your damned eyes shut not to have noticed they were up to this!' he said, and suddenly remembered Dora questioning him on Harry's tiredness. No damned wonder. They had him out every night helping them, that was why. He threw the memory behind him before it could be detected in his eyes and Dora, stiff-faced, came in with the tea, but deliberately without milk. Hill and Murray courteously stood and as she put the tray down on the table, she heard her pacing husband say, 'You realise that theft is the only thing the damned bull isn't covered for in the policy! Every run in the Colony must know about it by now. They couldn't sell it anywhere. They've done this just to try and ruin me! Well, by God, we'll see who's going to be ruined. It's the end of a rope for all of them!'

Dora turned to Hill for a moment. 'I would prefer it, Jim, if you didn't spit in the house,' she said, then made her way out.

Hill looked embarrassed. He had never spat in the house and never had any intention of doing so. If he was chewing tobacco there and had to spit, he always went outside. The bloody woman knew that. She was just showing her displeasure with Don and trying to take it out on him. No woman talked like that to him and he would say so. He didn't. Instead, he kept his mouth shut and sat down again. Not so long ago, it had been quite good working on Albert Downs. If it hadn't been for the excessive heat, even pleasant. Life had been smooth and easy. Now, it was all turmoil and trouble, and as Head Overseer there was no way of avoiding being right in the middle of it. It was enough to make a peaceful man hang up his horse for good and find a job in a lolly shop.

'Don't worry, Don, we'll get them,' Murray said, and poured the tea.

It wasn't until three hours later and the sun was up when Wooly walked back into the homestead. That he'd had to walk all through the night made no difference to McKenzie who had been waiting impatiently for him. He immediately directed that the blacktracker be fed and while Wooly was squatted outside eating, he approached him with Hill and Murray still in close attendance.

'Tell him,' he said to Hill, 'that I want him to go on tracking until he finds where the mob of cattle and big white bull have gone. Tell him I won't only give him a lot of flour, tea and sugar but new trousers just like the ones he's wearing.'

Wooly had observed this strange ritual amongst white men before where one boss directed another to repeat what he had said, as if he were deaf to one mouth but not another. It could only have had something to do with their Gods. But the thought of a brand new pair of tartan trousers made him grin widely. They were a treasure and gave him great importance. Even before Hill had finished speaking, Wooly was on his feet, still grinning.

'Him call 'im pella Wooly track 'im pella bull, boss,' he said.

'Tell him,' McKenzie said, 'that I'm going to give him letters in a pouch and that if he comes across any boss man on the way, he's to give one of them to him.'

Murray's face dropped in disappointment. 'Don't you want me to go with him, Don?'

'No, I don't want you to go with him. He'll be faster on his own and he can live where you could die.' And he turned to Hill again, 'And ask him if he can give a clearer indication of the size of the mob than just plurry plurry plenty plenty.'

Further instructed and asked the question, Wooly

began to understand. He looked around, spotted the wood-pile where for years Harry had chopped with his axe for the kitchen range and began to walk there, McKenzie, Hill and Murray following him in curiosity. At the wood-pile, the blacktracker put down his spear and throwing stick, scraped wood chips into a pile in both hands, moved to a clear patch of ground and scattered them. McKenzie stared. If the blacktracker was trying to tell them that was how many head there were, it was certainly more than a couple of hundred. He turned to Murray. 'Count them,' he said. But Murray had no faith in any black having such intelligence and tried to protest.

'He's only trying to say it was a big mob, Don.'

'Count them!'

Feeling he was being humiliated in front of a black, Murray was nevertheless forced to go down on one knee and start counting, scraping wood chips away with his hand as he went so as not to get mixed up, particularly as the patch contained bits of dead grass. Wooly backed away to squat on his own a few yards away while McKenzie and Hill watched Murray. Finally, the young Overseer rose to his feet.

'He's lying, Don, if he thinks there's this many.'

'How many?'

'If you mean wood chips, about a thousand.'

'A thousand!' McKenzie turned and stared at the blacktracker. He was squatted there looking as if he'd lost all further interest in the size of the mob he had been trying to express for them. In his time, McKenzie had seen aborigines do some surprising things but never anything like this. He had to make up his mind whether Wooly's display was simply a symbolic gesture or that he did actually have some idea of numbers. The pessimistic side of his nature made the decision for him.

'In the name of God,' he said in shock, and for the second time that morning, blood drained from his face.

Although Jim Hill was of the same opinion as Frank Murray, he was determined to play it safe and make no comment. It was left to Murray to try and give comfort.

'Four men couldn't have handled a thousand, Don. Three if you count Walford out. It's impossible.'

Impossible or not, McKenzie was believing it, and looked at his Overseers. 'Well don't just damned well stand there doing nothing!' And he jerked an arm towards the squatted Wooly, 'Get him after them! Now!'

Shortly afterwards, with the promise of new, plaid trousers as his spur, Wooly trotted off across the wide, hot landscape towards the west, carrying only his spear, throwing stick and a leather satchel containing four identical letters addressed 'To Whom It May Concern'. He would have no difficulty in picking up the tracks of the great mob of cattle and the big white bull. What had not been explained to him and what he was quite unaware of, was that he was also a messenger to bring four men to the gallows.

When he returned into the house, McKenzie felt a little better at the chase being under way and was confident that it would not last long. There were few places the blackguards could go. He found Dora cleaning and dusting like a servant girl, but she was still unhappily poker-faced and he went to her to give consolation. With no one else there to see, he put his arms to her to stop her working and held her.

'I know how difficult it is for you living here,' he said, 'but it won't be forever. And as soon as this damnable mess is sorted out, I intend to invite some of our friends to stay who can give some pleasurable company. Or, if you prefer, we can go down to Bari or even Brisbane for a while. You can see people and shop for clothes and other things you want.'

Normally, Dora glowed with delight when Don made such tender approaches and knew he was not so hard as he tried to make out to men. But this time, her arms did not respond, and her body stiffened, too, under his touch and she did not smile.

But it was not until a mostly silent dinner – some of it half-cooked, some of it cindered by old Charley – was well over and McKenzie retired to bed, that he realised the full extent of his wife's rejection. She wasn't there. It didn't take him long to search the house and he saw the chink of light under the door of what had been Lilly's tiny room. He opened it and saw Dora in the single bed, reading a book. She did not look up.

'What in the hell do you think you're doing?' he said, amazement all over him. Dora didn't remove her eyes from the page.

'Please do not swear.'

'Come to your bed like a decent woman!'

Dora knew only too well that it wasn't decent he was thinking about. When Don was under stress, he used her body simply to try to ease his pain and help him sleep, not to love.

'Not until you admit that Harry had nothing to do with it,' she said; the only one left still calling him by his Christian name. McKenzie struggled hard to hold his temper and tried for sympathy.

'I could lose my position over all this.'

'That's a much more comfortable circumstance that sordidly dying,' was all he got, and she didn't even lift her eyes to him for the giving. McKenzie stood burning. The preposterous woman had taken marriage vows to honour and obey. It was bloody sacrilege.

'I demand you come to your bed! Now!' But to that, Dora didn't answer and she heard him soundly curse her before striding out and slamming the door with such force that her bed shook.

Purdy and Spence had been becoming more afraid and discontent the further they went and their efforts at breaking Bluey's loyalty to the yellow bearded rouse-about had been difficult. Only when they got him to see that Harry didn't know where he was, or what he was doing, that they were all lost, going in the wrong direction and might never find a way out, did the Irishman start to waver to their side.

In truth, Bluey had been getting every bit as confused and anxious as they were, and even when Harry headed his big white bull and the huge mob towards the south, it didn't make any difference.

For a week they had been travelling over the searing heat of a reddish brown landscape of rocky ridges with occasional huge, rough outcrops with flat tops and Harry was behaving more like a real boss drover than ever, telling them all when to ease the great mob up, when to stop, when to move, sending them ahead to search for water and report on the state of the feed which was mostly saltbush but on which, Harry noted, the cattle appeared to be thriving.

Harry rode a happy man, his whip coiled over his arm. There was little need for it now. The big mob had become quiet and obedient and moved as they were bid. Even at night, the tension had gone and although he insisted that the riding round went on, there was less and less need for that, too. But it was with a false confidence that he no longer looked over his shoulder. A blacktracker far to the north-east on his trail didn't even cross his mind.

A worried looking Bluey rode up alongside him.

'Jack an' Dan says if we don't turn back east soon, we's never goin' te find a way out, Harry,' he said, but Harry just grinned at him.

'Don't listen to 'em, mate. This is gotter be the way.'

'T'e way to where, Harry, t'e way to where?'

'To safety, mate.'

'Begod, ye can't be safe an' dead all at t'e one time, Harry.'

Harry pointed to the big white bull away out ahead of the huge mob that was pouring slowly over a rocky slope. 'Look. He's in better condition than he was when we started. Stronger. We hayn't lost one single head an' nobody's dyin'.'

'T'ey's sayin' if we don't turn now, it'll be too bloody late.'

'They agreed ter go where I said before they come in, didn't they?'

Bluey knew there was going to be no shifting him and his confusion remained. Although he was almost certain that his friend didn't know what he was about, a little bit of his Irish imagination niggled at him that there might be something akin to magic going on. Some kind of 'little people' that only revealed themselves to Harry and were leading him. Harry had already amazed him several times. It was only that which kept his loyalty from breaking down completely. Bejasus, if you annoyed the 'little people', they could bring God knows what down on a man's head. Make it rain bloody snakes.

'T'ey's goin' te make trouble for ye, Harry,' he said, and for once saw Harry look worried himself.

'I know.'

It was trouble that was not too long in coming. By the end of the day, the rock began to turn to red sand. Ahead of them, they could see what looked like desert and the huge sandhills were not only red but crimson and black in the dying sun. Harry rode on ahead of the mob, then stopped to gaze on it. As his eyes moistened with emotion, he was pleased he was alone. It would have been difficult to explain why its splendour and magnificence moved him so. Had he been forced to try he might have said that here, he sensed, was somewhere on earth that was pure and untouched, uncorrupted ever since God had first created it and on which no man had left his mark.

It was the cracking of whips that brought him to and, puzzled, he swung his horse to start riding back at a canter. As he got closer, he could see Purdy and Spence turning the big white bull back through the head of the mob towards the east, the falls of their stock-whips cutting at the animal's hide. By the time he reached them, half the mob had turned.

'What d'er think yer doin'?' he said to them.

'We got an hour er light left an' we's takin' 'em east,' Purdy said, and Harry felt a fury rising in him he had never felt before.

'We's goin' where I say.'

Purdy had got himself worked up at the sight of the red sandhills and was angry at having allowed himself to be taken so far into country that could only end in the bleaching of his bones.

'We's goin' ter New South Wales an' you can go and crawl up yer jack,' Purdy said.

'It's what we says goes now, yer mad bastard,' Spence said in support, and Bluey rode into the affray to add his opinion.

'Listen to 'em, Harry. Yer can't go into t'at.'

The four stopped riding, circling, shouting at each other, Harry trying to point out that if they went into New South Wales they would only get caught and end as dead men and that they were breaking their agreement with him.

'You go an' perish on yer bloody own, it'll save us a bloody bullet!' Purdy shouted, and Spence laughed.

'We'll give yez a stupid bloody old cow so yez'll have one er yer own ter poke borak at.'

And they turned their backs on him to ride off again, cracking their whips. Bluey, not knowing what to do, watched Harry sit still on his horse for a moment. Well, not quite still as his whole body appeared to be trembling as he looked on the mob and the big white bull being taken away from him.

The suddenness of Harry's move took his friend by surprise. One minute he was there, the next his spurs were in and his horse jumped forwards in a leap as he went after them. He was still going at a full canter when he reached Purdy and he sprang at him from his saddle with the agility of a tiger, knocking him right over the other side to the ground. And there they rolled, fighting desperately. In moments, Spence was off his horse, too, to help his mate and Harry was fighting both of them like a man possessed.

Bluey, both amazed and held in fascination, at least had the presence of mind to grab Purdy's rifle from his saddle and squatted with it, looking on wide-eyed.

There were no rules to the battle, for battle was what it was. With Spence on his back, trying to choke him to death, Harry swung and kicked wildly at Purdy who was trying to butt him in the face. Then they were all rolling as one on the ground again over rock, sand and dust, wrestling, tearing and punching before finding their feet again, Purdy this time springing on Harry's back to try and hang on to his neck as he smashed at his head while Harry fought and struggled with Spence at his front. Crunching blow after crunching blow went in from both boot and fist but Harry fought like two men and they might have known both his strength and stamina from the things he did on Albert Downs and from the sheer determination he had shown not to lose a single head on their first few days out.

The squatted Bluey winced as if feeling the pain each time his friend was struck hard, and was quite unaware that his clenched fists were twitching at the air in symbolic participation against his foes.

It lasted a long while but once Purdy was down, blood spattered around his mouth, not to rise again for lack of breath, Spence, blood pouring from his nose, was soon to follow.

Bruised and battered, but with no signs of his own

blood running, Harry finished exhausted on his hands and knees. He stayed like that panting, looking on the two prone bodies in case they got up again, and when he was sure they wouldn't, he turned his head to see Bluey squatted there with admiration and found enough air with which to speak.

'Where were you, then?' he said.

'Begod, Harry, I never seen a greater fight in me life. If I'd joined in, begod I'd er missed it. An' did I not have to keep a tight hold on t'e gun in case t'ey used it?'

Bluey might have expected Harry to have been annoyed at that, but he wasn't and not at all surprised when he saw the yellow beard part into a grin from a swelling mouth.

'You still with us, then, mate?'

'I's wit' ye, Harry, I's wit' ye.'

Harry rose to his feet and went to stand between Purdy and Spence who were only a few yards apart, the hurt of their humiliation in defeat even greater than their pains which they were just beginning to feel with the cooling of their blood. Purdy managed to raise himself first and sat bowed over, eyes of anger on the ground.

'I's givin' yez enough supplies ter see yez through,' Harry said, 'then I wants yez ter go.'

Purdy and Spence didn't waste any time. Without having to say it to each other, both knew they had made a very big mistake in their estimation of Harry and didn't intend waiting around to make another one and although darkness was already on them, they mounted with their supplies and rode off to retrace their steps, shouting back when they felt safe enough to swear their intentions of vengeance.

Bluey found enough scrub with which to make a fire, but many of his worries had returned and a new one was now added.

'T'ere's only two of us, Harry, an' fifteen hundred

head. You sure we can handle t'em?'

'We've got to an' that's all there is to it.'

'An sout', Harry. Bejasus, t'ere can be nowhere sout'.'

'South Australia,' Harry said casually, and Bluey's mouth just fell open. It was the first time Harry had ever mentioned such an impossible idea and Holy Mot'er of God, was it not as well? He might have come from Ireland but he had been long enough in the Colonies to know there was no way from Queensland to South Australia, except by ship or along the coasts. Was all that Jimmy Case, the blacksmit', said about his friend true, t'en? Jasus, Mot'er an' Joseph help us.

'Harry,' he said when he found his voice, 't'ere isn't no way to Sout' Australia.' And Harry found yet another, sore smile of reassurance.

'There's gotter be, mate. There's been two good seasons back up there an' this is gotter be the way the water goes. An' water goes ter water. As long as the mob's alive, we is alive an' I don't intend ter see any of 'em dyin'. Nobody'll ever find us this way. Nobody'll ever know we went ter Adelaide because they don't know there's a way either. But we's goin' ter find one. So don't worry. An' remember yer said yer would trust us.'

'So I did, I did, Harry, so I did.'

The way Harry had put it sounded calm and reasonable, not the yabber of a man who had lost his mind. It made Bluey feel much better and, once again, he surrendered himself into the hands of his friend. Had he known what lay ahead of them and that a blacktracker sent by Albert Downs was in hot pursuit, covering the ground twice as fast as they had been able to, there is little doubt that he would have fled after Purdy and Spence right there and then while escape was still a possibility. But he was not to know.

In the morning, the big white bull walked out into the sandhills, the two men pushing up the great river of cattle behind it.

Five

It was late afternoon when McKenzie, accompanied by Hill, Murray and a group of station-hands, returned to Albert Downs homestead from his second visit to the gully into which the stolen mob had been mustered. He had gone in the hope that a more careful search might have revealed something they had previously missed. Not only was he desperate to get the bull and cattle back before he had to write to London, but to find some evidence that Walford had been a willing participant. The fool had said to him he knew cattle and it probably didn't take much for the damned thieves to talk him in to helping them. It was more than disappointing that no such evidence had come to light because until he could present it to his wife, his marriage was never going to return to normal. Despite all his pleadings, his patience, his tolerance and attempts at kindness, the damned woman would still not come back to her bed. Could she not see that his life was on the verge of ruins? No. She damned well couldn't!

As he approached the house, he saw her come out, and he dismounted for one of the hands to take his horse. Dora knew by his face he had nothing to offer her and as he reached the gate, she said, 'There's a Sergeant

Willis here from the Bari Police. He arrived over an hour ago and I put him in your office.' And she turned away to go back inside, leaving McKenzie to follow.

He found the travel-dusted Sergeant Willis sitting where he had been left. He was a hard-faced looking man with side whiskers and a scar on the left side of his chin which was highlighted by not having shaved on his ride from the railhead. He stood to shake hands but didn't smile.

'I got the first train out of Bari after I got your message, Mr McKenzie,' he said, 'and a search by the Native Mounted should already be under way to the south.'

McKenzie told him about the blacktracker and the letters but Willis showed no sign of being pleased by it. He didn't trust blacks and only ever used them when his Sub-Inspector ordered him to.

'He seems to think that, apart from our bull, they took a thousand head,' McKenzie said, and Willis stared at him in amazement. A theft of such numbers was unheard of anywhere, but McKenzie thought the Sergeant was due an explanation for not having been sent another message to that effect.

'At least, that might have been what they started with but they wouldn't have had them long. Of the four men, only one, the Irishman, was of any account and I'd be surprised if they were left with any more than two hundred after the first few days. The bull is a different matter since it was used to being led along on a rope.'

Willis didn't comment and it was only then that McKenzie noticed the surface of his desk. It had no signs of hospitality.

'Haven't you had tea?' he said.

'No, not yet. But I've spoken to your wife – or rather she spoke to me – and she seems to hold her own opinions on the criminals responsible.' McKenzie was embarrassed by that.

'We're shorthanded at the moment, and my wife has been under a lot of strain over it all. You mustn't listen to her. Excuse me,' he said, and went off to get old Charley to make tea, nursing his anger.

Dora was in the kitchen putting on what had been Lilly's apron, evidently intent on setting about the polishing of copper pots arrayed on the table in front of her. It infuriated him the way she kept doing things like that as if in self-imposed penance, and as old Charley had gone out to get water, he was able to speak freely.

'In God's name,' he said,'he's travelled the best part of a week to come here to try and help us. Why couldn't you have given him a cup of tea?'

Dora looked at him squarely and honestly.

'I'll tell you why,' she said, 'because there's a cruelty in that man's eyes like I've never seen and, believe me, I have seen some.'

'What absolute nonsense, woman!'

But there the discussion had to end as they heard old Charley return with the water. McKenzie waited just long enough for him to come in.

'We'd like some tea, Charley, please,' he said, and went.

He returned to his business with Willis who produced charge sheets for him to sign against the four men, and once that was done, the Sergeant sat back a little.

'Without doubt, they'll hang,' he said, 'all four of them.' And although there was no expression on his face, there was a sensual pleasure lying behind his words so strong that, for a few brief moments, McKenzie felt a disturbance in his soul, then dismissed it, and reached for written papers.

'My Overseers have written out reasonably accurate descriptions of them all,' he said, and handed them over. As Willis scanned them, old Charley came in with the tea and put it down and Willis raised his eyes to him. He didn't have to ask his name. At the railhead,

Eddie Giraldi who'd never had so much to talk about in his life since he'd tapped out the telegraph message Rudd had brought in, had told him the names of everyone on Albert Downs and what they looked like without him having to ask. And he knew all about the servant girl who had been left a fortune and had gone. He caught a whiff of drink.

'Where do you come from?' he said, and old Charley raised his eyebrows.

'Come from, sir? Why, here and there. Nowhere, really. I'm of no interest, I'm afraid.'

'You're wrong,' Willis said, 'the most interesting people come from nowhere. They have a lot to tell.'

Old Charley excused himself and went, Sergeant Willis's eyes following him out. It was a curious questioning, underlined with undoubted suspicion and McKenzie hurried to correct it.

'I'm sure old Charley hadn't the slightest knowledge of what was going on,' he said, and Willis turned to him.

'I didn't say he did, Mr McKenzie, but the man has things to hide all the same. I can always tell.'

McKenzie began to dislike the man, but not for the ridiculous and fanciful reason Dora had tried to give him. But damn it all, if he was going to waste time by trying to delve into every man's private business while the big white bull and his cattle were being taken further and further away from him, he wasn't going to be of much bloody use. Better employed out with the Mounted than damn well sitting here as if he owned the place. Thank God he'd found the tracker. His best hope was that the black met someone soon and that a message was got back to say where they were, or at least in which direction they were headed.

'How long will you be staying?' he said.

'A couple of days, Mr McKenzie. To look around, talk to your employees and make out my report.'

McKenzie decided there and then that it would be

best for the Sergeant to be put up with Jim Hill in his hut, and it was to be two of the most tortured and hard chewing days of Jim Hill's life. In the constant and questioning imprisonment of Sergeant Willis, he went through as much tobacco as he normally did in a month. It was bad enough having to go around with him during the day, and all the way out to the gully. At night, totally alone with him, the only solution was to get himself drunk as quickly as possible. And, unlike other men, when Hill drank, he spoke less and less, ending as silent as a long dead clam from which God himself could not have dragged a word.

'Mr Hill, the Head Overseer, obstructive.', Willis wrote in anger and frustration in his book. 'Does not appreciate the enormity of the crime that has been committed here. Suspect he may know more than the little he says. Would be well worthwhile questioning in the more appropriate surrounds of the Station at some future date.'

There was more desire than reason in the last sentence but had Hill seen it and known of Sergeant Willis's practices and pleasure in extracting information from suspects on his home ground, he would have had good reason to go looking for his lolly shop right then. As it was, when Willis finally rode away back towards the railhead, he was filled with the joy of overwhelming relief.

Little relief came to Don McKenzie as he scanned the horizon to both the west and the south in the hope of a message from the blacktracker. His time was beginning to run short. Sooner or later, despite the police request of wanting to keep the matter quiet for the sake of the good name of the Colony, at least until the men were caught and made an example of, the newspapers in Brisbane were going to hear of it. And if that happened, the news of the great cattle robbery that had taken place on Albert Downs might reach the ears of his employers in London before he had written. For that alone, they could condemn him for being utterly useless. Damn everyone who had got him into this mess to everlasting hell! And damn the Police Sergeant for upsetting Dora more than ever! Brushing flies angrily from his face, he turned back from the western edge of the homestead from where he had been looking in hope but in vain.

'Mr Murray!' he shouted as he walked, and Murray was hurrying to his side.

'Take a man and ride to Mount Evans,' McKenzie told him. 'Find out if they've heard anything there. And don't waste any time.'

Mount Evans was the northerly out-station to another cattle run and lay a bit over two hundred miles to the south. It consisted simply of a single small hut and some roughly made yards, but two or three men were usually based there.

Murray felt sure that if they'd heard anything at Mount Evans they would have sent someone up, but he didn't say so. He quickly chose a hand who was easy to handle and, within the hour, was heading south, pleased at having been given the job, and pleased, too, at the prospect of having Don off his back for a while.

There was nothing else McKenzie could think to do. If the Native Mounted Police were on the job, they still had an enormous amount of country to cover and they would take time. As he saw it, his whole life, his marriage, his reputation, his job, his future, lay in the hands of a bloody black in ragged trousers called Wooly and he didn't even know if he could trust him. He tried not to think of the black having given up, gone walkabout, and headed back north to his tribe.

Wooly had never had a dilemma in his life, but he had one now, and it was properly the white man's, not his. He struggled to think what the white man might want him to do and thoughts tumbled confusingly over in his head. A decision had to be made and his new tartan trousers were at stake. A lot of white men couldn't be trusted but he trusted the boss man of Albert Downs from his face. He had come a long way and had met no one to whom to give a letter and was now in a quandary as to what to do.

He squatted by the old fire where the men with the big white bull and the huge mob had camped, and where Harry had fought his battle with Purdy and Spence, gazing out into the scorching desert-like country of red sandhills. The tracks and droppings were still reasonably fresh, only a few days old, and led south over the horizon. And he knew by the signs he could see there, that there had been no rain in a very long while. What puzzled him was that although he himself would have been able to live in traversing such country, the white man and his beasts could not survive. Days without water and they would be dead.

It was the day before when he had reached this spot, but, curious about the tracks of two horses with the weight of men on their backs going away in the opposite direction, he followed them. For more than half a day he had done that, but as they kept on going roughly towards the north-east, he returned to the edge of the sandhills.

He rose, and for two hours tracked a small goanna to a hole, dug it out, caught it and killed it. Then he scraped enough vegetation together to make a fire and got it going by spinning a stick with great speed and skill between the palms of his hands, boring it down on to another. He roasted the goanna then ate it, again gazing towards the south. The boss Hill or the boss McKenzie hadn't told him what to do when he'd tracked down the big white bull. He couldn't bring it back to them. His meal finished, he found a likely depression in the ground nearby. Although there was not a single sign of any vegetation near it, he dug down with his hands.

In less than three feet, he came on some brackish, muddy water and drank. And the dilemma receded. With spear, throwing stick and satchel of letters, he headed back the hundreds of miles he had come, supported by the promise of his new tartan trousers. And his sweet, sweet sugar and flour, and his tea.

Harry and Bluey had been only twenty miles on from that camp when Wooly had squatted there and the blacktracker could have reached them in much less than a day. They were quite unaware that they had been followed, or that by having met no one on his way and turning back, their pursuer had given them a reprieve. As it was, things were bad enough for them.

Although Harry had found some useful feed for the herd amongst the sandhills in the way of what was an edible spinifex and occasional patches of saltbush, water had eluded him. And without water in that searing, dry heat, he, Bluey, the big white English bull and the great mob of cattle were all on the track of death. It would not be the first time white men tried like the more knowledgeable Wooly had, to dig in their final agonies of thirst, only to be found dead with the flesh of their fingers worn right through to the bone.

'We got to turn back, Harry,' Bluey said for the tenth time that day in the blistering heat, but Harry had simply directed him to let the big mob spread and forage for whatever they could find while he rode off ahead in search of water. And returned in silence.

During that night, Bluey awoke from an anxious and restless sleep and opened his eyes. Some good way off under the stars, he saw Harry, hatless, kneeling in prayer. Never had he seen his friend do such a thing before and it only made him feel more afraid. Not once had he ever doubted God, the Holy Mother, Holy Jesus, Joseph or any other of the religious hierarchy. What he doubted was Harry's relationship with them. Any of them. For himself, he felt he could not rightly ask for deliverance until he had confessed his sin to the proper authority and been given absolution. And he suspected that the theft of as many as fifteen hundred head of cattle, if not an English bull, might be considered more mortal than venial.

He turned his head away from the praying Harry and looked to the darkness of the sky. There was not a single cloud in sight. The only escape from such torture was the oblivion of sleep, and he closed his eyes to try and return to it.

At dawn, Harry stood with his saddled horse looking down on the curled up, sleeping figure. It wasn't easy for him to keep on reassuring his mate when his own anxiety was deepening, but he had made up his mind long before this that there was to be no turning back, either with the mob or without them. He was no more prepared to perish than Bluey was but the responsibility for keeping both themselves, the big white bull and the mob alive was his alone. He had to show confidence and keep on showing it.

Bluey woke, saw him standing there, and sat up, his mouth dry with thirst. Harry handed him his water bag. There wasn't that much left in it.

'Here, have a swig, it'll make yer feel better.'

Bluey took it and drank, then glanced around. It was no dream, he was still there amongst sandhills.

'We got to try an' save ourselves, Harry,' he said, but Harry only grinned.

'That's just what I'm bloody doin', mate. Just let the mob look for what they can find. All yer have ter do's watch 'em. I'll be back before dark.'

And with that, Harry turned, swung himself up on to his horse and began to ride out towards the south again.

'We'll bloody die here!' Bluey called after him.

'I'll carve yer headstone in solid gold, mate!' Harry called back jokingly, and Bluey was alone once more. The bloody man was mad! More eejit an' stubborn t'an a bloody pig! A t'ousand bloody pigs! A friend of no man's! An' bejasus, if he lived long enough, he would bloody tell 'im t'at!

The heat of the day was even more fierce than the one before and although the big white bull wandered further ahead in the line Harry had taken, the rest of the mob was scattered over miles, the horses, too. Bluey didn't even attempt to mount up but made a tiny shelter for shade and lay in it to try and conserve his body moisture. If he drank like he wanted to, there wouldn't have been a drop left. Once, he gathered enough energy to stand and, close to tears of fury, shout around, 'You God-forsaken, cursed land!' several times, then retreated.

It was dusk when he saw the exhausted figure of Harry on foot leading a tired and thirsty horse. Half the day, Harry had walked and Bluey did not have to be told by the forlorn sight that they were now worse off than ever. He watched in silence as his friend unsaddled. Harry looked as if he could not have gone a single step further. His lips were swollen and the skin on his cheeks and the backs of his hands was beginning to look as if it was starting to rot. Bluey felt shame at his anger. By comparison, his own day had been easy. The only good thing was that he was sure Harry would now see that to turn back was the only thing left for them.

Harry had to take a drink of the fast depleting water before he was able to speak, then he said, 'David don't come down around these parts too bloody often, does 'e mate?' And he lay down and was immediately out to it.

It was the middle of the night when something woke the thirsting Bluey and he didn't have to open his eyes to know what it was. It was a strange smell. His head close to the ground, it smelt like earth, a sweet, scented smell. He sniffed at it and filled his nostrils, then opened his eyes and raised his head. It was very dark but he could just make out what had to be the kneeling figure of Harry a little way off. He rose to his feet and moved slowly towards him to see him better. Then he felt it and stopped. A single, tiny droplet of water had lightly touched his face.

As Harry knelt, a heavier drop fell on his yellow, matted hair, then another, and another. The flash of lightning lit him up, followed by a clap of thunder. Bluey just stood there transfixed. A miracle was taking place around him. A miracle. In what seemed only seconds, the heavens began to open up and water was running down over Harry's hair and face and beard. The slender thread that held the life of man and beast to earth swelled to a sky-borne river.

Harry raised his head to it, got to his feet and laughed. Then he turned to the transfixed Bluey, standing there being soaked.

'An you took us for another bloody heathen, didn't yer?' he roared in delight, and Bluey was shaken from his spell.

They ripped the boots and Alberts from their feet, then, in the darkness and the pouring rain, splashed the ground as they danced and jigged together with whoops of joy.

Away, almost sixty miles back towards the north-east that he had already covered, Wooly lay undisturbed in his rest. He didn't see the lightning of that local storm and, not knowing of it, would be unable to tell that it had happened.

Amongst the sandhills, the cattle and the horses drank deeply from the small pools that formed around them and all the water bags were filled. And, in the morning, Harry and Bluey cracked their stock-whips and rode far to bring the huge mob together again and start them moving, the big white bull at their head.

It was only six or seven miles further south when Harry, riding far out on the right flank, accidentally came on a large water-hole and stared at it in amazement. It lay just over a sandhill and there was no vegetation or trees or any other such sign that might give it away. And, after examining it, as he suspected, he realised that it had not been created by that one, sudden local storm but had been there all along. Twice, he had passed within a few hundred yards of it in his desperate searches and not seen that sandhill's hidden secret. He could have perished within ten minutes of it and never known. There was no point in dwelling on the irony of that now. For the first time in many years, he had learned something new about the country into which he had been born that hadn't come from other men's lips, and he felt an uplifting surge of pleasure in that.

It was a windy but sunny day as Lilly Boyd alighted from the train at Adelaide with her small, cracked leather bag that she'd had ever since she could remember. That and the few valueless things in it were her sole possessions and, like a little girl with a beloved doll that gave her the only security she knew, she had clung closely to the handles from the moment she had left Albert Downs.

'When you get to Brisbane, take a ship,' were McKenzie's last words to her but she had no intention of drowning at sea before she'd had time to become a lady and had travelled by land.

It had been a very long and tiring journey, all the way down the coastal routes of the different Colonies by train and at times by horse coach. There had been many long waits and delays and many more overnight stops at inns than she would have wished that had cost her more money. There were even moments when she had despaired of ever reaching Adelaide, and moments of danger, too, when drunken men back from gold fields had tried to touch her and she'd had to run to some other woman for protection, feeling terror. What could be said was that her experiences had made her a little wiser about men than she had previously been, and she had learned never to return a glance from any of them. She also learned that she was much more vulnerable because she was dressed as a servant girl.

All that was behind her as she emerged from the railway station, buoyed up by excitement again as she set off in search of good accommodation.

'Only stay in Temperance Hotels,' Mrs McKenzie had warned her, but there had been little chance of finding any up until now.

When her train, which consisted mostly of loaded cattle wagons and only the one small passenger coach, had pulled away from the railhead and she waved to Mrs McKenzie standing there alone, getting smaller and smaller, she had felt sad and very close to tears for a while. There had been some happy moments at Albert Downs and she was sorry that, in the end, she was still tongue-tied over what she had wanted to say. In view of the good fortune that had come to her so soon afterwards, it had been silly of her to get so upset about the curtains. The needs of those poor blacks without a stitch had been much greater than her own. And she shouldn't have shouted at her mistress like that in anger. It was just that she felt they were trying to take her inheritance away from her before she'd even got it. It had made her feel deeply ashamed when Mrs McKenzie had come to her and, instead of striking her as they would have done at the Orphanage, had insisted on giving her a loan of thirty shillings to add to her savings so that she could present herself to the solicitors more in keeping with her new position. She had been so taken aback, she had failed to thank her. It wasn't until the break had been made and she was on her way to Bari that all the words she had wanted to say flooded through her mind and she determined to write and say them all as best she could once she had collected her inheritance and was able to return the money.

She turned into a wide street, busy with the traffic of wagons, cabs and even private carriages. Bits of straw were being whisked along in the strong wind and she found she had to use a hand to keep her skirt down.

'Pardon me,' she said, stopping a passing couple, 'but do you know if there's a Temperance Hotel here?'

The well-dressed woman just looked back at her with pursed lips in silence but the man pointed up across the street.

'I think that's one,' he said, and they moved on.

Lilly stood on the pavement for a while in fear that she might be knocked down in trying to cross then, plucking up her courage, made a dash for it.

She walked up to where the man had pointed. It was more like a large house than the other hotels she had seen but the sign outside read 'Balmoral Hotel' and another, much smaller notice by the side of the door did indeed declare it to be a Temperance one, under which was printed, 'Proprietress, Mrs A. Googe. Member of the Christian Union Society.'

It was clearly a very safe place in which to stay. Unlike other hotels, not just anyone could walk in off the street for, as she tried the door, she found it locked, and felt that Mrs McKenzie would have been pleased by her finding such a place. She pulled at the bell, heard it ring inside and waited, her clothes blown by gusts of wind. After a while, the door came cautiously ajar before opening wider to reveal the figure of Mrs Googe. Her dress was gravely black with a white lace collar up to her chin and Lilly took her as a widow. The only curious thing about her was that the lips of her squarish mouth were a little over-red and couldn't have been entirely natural. But her speech and genteel manner quickly dispelled any suggestion of impropriety.

'Yes, my dear?' she said kindly enough.

'I'd like a room, please, m'am.'

'A room?'

Lilly was only too aware of what she must have looked like to the lady, particularly after all her journeying.

'I know maybe I don't look like I can pay, m'am, but I can. I've got money. See, I've been left it an' have ter see the Solicitors.'

The red mouth twisted into a smile.

'Goodness gracious me, my dear, I didn't doubt you for a minute. I know an honest face when I see one. Come in, come in.'

Lilly smiled in return and entered while Mrs Googe closed the door securely against the wind.

Just inside on a wall was a notice of tariffs and the information that if a bath was required, a booking for it had to be made at least a day in advance, for the additional charge of a shilling, fresh towel supplied. At that price, cleanliness was clearly not encouraged. Godliness was. Opposite was a framed needle-work tapestry in many colours reading: 'Be righteous and the Lord will hear thy prayer'.

'This way, my dear,' Mrs Googe said and made for the stairs. As Lilly followed her up, she thought she could smell scent coming from Mrs Googe's dress but there was nothing wrong with that. It was pleasant.

The room was as plain and Presbyterian as the hall, but to Lilly it was luxurious. She put down her bag and went to the window with delight. It faced directly out on to the wide street, and all the business of life was passing by down there. Now that she had found such good accommodation, she was eager to be back out amongst it and shop for her new clothes. Mrs Googe watched her excitement.

'Well, it is nice, I must say, to meet somebody who's had good fortune. Solicitors did you say, my dear?'

Lilly, drawn by Mrs Googe's interest in her, turned with a smile and explained the letter she was carrying.

But instead of leaving it at that, Mrs Googe expressed further interest still in Lilly's affairs and Lilly, only too pleased to have someone with whom to talk and show friendliness, willingly obliged her with answers. By the time Mrs Googe was satisfied, there was very little left of Lilly Boyd's life to know.

For Lilly's part, she found out nothing at all about Mrs Googe but still presumed she was a widow, otherwise her husband would have been the proprietor.

'But I'm stopping you from going out to look at the shops,' said Mrs Googe and Lilly appreciated that. Minutes later, her heart light and full of expectation, she was on her way out again to a shop that Mrs Googe recommended her to try.

Shortly afterwards she stood buffeted by wind outside the purveyor of women's fashions called 'Mademoiselle Cooper', her excited face almost pressed against the window to see better through the reflection of the late afternoon light. There were two dresses draped on display, both of them beautiful, but there were many more hanging inside. And there, too, she thought she caught sight of the wondrous shiny boots she had always wanted. All her dreams were coming true and she felt almost rapturously drunk with it.

The woman inside saw her, moved to the window and, with severity of face, gestured for her to go away. It wasn't good for business to have street urchins and impudent servant girls smearing her glass and gazing on her costumes. It brought the tone of her establishment down. 'Go away, go away, go on,' she said as she waved, but instead of moving on, the girl began to make for her door. Perhaps she had come to pick up something for her mistress. That sometimes happened, but she had never seen this girl before.

Lilly had not been surprised by the woman's reaction, but it was because of it, in her state of ebullience, that she felt bold enough to have a little fun at her expense.

She walked in, closed the door behind her and said, 'I'm not who yer think I am, madam. I'm Miss Lillian Boyd an' I'm in disguise. My friend, Mrs Googe, of ther Balmoral Hotel thought I'd get what I wanted here.'

The woman looked at her in surprise, not at all knowing what to make of her, but once Lilly had opened her purse to show she had money, her manner changed.

'Why, of course, miss,' she smiled, business being business, no matter who this country girl was who'd clearly been sleeping in her cheap and nasty clothes.

The next hour and a half before the shop was due to close was the most wonderful Lilly had ever known and it was obvious to her that the good name of Mrs Googe helped enormously. Although a few other customers came and went, she was attended to like a queen. She tried on dress after dress and petticoat after petticoat until Mademoiselle's stock, but not her patience, was exhausted. It was very difficult, but with Mademoiselle's help, she eventually made up her mind and stood joyously before the mirror. She was almost unrecognisable to herself in the fashionable green dress, black shiny boots and hat, her hair all pinned up like Mrs McKenzie's. It was hard for her not to keep grinning at herself and she had to suppress a hysterical little giggle. It was a transformation. Poor servant girl to lady of importance. That's me. Lilly Boyd. Just look at us! Nobody would know us at Albert Downs if I walked right up to them! If they could see 'er now, they wouldn't believe it!

It was impossible to even think of getting back into her own clothes piled on a chair. They had taken on the appearance of old rags and had become embarrassingly awful.

'I don't want those,' she said. 'Could yer throw them away for us?'

'Very well, Miss Boyd, I'll give them to charity.'

The new outfit cost Lilly every last penny she had

left. Four years of life savings plus Mrs McKenzie's thirty shillings which had covered only the cost of the boots and hat. But that didn't matter.

A smiling Mademoiselle Cooper saw her out and she hurried back to the Balmoral Hotel, holding down her hat and sure that everyone was looking at her.

She rang the bell and when Mrs Googe opened the door wide enough to be seen, she looked appropriately amazed.

'Is it you, my dear?' she said.

'Yeah, it is,' Lilly said with delight and went in to be admired.

'Well, I never! I only hope, Miss Boyd, now you're a lady you'll still think our little hotel's good enough for you.'

'Oh, yes, Mrs Googe. I love it here already. I wanter stay until I make up my mind what ter do. I thought maybe yer could help us with that, seein' as I've got nobody.'

'I'd be only too pleased to, dearie.'

'Thank you, Mrs Googe.'

And Lilly ran up to her room to admire herself all over again in the small mirror behind the washstand. It didn't strike her as at all unusual that she hadn't seen any other guests around as yet, but the truth was that Mrs Googe didn't actively seek business for her small hotel. The fewer guests she had, the less likely any of them were to create trouble and attract unwanted attention. The Balmoral, under her management, was of unblemished reputation and that was the way she wanted to keep it. She was very careful in choosing her guests. Many she turned away on the excuse that she was fully booked.

That night, Lilly hung up her new clothes carefully, but despite her tiredness, her great excitement made it difficult for her to sleep. Once, she heard the front door open and close and a horse and wheels drive away in the late night silence, but only for a few moments did she wonder who could have been going out of the hotel at such an hour.

In the morning she washed, did her hair, got dressed and went down but Mrs Googe did not appear and she was too shy to knock on the door marked 'Private' near the foot of the stairs that Mrs Googe had pointed out as her own.

She went out, and it was with nervousness that she approached the offices of Huggert and Huggert, Solicitors, and when she reached them, found that they were not yet open.

She walked around the streets that were already busy with carters, returning to the Solicitors every fifteen minutes but it was another hour and a half before she found the door open. She went in to be confronted in an outer office by a clerk.

'I'm Miss Boyd,' she said, but the man didn't seem to have heard of her and she produced the letter that had been so much read it was already splitting along one fold. The clerk read it, handed it back, and checked a book of appointments without any reaction whatsoever, not so much as a polite smile. Lilly hadn't thought about what to expect when she presented herself but she hadn't expected to be so ignored and felt a little let down by it.

'I come all the way down from Central Queensland to see yer,' she said, but the clerk, running his finger down the book, ignored that, too.

'Mr Huggert may be able to fit you in at eleven o'clock but I can't promise. Would you like to make an appointment for tomorrow. Or, better still, the day after.'

Lilly, feeling as if tomorrow or the day after might as well have been next year and with no money left to eat or buy anything else, clutched quickly at anything she could find in defence.

'I'm only in Adelaide for the day,' she said, and the man picked up a pen and dipped in ink, taking his time.

'What did you say your name was again?' he said.

'Boyd. Miss Lillian Boyd.'

The clerk neatly wrote it, put down the pen, blotted the ink and closed the book before looking up again.

'Try eleven, Miss Boyd,' he said, and took up some other work.

Lilly returned to the streets. It would have been nice to have returned to the Balmoral and shared a cup of tea with Mrs Googe but she wanted to go back with the happy news of her inheritance and not before. Before would somehow have spoiled it. She walked around the main part of the town, gazed on shops and churches, and looked longingly into a tea-house that smelt of delicious, freshly baked cake. For a few moments, it amused her to think of herself wearing so much money on her back, yet unable to afford to go in. At Albert Downs, she had been able to make herself a cup of tea any time she liked if she wasn't busy, but in towns she was beginning to realise that everybody wanted money for everything. Well, she would go back to that tea-house and show them that she could pay as easily as all the other ladies in their white, lace gloves. She walked on, aware of men's glances and ignoring them.

Eleven o'cock was an eternity but it finally approached and she found her way back to the offices without too much difficulty.

The unsmiling clerk looked up at her. 'I'm afraid, Miss Boyd,' he said, 'that Mr Huggert can't see you for another half hour.'

That was a disappointment but she felt pleased that this time, the man at least knew who she was.

'I'll wait, then,' she said.

That didn't seem to please him at all, but he did get her a chair and she thanked him and sat, doing her best to look as prim and ladylike as possible.

It was another eternity in which time had almost come to a standstill. Once, a messenger came and went but it was a brief diversion. Apart from the sounds of the street drifting in, the most dominant noises through the heavy silence were the ticking of a clock and the scratching of the clerk's pen.

When the door from one of the inner offices opened to reveal what was obviously a Mr Huggert, grey-haired, slight, stooped, peering at her over his pince-nez, it came almost as a surprise.

'Miss Boyd?' he said, and Lilly smiled then got to her feet. But the smile quickly turned to a grimace. It seemed that she had come all the way across the world for this and now that the moment had arrived, the most important moment in all her life, she found that she had pins and needles in her left leg and could hardly move. Mr Huggert waited, impatiently.

'You can come in now.'

The clerk was looking at her, too. She felt stupid and embarrassed and she blushed. It wouldn't have been ladylike of her to admit to her disability. Her face set against the pain, she limped towards Mr Huggert's office, a step at a time. But, fortunately, once she got in there, it began to ease. Huggert gestured to a chair and she thankfully sat again.

Huggert took his place behind his desk, sat, and said, 'I believe you have a letter.'

Lilly handed it to him. He opened it, adjusted his pince-nez and took ages to read it before putting it down on his desk that was littered with files and papers, much of it tied up in narrow, pink ribbon. The window sill was the same, the shelf of the bookcase, too. The whole place smelt of paper.

'Do you have any other identification, Miss Boyd?'

Mr Huggert was clearly not going to hand over Aunt Aggie's money to an imposter and Lilly silently thanked Mrs McKenzie for having thought of it. To that end, she had got Mr McKenzie who had been in a frantic state over his missing bull, to sit down long enough to write a note for her. She handed the note over. It was sealed in an envelope and Huggert began a search of his desk for his lost letter-opener. It took a long while for him to find it, then he opened the note and read.

It was some time before he seemed satisfied, then he looked at her over the tops of his glasses again.

'You realise, young lady,' he said, 'that you're very lucky in being able to see me today. We are very busy people here.'

Lilly was rather astonished by that. If Mr Huggert thought this was being busy, he had obviously never set eyes on men branding and marking on a cattle run, sweating, cursing and struggling to throw large, horned beasts from daylight to dusk. He had never drunk dust and been torn and bruised. There were two entirely different kinds of people in the Colonies and, already, she was beginning to become aware of it. But she said nothing.

'Now,' said Huggert, and having disturbed the file he wanted in his fiddle-digging for the letter-opener, began to search for that, too, and as time went on, looked as if he was never going to find it.

'Ah, yes,' he said at long last.

It was bound with ribbon and he began to untie it carefully with his finger-nails. But once that had been done, he began to search amongst all the papers in it, again not being able to find what he was looking for. Lilly, on the edge of her seat, forced to be so long patient, was having a struggle to contain herself. The man had only two speeds. Dead slow and stop. He still searched and fiddled.

'I take it, Miss Boyd,' he said, 'that I need only read the clause concerning yourself, although I can read it all if you wish.'

'Oh, no, no,' said Lilly hurriedly, 'just about meself'll

be enough, sir.'

Then, he found it. 'Ah, yes,' he said with self-satisfaction, and began to peruse the document, quietly mumbling to himself as he read it through, following the words with his finger. 'Ah, yes, here we are. Here we are. Well then. Here we are.'

He read slowly and precisely so that there should be no mistake or misunderstanding. 'To my niece, Lillian Boyd, last heard of working in service at Galgeela Station in Southern Queensland, as a small token of remembrance, the sum of five pounds.'

Finished, he looked up at Lilly and smiled, but the words ending there were meaningless to her as they had not sunk in. The first stab of a sudden and unexpected knife is not necessarily felt. She waited for what was to come, not a token but an inheritance and watched with further expectancy as Huggert began to rummage through papers again in yet another search across his littered desk. Finally, the hiding culprit was in his hand, and, as he studied it, his manner became almost one of humility.

'Unfortunately,' he said, 'there are small costs involved, but we have kept those to an absolute minimum, Miss Boyd. Say six shillings. That leaves the net amount of four pounds, fourteen shillings.'

Only then did it begin to sink in to Lilly that this was all there was, and the knives began to strike at her heart and her stomach and her throat. And she was stunned by them, unable to speak.

Huggert looked on her wounded and disappointed face and felt angry. The ungrateful wretch of a girl had obviously expected more. A man of mean spirit, he was fond of condemning people of greed and sought to say so now. And the tone of his voice was as severe and chastising as he could make it.

'I didn't know your late Aunt,' he said, 'but she was clearly a very worthy and Christian woman the likes of which are few enough amongst us. Let me tell you, young woman, that the bulk of her Estate amounting to almost five hundred pounds she left to a charitable trust caring for poor children.'

Lilly felt the bitterness of the salt but could only stare at him, and Huggert felt assaulted by her attitude. A servant girl wearing such bright, fashionable clothes that must have cost a pretty penny was more suggestive of a digger's tart from the Colony of New South Wales than any decent woman of Adelaide. There was only one other matter to be resolved before he could be rid of her.

'Do you want it as a cheque or in cash?' he asked brusquely, but Lilly, choked, was unable to reply and he went to the safe, opened it, impatiently counted out four pounds and fourteen shillings, locked up the safe, and held out the money to her.

'When you sign for this, I believe our business will have been concluded.'

Lilly, feeling weak and faint, had difficulty in finding her feet, but got up, took the money, scribbled her name where she was directed and managed to remain upright. Huggert then opened the door for her and she managed to walk out past the back of the unsmiling clerk to the other door and the clouded street. For a few moments she stood fighting to hold back her tears, then began to walk in a daze back in the direction of the Balmoral Hotel, self-pity, self-accusation, remorse, anger and despair pouring from her wounds all at the same time.

From the downcast face with the trembling lip that Mrs Googe opened her door to, she knew without telling that disaster had befallen Lilly Boyd and guessed that what she was still clutching in her hand was her inheritance. All of it. It was written all over the girl.

Lilly entered, avoiding looking at Mrs Googe, ran straight up the stairs to her room, sat, opened her fist, looked at the remains of her fortune, then wept in her shame and stupidity.

Mrs Googe looked up the stairs in thought. There was much to think about and several possibilities to the outcome of such a situation. She smiled to herself with that. If she was careful, she could make this girl her own. But the first thing to do was to see to it she got her share of whatever the girl had before it went elsewhere. She would ask her for a week's rent in advance. That would be a start. She crept up the stairs to Lilly's room and listened at the door. As she expected, the girl was sobbing. She waited a short while, then knocked.

In her room, Lilly wiped her eyes and struggled to pull herself together but even before she had opened the door, Mrs Googe had decided to raise her sights.

'Is it all right to come in, dearie?' she said, but whether it was or not, for Lilly simply turned away to sit again, she went in and closed the door behind her.

'I don't know if I told you,dearie, but it's normal for my guests to pay two weeks in advance if they mean to stay that long. That's all right with you, isn't it?'

She watched Lilly reach for the money to pay her which she had put down on the little table and was somewhat taken aback that the girl made no attempt at a protest against her outrageous request. And she quickly noted that the money there amounted to less than five pounds. No wonder she was crying. Her clothes must have cost almost that much. She felt obliged to appear sympathetic and give advice but she sensed as well as hoped that it was advice that would not be taken.

'If I was you, dearie, and things hasn't worked out as well as you thought they would, I'd go down on my bended knees and write to your mistress and beg for her mercy an' ask 'er ter take you back.'

For the first time, Lilly looked at her.

'I can't do that. I can never do that. I'm stupid. They warned us. They'd all laugh at us. I can never go back there. Never.'

In her distress, Lilly hadn't noticed the slight breakdown of Mrs Googe's genteel accent to something more akin to her own. Instead, she looked as if she were about to break down again and Mrs Googe took her softly in her black-clad arms, winding them around her. And Lilly accepted the comfort with gratitude.

'There, there, Lilly,' Mrs Googe said, 'you don't mind if I call yer Lilly, do yer? Things is not so bad. You're young, you're strong. You'll be all right, you'll be all right. You don't have to go down on your knees an' beg ter that woman if you don't want to.'

And Lilly clung to her as the only other human being on earth who appeared to care and understand what had happened to her. It wasn't her fault that she failed to see Mrs Googe with her red stripe of a mouth and black covering as something more resembling a red-back spider with a poisonous sac, for there were many more mature and honest ladies of Adelaide who didn't either. A little eccentric she may have been but she was as respectable as any of them, was to be seen in church twice a week, regularly attended meetings of the Christian Union Society and gave generously to charities.

And yet, the people of Albert Downs and the entire Colony of Queensland may never have heard of Lilly Boyd again had she not walked into Mrs Googe's web.

Jimmy Case woke fully dressed from a drinking spree the night before and his bladder demanded that he get up. He went outside into the first light of dawn, but as he peed, he noticed what looked like a dark shape bundled against the wall of the eating hut. Finished, curiosity drove him over to see what it was. It was a surprise. It was Wooly, lying there fast asleep, his spear, throwing stick and leather satchel beside him. Never had an opportunity like this presented itself to Case to be the bearer of important headlines since Harry

Walford had buried his bloody dog. He put out his boot and kicked the black awake. Wooly sat up, his back against the wall and glanced up at him. The blacksmith's manner was menacing and he didn't like it.

'Did yez find 'em?' said Case, keeping his voice low, but Wooly didn't immediately answer.

'I's talkin' to yez, yer stupid black bastard,' Case said threateningly. 'Answer us or I'll put a boot inter yer guts.'

Wooly understood the meaning and wasn't in a position to get quickly out of the way. He knew black men were often shot for nothing by white men like this. And there were his tartan trousers to think about.

'Pella call 'im Wooly find 'im, boss.'

Case was delighted by that. 'Where?'

Wooly pointed towards the south-west, and Case gestured with his dirty fingers at his chin.

'Was there a fella with a yeller beard with 'em?' he said, 'A yeller beard?'

Wooly had been tracking a big mob of cattle and a large bull that they had indicated to him was the colour of Boss Kenzie's trousers. He knew nothing of a yellow beard. He looked blank but it was enough for Case. He could hold himself no longer. He ran towards the main house and when he got close enough, started shouting.

'The blacktracker's found 'em, Mr McKenzie! The blacktracker's back! He's got 'em, Mr McKenzie! He's got 'em!'

Within minutes, everybody on the homestead was awake and coming running, Case, the centre of attention, telling them all he knew and a lot he didn't.

McKenzie, who was still having to sleep alone in his stalemate with Dora, dressed as hurriedly as he could. He had been going frantic for the lack of news and Frank Murray was overdue in returning from Mount Evans. And apart from all his other problems, he was due to start a muster for fats to get them to the railhead and the market.

When he reached the group clustered around both Jimmy Case and the now squatted Wooly, Jim Hill was already there starting his job of questioning. McKenzie ordered him to send the groups back to their huts and a detailed enquiry of all that the blacktracker had found out began in earnest. Not only that but, true to his promise, he caught sight of old Charley and instructed him to produce the pair of new tartan trousers that had been obtained for him.

There was a short delay while Wooly stripped himself of his old ones to complete nakedness, right there and then, and put on the new, for all he could do was grin widely in the process. And Dora, who was trying to look on anxiously from the gate, had to turn away.

'Go plurry plurry dry, boss,' Wooly said so many times with dust held in his hand, that there was no doubt in the end that he meant the big white bull and the mob had headed into desert, and that didn't make any sense to start with. There was nowhere to go there. Nowhere. And it was far from the only thing that Wooly told them that stretched both McKenzie and Hill's belief.

Four quart-pots of sweet tea, pounds of grilled steak and a whole damper later, and with the sun pushing well up into the sky, they were still at it, and with his stomach filled almost to its full capacity, Wooly looked as if he wanted to sleep again. A new pair of tartan trousers and an unhunted feast were enough for any man.

'Ask him again, how many he thinks there were,' McKenzie directed Hill, but Wooly who had already answered this more than a dozen times didn't give Hill time to repeat it, although there was not the slightest hint of impatience in his words.

'Plurry plurry, plenty plenty, big mob, boss,' he said directly to McKenzie and McKenzie's instincts told him the black was not trying to lie, not even for another pair of trousers.

'It's impossible, Don,' Hill said, hoping to ease McKenzie's ever increasing anxiety, although it was what he actually thought.

'Why the hell is it impossible!' McKenzie shouted back at him. 'Either we believe all of what he's trying to tell us or we believe nothing. You got him. Are you trying to tell me now he's no bloody good?'

Flies crawled undisturbed across Wooly's face and around the golden brown ends of his matted locks. What he was asking boss McKenzie to believe seemed utterly incredible: that the big white bull and a mob he was still making out to be a thousand had been taken by only four mounted horsemen far to the west, then to the south, had got to a desert where two of them turned back, leaving only two to push on in there with them. And without sighting one single dead carcass in all that way along their tracks. McKenzie had to make a decision.

'Going into desert could have been a trick to cover themselves and make sure,' he said. 'They could have gone in just a way and turned back out east further down. Tell him I want him to go back and keep on tracking until he finds them dead or alive, no matter where that is. Tell him that while he's away I'll send up to his family all the tea, sugar and flour they can eat.'

At that, Hill felt obliged to warn him. The blacks always shared whatever they got amongst themselves. For many thousands of years it had been necessary for their survival and was ingrained in them.

'He'll name his whole tribe, Don,' he said out of the corner of his bushy moustache.

'Don't you think I damned well know that?' McKenzie snapped. 'Tell him!'

Wooly grinned at the generous offer and showed his willingness to take it up.

'Pella Wooly track 'im pella bull, track 'im plurry plenty mob, boss,' he said, and listed to an unhappy Hill no less than forty names who were to receive rations. It was going to mean sending a bloody wagon away up north – and then bloody finding them. He only wished the men could be caught, hanged and the whole damned business be got over with. It had made Don go out of his mind. Believing everything the black had told them was sheer, bloody stupidity.

There was something else Hill would have not believed. To Wooly, distance was more of an abstract than a reality and he had made no attempt to describe the vast mileage he had already covered in the time. As a result, McKenzie and Hill visualised the bull and the mob to be much closer than they were. Although they knew there was nothing but the Wild Heart to the south-west and no known route there, they had never seen the sandhill country into which Harry had gone. The concept of taking a huge mob of cattle to South Australia was not even a consideration in their minds. It would have been as absurd as suggesting that two men had taken their cattle to the moon.

'Pella Wooly go, boss,' Wooly said, and lay down in the narrow shade against the hut wall to go straight off to sleep right in front of them.

'Get him moving again as soon as he wakes,' McKenzie said and walked away to the house. He could put off his duty no longer. He had to write a long letter to London, pray that they hadn't already heard, and hope they might understand at least a little of his overwhelming difficulties. He would tell them that he was doing everything humanly possible and that he would not rest, day and night, until he found out what had happened to the new bull and the stolen mob, and until the murderous, villainous bushrangers, the likes of which the Colony had never known, had been brought to justice on the gallows. He would also explain that, to that end, he was having to search an area as large as the whole of England and Scotland put together. They just might see that. On no acount would he mention the blacktracker. That would be like trying to tell them that the best chance of retrieving their valuable property was not, as they might have thought, in the hands of a huge army of troopers marching abreast in their hundreds across a continent but in those of a single black, almost naked savage armed with a primitive spear who could not even speak the Queen's English. That, they would not have understood at all.

'Well?' said Dora, deeply anxious to know what had happened. It had taken all her self-control not to rush out and listen to the questioning that had taken hours. But she had been clever in making her life appear normal in the house. She had gone about her domestic duties, seen to all Don's needs, except the all-important one of sharing his bed and giving her body, and otherwise spoken to him as if nothing between them was wrong. A stranger would never have guessed she was on matrimonial strike.

Don, also careful to keep up this appearance for the sake of his own respect and dignity, told her the essence of what Wooly had said and began to make for his little office, but not before noting some sense of relief on her face.

'Harry's escaped from them, that's what's happened,' she said after him as he went. 'He'll turn up now and be able to tell us for himself. Then you'll see.'

McKenzie made no reply to that, reached his desk, and sat down to write the most difficult and embarrassing letter of his entire career in property management.

It was evening of that same day when Frank Murray finally returned from the out-station at Mount Evans and Wooly had already gone. He went directly to the main house and, told by old Charley that McKenzie was in his office, went straight in there.

McKenzie was surrounded by sheets of torn up paper, and had just begun starting all over yet again. He did not welcome the interruption and looked up at the hot dusty figure.

'I'm busy, Frank,' he said, and Murray couldn't understand it.

'Don't you want to know what I found out?'

'You found out nothing.'

Frank Murray looked astonished.

'How did you know that?' he said.

'Because you were looking in the wrong damned place, that's why. They went south-west and have gone into desert. Now, for God's sake, let me get on with this. And get yourself ready to go out mustering in fats starting in the morning.'

McKenzie started scratching away with his pen again and a hurt and mystified Murray had no alternative but to leave. On his way to find Jim Hill, he was annoyed when Jimmy Case caught him and tried to tell him the whole story.

'Shut up!,he said, 'Mr Hill will bloody tell me.'

That took a while and not only was Murray angry that he had missed out on the day's events but because Don had believed the black's impossible story. It had to be his dreams, his fanciful imagination.

What lay at the root of Hill and Murray's disbelief was their fear that it might turn out to be true. For two lazy malcontents, an Irishman whom they had looked on as still a Johnny Raw and a half-witted rouseabout to have carried out such a droving feat would have been a humiliating reflection on their own abilities as Overseers. To have believed would have been an admission of their own inferiority as cattlemen.

'All blacks are bloody liars,' Murray said. 'They only say what they think you want to hear. Don's a bloody fool.'

But the truth and the lies of the situation were about

to raise their dual heads away down to the south-east in
the town of Bari.

Six

Constable Hackett peeped into a cell at Bari Police Station, keys in hand. Inside were four men. One was a dark-haired youth with a squint in one deep-brown eye which gave him, to his misfortune, an unwarranted evil look. Another was an old man in rags with a stained grey beard, a rum-bibber known locally as Jackshay Jack. It was his habit to wander about with a billy-can tied around his neck with string in the hope that some merciful being might accidentally drop an odd penny into it to supply him with more drink. Since he didn't ever actually ask anyone for money and carrying a jack-shay was not a crime in itself, magistrates were forever having to let him off on charges of begging for lack of proof. The other two men were a pair and had clearly been on the track for a good while looking for work. Both had heavy, dark stubble on their faces and could have done with a good scrub.

The youth, the old man and the pair of strangers who had only arrived in town the previous day had been picked up as suspects following a complaint of a saddle having been stolen from the verandah of a house the previous night, but the Constable had been unable to find any evidence against them. And, indeed, all were innocent.

The two strangers had remained very quiet and shown signs of nervousness, but arrested men often behaved like that so there was no reason to connect them with any other crime. They had given their names as Arthur Watson and Joseph Green and Hackett had not even given thought to the idea that they might be Jack Purdy and Dan Spence. The news that Wooly had brought back to Albert Downs had not yet reached him and Bari was the last place he would have expected any of the cattle robbers to appear. These men drove no stock and had no money from the sale of any. Certainly, there were descriptions of the four men involved in the great cattle theft in the desk, but apart from the loppy who was distinguishable by his yellow hair and beard, the others could have fitted half the men in the Colony.

He unlocked the door and swung it open.

'All right, you can go,' he said, 'and you can count yourselves lucky this time.'

Purdy and Spence had never heard truer words spoken. They had been devastated by being arrested within a day of arriving in Bari and the new names had come quickly to their lips. Both had sweated it out in terror in that cell and although both the youth and the old man had tried to be friendly to them, they had sat in a corner by themselves and refused to respond or be drawn. The relief on being released felt like the Constable's boot being withdrawn from their throats and Purdy who very rarely ever smiled except in a sardonic smirk, grinned.

'Thank yer, sir,' Purdy said, and Spence added to it.

'We's won't be given yez no trouble, sir. We's honest men can be vouched for.'

Hackett wasn't too sure about that and as he handed back the few possessions they had had in their pockets, gave them a reminder of his leniency.

'You know I could hold you on having no visible

means of support, don't you.'

That wiped the grin from both of them.

'Yeah, we knows sir, we knows. It's very kind of yer, sir,' Purdy said.

Outside, Sergeant Willis, hot and dusty, dismounted from his horse in the evening sun. Frustrated by getting nothing but negative reports in from the Native Mounted he had cursed them for their blind inefficiency. Not for the first time, he had ridden west for several days to call on as many outlying properties as he could in the hope of picking up information for himself. To bring such gully-rakers in, get them personally into his hands and then have the enormous pleasure of experiencing a multiple hanging had become an obsession with him. Almost all his other work had gone neglected. Having to return from another trip without a scrap of anything had put him in a foul mood.

As he strode towards the front door of the Police Station, he saw Jackshay Jack come out, already replacing the can around his neck. The bugger of a man had been in again. A bloody nuisance taking up his important time. He approached the old man, tore the billy from his neck and crushed it under his boot, pushed the squint-eyed youth in his path aside and almost bumped right into Purdy and Spence as they came out of the doorway. As they were strangers to him, his curiosity was immediately aroused and he watched them go.

Purdy and Spence did their best to look casual about their departure and appeared to be in no hurry. Willis stepped into the Station.

'Who were they?' he said, and Hackett briefly explained their presence and the lack of evidence against them over the missing saddle, but Willis turned back to the door, hesitated for a moment, then walked outside to go after them.

'Hey, you!' he called, when they were well within earshot and Purdy turned his head to look back. 'Yes, you! Both of you!'

Purdy and Spence stopped and turned, and Willis went up to them. They had never run into Sergeant Willis before and had never heard of him. All the same, both felt a great temptation to try and make a bolt for it, even though they knew they would not have got far.

'We ain't done nothin', sir,' Purdy said.

'We got saddles of our own, sir,' Spence added.

Willis stood taking them in. He knew bloody liars when he saw them. All men had something to hide and these two were no different. The bloody saddle didn't matter.

'I want to talk to you,' he said, and nodded for them to start walking back to the Station. Purdy and Spence, terror striking at them once again after such short relief, had no alternative but to comply. Willis could smell fear like Hackett couldn't. And he smelt it now. It was as attractive and heady as evening jasmine to a girl in love.

Back inside, they stood at the desk, Hackett looking on. Although the Constable was not a squeamish man, he only hoped that the two men were indeed innocent of any crime for he knew his Sergeant's moods well and neither liked nor approved of his methods. With Willis, it was more like a deep desire for self-satisfaction than a search for truth.

'Names,' Willis said, and Purdy and Spence gave them as before as Watson and Green.

'Who can identify you?'

At that, Purdy and Spence exchanged quick, surreptitious glances but it did not go unnoticed.

Willis pressed them for the names of friends or anyone in town who might know them but, in the end, Purdy as the main spokesman, had to admit defeat.

'We dunno nobody, sir, we's just passin' through and we's not done nothin. We's goin' in ther mornin' an' is not lookin' fer no trouble.'

A man without friends was like the taste of nectar to

Sergeant Willis. He ordered them to empty their pockets and gazed with pleasure on the two pocket knives, a couple of whip falls made of horse hair, a needle stuck in a piece of cork and a few other valueless bits and pieces. No visible means of support.

'Lock them up,' he said to Hackett and Purdy and Spence looked appalled, 'separately.'

'We ain't done nothin'!' both tried to protest.

'We got friends down south, sir!' Spence tried to tell him, his anger rising but fear was the overwhelming emotion in both of them.

Hackett obediently shoved them towards the cells, locked them up separately, and returned to the desk where Willis had removed his hat and jacket and was rolling up his sleeves.

'What charge?' Hackett said in apprehension.

'We're about to find out, aren't we, Constable? They could be two of them.'

Hackett was amazed by that. Willis had no more reason to believe that than he had, but his obsession had consumed him. He was ready for one of his pleasurable sessions and nothing was going to stop him. Hackett knew exactly what he was going to say.

'Strip them and tie their hands behind their backs.'

'Sergeant . . .' Hackett tried to get in with a plea.

'Do what I damn well tell you!' Willis ordered and Hackett returned to the cells to do what he was bid.

'What the hell's yer doin'?' Purdy wanted to know, beads of sweat starting to run from his forehead, and Hackett had to pull his baton to make him strip right down and have his hands tied.

Willis came in, smiling. His shirt was unbuttoned almost to his waist and his baton swung from his right wrist on its strap. Purdy stared at him in horror. Twice, he had served short sentences, once in Victoria and once in New South Wales. He had known manacles and leg-irons and had been struck several times without good reason but it had never been like this. Funk and panic devoured him even before the Sergeant's big hands made their drive towards his genitals.

'It was Walford!' he shouted, 'Walford!' and the hands twisted and the scream was one of extreme and unbearable pain.

Such was Willis's preoccupation and delight, that the name spoken didn't sink in until the scream was dying to a whimpering sob and he stepped back for a moment, staring at the doubled up, naked figure, staggered by the revelation. He had not really expected these victims to be who they were but Walford was the name of one of them and it took him completely by surprise. He glanced at Hackett. He looked surprised, too.

'Get your notebook,' Willis said to him and Hackett went to fetch it.

'I'll tell yez, I'll tell yez,' Purdy just managed to get out, but Willis smiled again. He was not going to be deprived of his pleasure. He knew how to torture a man without leaving a mark so that he could always deny his method of questioning a suspect, there being no visible evidence to show, but he was not concerned about marks now. He knew he had two of the right men. He rushed at Purdy again, and, once more, Purdy's scream rang out. There would be many to follow and when Hackett returned, it was difficult for him to pick up what Purdy was trying to tell them as pain piled on his pain, but Willis wouldn't stop and the pleasure the Sergeant was getting sickened him.

The story Purdy told was not all the truth for despite the excruciating agonies that over and over took him close to unconsciousness, he was still trying to cling to life. What Constable Hackett noted down was the information of it being all Harry Walford's doing; that it was Walford who had planned it and had forced them to come in under threat of death; that, during the day, he had kept a rifle on them and at night had tied them up.

It was while Walford and the Irishman, McGuirk, were both asleep on the edge of the desert that they managed to escape.

'He took fifteen hundred,' Purdy sobbed through the extremities of his pain, and Willis stepped back again for a moment in incredulity. It was the first time the real size of the stolen mob had been mentioned, and as he had worked as a drover himself at one time, he wondered, just for a brief moment, what kind of man this Walford might be.

It also emerged from Purdy's shuddering and bleeding lips that Walford had also planned to steal the big white bull from the moment he set eyes on it and although he, Purdy, had pleaded with the madman to let it go, knowing how valuable it was to the cattle run, Walford had just threatened to shoot him if he didn't shut up.

In the other cell, Spence sat trembling in a cold sweat, wishing he had never met Jack Purdy. He could hear not only the terrible screams but everything that was said, and he knew his own turn was coming. He also knew that if he stood any chance at all of saving his neck from the rope, his story would have to be the same. And as another tortured cry came from Purdy, seated alone and as yet untouched, he felt as if he might faint.

What Sergeant Willis found most difficult to believe was his own bloody luck. He was not usually a lucky man but while others searched the back-blocks all the way through into New South Wales for the four cattle-duffers, two of them had come to him and fallen right into his lap. He could hardly wait for the ring-leader about whom he had clearly been misled, and the Irishman, to be delivered to him and thought it would not be too long.

Harry had been lucky, too. When the situation in the

sandhill country again looked desperate, he had ridden out and found a small area of good feed and water. There he had rested the white bull and the great mob to let them build up their weight and strength. Some of the edible vegetation he had never seen before but he closely observed what the cattle preferred and what they did well on. Had he known that a blacktracker who had already given him a reprieve was once again on his tracks and that Purdy and Spence were in the hands of the police, he would not have stayed so long.

'We's goin' ter make it, mate, no question,' he had said to Bluey with a confidence that would have surprised those who had previously known him.

They would have been even more surprised to see him come out of the sandhill country, seated on his horse, gazing out across the land into which he fully intended going towards his goal. Bluey just gaped at it in fresh, rising anxiety and awe.

'Holy Mot'er of God, Harry, no man nor beast can go on inter t'at,' he said, but knew even as he said it that it was where Harry was going to try to take him, and that no pleading or argument was going to change boss drover's mind. It was the most forbidding sight either of them had ever set eyes on and only a handful of men had ever seen it.

Stretched before them for as far as the eye could see and going on into seeming eternity was a dead flat, rust-coloured plain thickly littered with rust-coloured stones. Not a bush, not a single blade of grass, not a drop of water nor any living thing could be seen. Here, it looked as if the continent of Australia itself had perished but that God had not been content until the bones of all life and every presumptuous rock and rise had been reduced to the same size to be given equality, then placed evenly across the surface in their own long-dried blood. If death was the Great Leveller, it needed no greater demonstration than this.

Harry was only too conscious of the deep concern that Bluey was feeling and from under the brim of his sweat-stained hat, he searched the full breadth of the horizon carefully for a sign of smoke in the hope that he might find something to offer. He had heard of men's lives being saved by smoke, because where there was smoke there were blacks, and where there were blacks there was likely to be water.

There was no smoke and he squinted up against the brightness of the sky. There, too, could be a guide; a bronze-wing or some other bird flying in a positive direction towards life-sustaining moisture.

But, apart from one single, feathery wisp of a cloud and the furnace of a sun, the sky, too, was empty. For Bluey's sake, he had to try and make light of it again.

'Well, no point hangin' around here,' he said cheerfully and turned his horse back towards the mob, Bluey after him.

'We'll die t'ere, Harry. Even if t'e Saints themselves came right up to us on heaven's horses, t'ey couldn't help us across t'ere.'

He watched Harry go up to the big white bull that was grazing on the very last bit of vegetation to be seen as if it knew what lay ahead of it. It was no longer any surprise to him to hear his friend talk to the animal as if it understood. He often did it and the bull appeared to respond to the sound of his voice.

'What d'yer reckon, fella?' he said to it loudly enough for Bluey to hear, and the bull raised its huge white head to fix him for a moment with a bold, red eye. Harry pointed to the south, 'No desert can go on forever. Is yer game?' Then he reached out with his coiled stock-whip and touched it lightly on the rump. The big white bull began to walk out into the stony desert and other leaders of the mob on seeing it, began to follow.

Harry, grinning, turned to Bluey. 'There, mate,' he

said with a laugh, 'now tell us. If an English bull is game, what the hell's the matter with the Irish?'

Calculated to raise Bluey's anger and help shed some of his anxiety and despair, it did just that and Bluey flared.

'T'ere's not'in' t'e matter wit' me an' t'at English bull's as stupid an' pig-headed as you are!'

'I'll tell yer what's wrong with yer kind an' kin,' Harry said more seriously to keep him going. 'Yer think so much about bloody dyin', yer ain't got no time ter turn yer mind ter bloody livin'.'

The words had their effect. Bluey swung his horse away to go further back on the mob, letting his coiled whip loose and raising it to crack it angrily at the air and help bring them on. No bloody yellow bearded friend of his was going to tell him what the Irish could and couldn't do. Sure the very worst of t'em was better than anythin' on legs t'at ever come out of bloody England. An' bejasus, did he not want to live as much as any man? Sure, a bloody sight more if it came to t'at.

'Hi, hi, hi!' he yelled at the river of beasts as his whip circled furiously.

Both men were hardly aware any more of the way they looked. It had taken all their time simply to keep the mob within a manageable area and no longer did they bother about stitching up rents in their clothing which was gradually becoming very much the worse for wear, while Stockholm tar was smeared on them in an unsuccessful attempt at curing their scurvied skin. Had they thrown away their whips, removed their spurs and hung their quart-pots around their necks, they would not have looked out of place alongside Jackshay Jack.

As they went on into the stony wilderness without any idea of how far it might be to the next water, or if there was any at all, Harry concealed his own fears well. With no real knowledge of where he was at any time and only the sun and his other friends, the stars, to go by, the directions he took, although he always made the decision appear positive and never hesitant, came purely from instinct.

It was exhausting, hot and thirsty work keeping the huge mob close together and on the move. Several times each day they changed horses to give them rest and rode ceaselessly from first light to dark. But all the time, the big white bull needed no bidding and kept well out in front as the leader, doing its best to try and place its hoofs between stones to make it easier.

At night, Harry and Bluey had to scrape stones aside to make enough clear ground on which to dig their hip-holes and put their tired bodies to sleep. And without enough fuel for a fire, they mixed flour with water from their water bags and ate the unbaked dough.

Four days later, Bluey rode up to Harry who was seated on his horse sadly looking down on the first beast to drop and die of thirst.

'It's over, Harry, isn't it?' he said. 'We's finished.'

'It's not over,' Harry said with a choke in his voice and rode off.

In dread of his sins never being forgiven and being condemned to an even more fiery place of torment through everlasting time, Bluey watched him go. It was too late to start doubting the sanity of his yellow beard-ed friend. He was trapped before the sulphurous jaws of hell with no chance of escape and the stench of death filled his nostrils. He could not have found his way out of there towards life on his own. And Harry was not going to leave the mob if he was the very last to die with them.

'Where ther mob an' ther big white bull goes, I goes,' he had said, making that perfectly clear.

Death waited unmoving in every cursed stone. It lay in the earth and in the sky, and in his thirsting mouth and throat. Somewhere, not too far away, it lay ahead.

Neither he nor Harry knew that, even if they lived, it

might be of no account for an unwitting messenger of death also lay behind.

There on the edge of the sandhill country where he had first turned back and now returned to, Wooly was gathering nardoo seed and gradually filling the pockets of his tartan trousers with it. It was dark before he had enough and he searched over the ground for two suitable stones, one flat and the other smaller and rounder. Between them he ground the seeds into a coarse flour and ate it. Although not as sweet as the white man's flour, it was satisfying. He would hunt for meat in the morning unless some unwary animal came near him in the night. He took off the leather satchel and, with both spear and throwing stick ready by his hand, he lay down to sleep.

When the telegraph message on the confessions of Purdy and Spence sent to McKenzie from Sergeant Willis in Bari reached the railhead, Eddie Giraldi was spellbound. Not since his wedding day had he had such excitement and he made the decision that no one but himself would carry such important information to Albert Downs. Although there were two other men around who could have done the job, he telegraphed back to say that with no messenger available, he was taking it himself, leaving his wife in charge.

'No, Eddie, no!' Mrs Giraldi cried in protest but in vain. That she was terrified of the alien telegraph machine, had always refused to touch it and didn't know how to operate it anyway, didn't make any difference to Eddie.

'You can learn, can't yer?' he drawled. He wasn't going to miss out. For the rest of his life he would be able to talk about his part in the biggest cattle theft ever known. Holy Christ! Fifteen hundred head! Two of them captured! The ring-leader, Walford! He knew that yellow bearded rouseabout. Had talked to him. What about? That was hard to say. Cattle mostly. They said he was a couple of links short but he knew different. Didn't fool him. The face of a born gully-raker if ever he saw one. People would remember Eddie Giraldi. And they would start right there and then. Before he packed a few supplies and had his protesting wife fill his water bag, he went out and drawled his information to all around, pleased to see the looks of amazement on their faces. Then, with the promise of more to come, he rode out.

His slow delivery of speech bore no relation to either the quality of the horses he kept or how he could handle them. In just over two days, he rode into Albert Downs homestead.

McKenzie was holding his horse outside the black-smith shed having Jimmy Case tighten a loose shoe when he saw Giraldi coming.

'They got two of 'em, Mr McKenzie,' he said before he had even stopped and dismounted. Then he pulled up, got off, took out the written message and handed it over. Case was nearly out of his mind with his desire to be the first to know but was forced to restrain himself. McKenzie would have blown his head off if he had opened his mouth. All he could do was watch McKenzie's face as he read and he saw fury mount on it. Eddie Giraldi was dying to talk his head off, but he was going to have to wait, too.

'Mr Hill!' McKenzie shouted in anger when he had finished, 'Mr Hill!'

But Jim Hill wasn't near. He had been on his way down from the yards when he saw Eddie Giraldi hurrying in on the track and had turned straight around to make himself scarce behind a mob of five hundred fats waiting to be shipped out. He knew well enough that Eddie wouldn't have ridden with a message about the availability of the railhead yards or the times of trains. It was trouble and he intended keeping clear of it until he found out what it was. It was a wise move.

McKenzie was too impatient to wait until Hill could be found. He would rather have had it come from Jim but Giraldi would serve the same purpose.

'Come with me,' he said to him and began to stride towards the house, Eddie Giraldi after him. Case hurried to the yards where the hands not out mustering were working, making the happy but wrong assumption that Walford and the Irishman had been captured.

The reason for McKenzie's fury was the information that it was Harry Walford and not the others who had brought the avalanche of troubles down upon his head. All these years the man had only been pretending to be a gentle fool. He had deceived him, cheated him, finally robbed him and pulled his happy marriage apart. The only good thing was that now Dora would be forced to see the truth and would hear of it not from his own mistrusted lips but from someone else's.

Giraldi followed McKenzie in and was surprised to see Dora cleaning the hall like a servant with old Charley, the book-keeper, helping her.

'Tell her, please, Mr Giraldi,' McKenzie said, and Eddie looked at Dora and old Charley looking back at him. There was something wrong here and it was something else he would be able to talk about if he could figure it out. Meantime, he suddenly felt like a skeleton at a feast and a bearer of bad news rolled into one. He hesitated.

'Tell Mrs McKenzie the message you've brought,' McKenzie said, becoming impatient.

'They've caught two of your men,' Eddie said, 'in Bari.' And hesitated again.

'Go on, go on,' McKenzie said, and Eddie Giraldi went on. Reluctantly.

'Purdy and Spence. They were caught by Sergeant Willis.'

He went on with the message which contained the

entire story just as Purdy and Spence had told it, but when he was finished, he was met with a solid block of silence. Dora's face was set as she waited for Don to speak while McKenzie waited for Dora. It was not old Charley's place to make comment of any kind and no one sensed the pride for Harry that was swelling in him. Droving one thousand, five hundred head without losing any, then having the audacity to head them into desert with only the Irishman at his side. It made no difference if Harry and the big white bull and the mob were all dead, and it made no difference either if no one knew it. It was Harry's dream and no one else's. That, he had achieved and no could ever take it back from him. He had probably gone into desert deliberately to end it there. Life's indignities could not touch him again. There was no sadness in that. Few men in death could ever be so fulfilled.

'Thank you, Mr Giraldi,' McKenzie said, and Eddie, taking his dismissal, thankfully made his way out to go and find more grateful ears.

'If you'll excuse me, m'am,' old Charley said and walked off to the kitchen, leaving McKenzie and Dora alone. He would have a little drink to Harry.

McKenzie stood holding his fury against Walford in check to make it easier for Dora to accept. Although the memory of his conversation with the man in his little office fleetingly returned once more, it would have been unbearable for him to admit to himself that he had been anything but reasonable and kind. That's what made it worse.

'All those years he deceived both of us,' he said. 'What damnable pretence. We should have known his cunning. Lying about his lack of experience with cattle when he first came here is proof of it. He'd probably been planning it carefully from the beginning and was only waiting for the right opportunity. Easily frightened men and the arrival of such a valuable animal as the

English bull gave it to him.'

It was not simply that Dora had been pushed into a position where she was being forced to save face, but that she genuinely sensed that there were faults both in the message and in all that had been said and now was being added to. The news had been a shock and she needed time to think.

'You might have offered Mr Giraldi tea,' she said as if none of it had got through to her.

'For God's sake, woman, don't you have ears?'

'Yes, and I have a mind, too, if only you'd allow me. And I can remember you telling me that the bull would be unsaleable anywhere. Even in New South Wales. You said it would be valueless to anyone else. Did these men explain that?'

McKenzie fought to hold himself. 'They didn't have to,' he said, 'Walford took it to try and destroy me!'

'Why would he want to do that?'

'I don't damned well know why!'

'Well, if you've been deceived, don't think I have. Those two men are lying. Or that Sergeant Willis is.'

McKenzie stared at her in disbelief. The evidence had been presented to her and she was still arguing. Nothing was going to convince her. God damned nothing! And the most worrying part of it was that if bloody Walford died in the desert, never able to make the admission from his own mouth, she might *never* believe it!

'In God's name,' he said, 'if they're lies, where are the cattle? Where is the bull? Where are Walford and McGuirk?'

'You're getting upset,' Dora said, 'I'll make you tea.' And she turned towards the kitchen.

'I don't want any bloody tea!' McKenzie shouted and strode back out of the house.

Dora didn't want to discuss it any further because she had made a decision. She would go to Bari and speak to the two men for herself and get the truth from them.

Don would refuse to allow her to go on her own on the pretence of shopping but he had promised the break before all this began and she would make him stick to it. As it was impossible for him to accompany her, he would be forced to let her go alone.

On Albert Downs homestead, Eddie Giraldi had never had such a time in his life, Jimmy Case hardly leaving his side lest he should miss anything. And there was plenty of scope for argument amongst the men, too, despite all the work that was going on in the yards and the paddock, with another mob of two hundred from which fats were to be cut out being held with difficulty just up the creek. It was noisy, hot, sweaty and dusty with a hundred flies to every man and beast and with Eddie Giraldi digging for every scrap of information he could get on Harry Walford in the midst of it.

But, 'What d'yer reckon on 'im, Mr Hill?' was a question that went unanswered not only to Eddie but to many hands as well. As far as Jim Hill was concerned, he was determined to keep his opinions to himself. He was the only one. It was left to Frank Murray to lead the group of disbelievers, Jimmy Case amongst them, and he had to do it without letting McKenzie know. When he learned that Rudd was another who was accepting the story, he immediately rode to him in anger.

'You pox-headed stupid bastard,' he said to him with McKenzie out of earshot, 'you're pissing down the bugger's bloody back, that's what you're doing', meaning that by accepting it, Rudd was only flattering the half-witted, yellow bearded loppy. 'And don't think I don't bloody know it.'

With that, Murray swung his horse away from him. That Walford could have done what no other man on Albert Downs could have done, including himself, was totally unacceptable to him. There had to be other men that Purdy and Spence were protecting.

It wasn't the end of shocks for McKenzie on that day. As the sun went down and eight hundred fats were in the yards ready for Murray and half a dozen men to start droving them towards the railhead in the morning, Eddie Giraldi managed to get hold of McKenzie as he was returning to the house. He already had enough to last him for more than a year but it wasn't sufficient.

'What chance do you reckon the blacktracker's got?' he drawled, walking his long, skinny legs alongside. McKenzie didn't want to discuss any of it with him, but the man was in a position to do him favours or be obstructive.

'Every chance,' he said. 'The only question seems to be whether he finds them still alive.'

'As long as he don't go near 'em, then, Mr McKenzie.'

There was some hint of danger in Giraldi's words and McKenzie stopped. 'What do you mean, as long as he doesn't go near them?'

'Well, they tell us he's one of that Jump up white feller mob,' Giraldi said and saw McKenzie's face darken like the eastern sky before he turned on his heel and headed back in the direction of the yards.

'Mr Hill!' he shouted, 'Mr Hill!'

Jim Hill appeared, knowing by the tone of voice he was in for something. Even keeping his mouth shut tight all day hadn't made any difference in the end.

'What the hell's this about the blacktracker being a Jump up white fellow?' McKenzie said, looking as if he might explode.

'They're blacks, Don, who believe . . .'

'I know what they are! Is he one or isn't he?'

'I thought you knew that.'

'Great God Almighty!'

There were many aborigines who had come to believe that white men were simply black men who had died, gone to some place they called 'Egland' and come back to jump up white pella with plenty sixpence. It wasn't the first time one of them had stood on the gallows with a rope around his neck and happily grinned in great expectation of the event. In Wooly's case, the implication was that if he caught up with Walford and McGuirk he might cheerfully walk on to the end of their rifle in order to receive a bullet.

'Do I have to be surrounded by idiots for the rest of my bloody life?' McKenzie said and strode away in a rage with yet another worry added, not even Eddie Giraldi daring to go near him again.

When Inspector Duncan from Brisbane walked into the Bari Police Station, Sergeant Willis was caught off guard. It was usual for even a Sub-Inspector to fore-warn of a visit, for the purely practical reason of ensuring the Sergeant's presence. But when Willis's telegraph message had come down the line, there had been concerned activity in other quarters outside the Police department, after which Inspector Duncan had been briefed and dispatched. And considering the purpose of his visit, he decided that it would be more discreet to make his call without attracting any more attention than was absolutely necessary. There was more than one Eddie Giraldi in the Colony.

Duncan was a tall, whiskered, dour-looking man who had been raised in India where his father had been an officer in the Bengal Artillery and the military bearing was well stamped on him. Neither did he waste time in idle chit-chat.

'Have you had any more information further to your message?' he said to Willis.

Willis was annoyed that the Inspector had just walked in off the train without giving notice. The Station needed a good sweep and a lot of work had piled up for him.

'You're lucky to find me here, sir. I've been having to

spend days away.'

'Just answer my question, Sergeant.'

'No, sir, nothing. The other two men and the cattle seem to have disappeared off the face of the earth. There hasn't been a single sighting and there's been nothing back from McKenzie's blacktracker, but it's only a matter of time, sir.' And he turned to Hackett, 'A cup of tea for the Inspector, Constable.'

Hackett hurried off to make it and Duncan glanced briefly around, taking in the condition of the place, Willis watching him. The bastard hadn't even congratulated him on catching Purdy and Spence. Instead, he was being silently critical of two peeling notices, the dusty floor and untidy bundles of paper.

'I want to see them,' Duncan said, and Willis picked up the cell keys and led him to the cell where Purdy and Spence had been put together. He unlocked the door and opened it. Duncan stood looking in but neither Purdy nor Spence looked up. They sat apart on the wooden board, manacled and leg-ironed, hunched and bent over in the dusty clothes in which they had arrived. Both were bruised and battered on their faces and hands and dried blood was thick around Purdy's right ear. Duncan didn't even have to glance at Willis to put his question.

'Resisted arrest, sir,' Willis said.

'And who was witness to it?'

'Just Constable Hackett, sir.'

Duncan nodded for him to close the cell door. It was just as he thought and his displeasure was written on his face. He turned away to return to the main room and Willis hurriedly locked the cell to go after him. It was an angry Duncan he faced.

'You don't realise the importance of your two prisoners, do you, Sergeant?'

'I certainly do, sir.'

'No, you damned well don't. And there are those in

government who would demand your immediate dismissal if they saw them as they are. You're a fool.'

Willis was completely taken aback by both the information and the insult. He wasn't even sure which government the Inspector meant; the Colonial Governor and the Queensland authorities or the Houses of Parliament in England but as it made little difference, he didn't want to invite another insult by showing ignorance.

'The government?' he said, 'what's the government got to do with it?'

'I shall say this only once, Sergeant, so listen. It's of great concern to some of them. The Colony is proud of its record of not having suffered bushrangers like New South Wales and Victoria have and you know as well as I do how impossible it is to police such an enormous area with so few men. And since it comes to us at a time when "Australia for Australians" is on the lips of many members of the public who have become unsympathetic to English ownership and English rule, they are determined that a hanging take place to set an example and a warning.'

'Oh, they'll hang, sir,' Willis said and Duncan noted the sense of pleasure in him.

'So, you're judge and jury in this community as well, are you, Sergeant?'

The acidity in Duncan's words stung Willis and he smarted. What the hell did they know about anything down in Brisbane? Upstarts. Politicians. If it hadn't been for him they would have had bloody nothing, but instead of getting thanks, all he was getting was the cracking of the whip. Anybody other than Duncan and he would have bloody told them so.

'No, sir,' he said, and watched Duncan glance around his station once more with disapproval on his face before resuming.

'What you have in your cell is Queen's Evidence. Or

will be when someone comes up from Brisbane to see them. I take it you're not in the habit of destroying or damaging such valuable witnesses for the Crown.'

Again, Willis smarted from the insult without being able to retaliate and felt angry at the rest of what had been said. He was being robbed. He wasn't going to see Purdy and Spence hang after all. They were going to be offered a lesser sentence for turning Queen's Evidence and held in custody without trial on the assumption that, at some time in the future, Walford and McGuirk were going to show themselves either in Southern Queensland or New South Wales and be captured. It was no longer important whether or not Purdy and Spence had told the truth. What was important was to make them stick to their story to satisfy the desired conclusion. It was clearly some higher authority's idea of making absolutely certain that the example be made by hanging the ring-leader. That was essential to show not only the people of Queensland but of the other Colonies as well. For lack of anything else, Purdy and Spence were the only two eye-witnesses they had who could attest to the outrageous cattle robbery, so even if Walford and McGuirk were picked up without a single head in their possession, it would still make no difference. They would still hang.

'The prisoners will speak to no one,' Duncan said, 'and you will speak to no one. You'll discuss the case with no one. And if you get any further information in, you won't send it down by telegraph but by messenger. Do you understand, Sergeant?'

'Yes, sir.'

'Get them washed, keep them shaved, attend to their wounds and see to it they get new clothing. I'll personally approve the expense. Good day to you, Sergeant.' And with that, he turned and walked out, Willis watching him go into the bright sunlight.

Hackett returned with the tea and was quick to

realise by Willis's stiff stance as he stood looking towards the open door that not only had Inspector Duncan gone but that his brief visit hadn't been a pleasant one. He also reasoned correctly that Duncan hadn't been pleased by the battered condition of Purdy and Spence. It was only a wonder that Willis hadn't been caught at it before. He only hoped that the Inspector didn't think he, Hackett, had any hand in it.

Willis continued to stand burning with resentment. It was the most important case he had ever had and he had expected a commendation for his part in it. It had never occurred to him that there might be political implications or that he would have to treat Purdy and Spence like bottled gold dust. He had looked forward to having further sessions with them, even although there was nothing left for them to say.

'I've got the tea,' Hackett said.

'Take it to the prisoners,' Willis said without turning and Hackett remained where he was, puzzled. Willis never made jokes but there could always be a first time.

'I said, take it to the bloody prisoners!'

'What?'

'Take it to them! You're going to crawl to the bastards! Crawl to them, because I'm buggered if I will! Go on, take it to them!'

Hackett, in total confusion as to what was really expected of him, began to move with the tea towards the cells, but Willis made no attempt at stopping him.

Willis could only console himself with the thought of Walford and McGuirk being delivered into his hands. He could make up for it then. No one would want to protect those two. He would show what he was really capable of and not even a doctor would be able to tell what had been done to them.

It was several days later when Constable Hackett, writing out a report at the front desk on an accident with a runaway horse, became aware of the shadow of someone entering. Although she was silhouetted for a moment against the sunlight, he knew immediately who it was. He had never spoken to her before but recognised her from her previous visits to the town with her husband. He expected to see him, too, but no one came in after her. She was alone.

'Good afternoon, Mrs McKenzie,' he said, concealing his surprise. It was unusual for any woman to come into the Police Station and even more unusual for someone like her. Females were not welcome here and not encouraged. Things happened here that would have shocked any decent woman into a faint.

Dora could both smell and sense it without having to be told, but had Hackett known it, it took a lot more than vomit or urine or cursing to make Dora McKenzie faint, and she was more in a fighting than a fainting mood. She had gone to a lot of trouble to get her way and get here so soon. Don had only given way in the hope that it might get her back on his side and back to his bed, but had insisted that the station-hand, Rudd, accompany her for her safety on the shopping trip to Bari. Once off the train, she had given the dull and boring man money with which to quench his thirst with beer and hurried here for her real purpose.

'I would like to see Sergeant Willis, please, if he's here,' she said, but there had been little need to ask. Willis had heard the name McKenzie mentioned from inside his little room at the back and appeared before Hackett could make a move to go and get him. Willis was far from pleased to see her and Dora turned to him. The man looked even more evil than she remembered from his call on them not so long before.

'Mrs McKenzie, m'am,' he said, politely enough.

'I've come down on my own,' Dora said, 'Mr McKenzie was unable to leave the property as you may well understand.'

Willis knew very well it was most unlikely that

McKenzie would have sent his wife with a message, even a highly confidential one, and he certainly wouldn't have sent her to the Police Station. The bloody woman was up to something. The sooner he got rid of her the better.

'You can tell Mr McKenzie, m'am, we've got nothing to report,' and he turned to go back into his room.

'That's not why I've come,' Dora said, stopping him, and paused. 'I'd like to speak to the two men, Purdy and Spence, you have here.'

Both Willis and Hackett looked astonished at her audacity but although Dora was well aware of their hostility, she looked defiantly back at them in turn.

'You can't do that,' Willis said.

'Why not? Because I'm a woman?'

Willis glowered at her, the scar on his chin looked white. Any ordinary husband would have given such a wife a bloody good beating, but Dora held her stance.

'What if I told you I'm here with Mr McKenzie's authority?' she said, but the Sergeant was not to be fooled by that. But instead of saying, 'I'd say you were a bloody liar, a cow and an interfering bitch', he said, 'It would make no difference.'

'We simply want to hear for ourselves what these men have to say.'

'No one talks to these men. No one,' Willis said and tried to turn his back on her once more. 'Good afternoon, m'am.'

But Dora was not finished with her attempt.

'As Manager, my husband represents the owners. Are you trying to tell me that not even the owners whose cattle they took have any right to speak to them?'

Willis, hardly able to restrain himself, answered only to get rid of her. Had she been a man, he would have had her outside by now.

'It's no longer their business,' he said, 'or yours. It's a criminal matter and solely in the hands of the police.

But don't be in any doubt – when the other two are caught, they'll hang.'

He disappeared into his little room, leaving Dora standing outside it, Hackett looking at her worriedly. She was clearly a little mad.

'You mean,' she said, directing her words through the doorway of Willis's office, 'that before they've even been caught and given an account of themselves, they've been tried, found guilty and sentenced?'

Willis replied to that by returning to his door and slamming it in her face and she caught a brief glimpse of the hate that was in his eyes. That frightened her, but it didn't dissolve the anger she was feeling. It wasn't only the rudeness, but there was an uneasy feeling that she was being regarded as a criminal herself and would not have to say much more before she found herself being charged with something. Gathering her dignity like a cloak around all her swirling emotions, she began to make for the front door, but before she reached it, she felt it necessary to say something more and turned to Hackett whose head was down, busily occupied with his report.

'I'd like you to tell Sergeant Willis I don't think I like the way you administer the law,' she said, with a sting in her words, 'I don't like it at all.'

Hackett, keeping well out of it, pretended he hadn't heard and didn't lift his head or stop his writing. Dora then made her way out, Hackett very relieved she had gone.

It was with great disappointment and a sense of defeat that Dora walked away from there. Living for such long periods in isolation on Albert Downs where, as mistress of the house, she was shown respect, even by her husband, she sometimes forgot the humiliations women of the Colony often had to endure. Even at the hotel, because Don was not with her, the owner paid scant attention to her needs. It was only with Don at her side she was anyone. Without him, she was nothing. Willis would never have dared behave like that to her with her husband present but she wasn't going to be able to tell him. It made her more conscious than ever of her position. In defence of the gentle and obliging Harry who she'd known for six years, she was entirely alone. For a moment she wished that he might be dead and had gone beyond the reach of all of them.

She would have been more than astonished to know, like everyone else would have been, that not only was Harry still alive, if only just, but that he was certainly beyond the reach of all but the blacktracker in his tartan trousers, and even Harry himself didn't know that.

The last hope for Harry and a Bluey who had become convinced that death was now upon them, lay in the gradual appearance of herbage. But the last drop of water had been sipped between them the day before. It seemed both impossible and pointless to go on but Harry went on and forced Bluey to do the same. Only the big white bull, the strongest of them all, needed no urging.

It was midday with the searing sun right overhead when Harry stopped, peering at the horizon directly ahead of them. For a moment he thought he might be imagining it but, despite the shimmer of heat rising from the far ground, it did not look like a mirage or some trick of distant cloud. To his red-rimmed eyes, it became unmistakable. A long line of faint, greeny-blue. They were trees. That did not necessarily mean that there was also water but it was only in his overwhelming excitement at the prospect of it that found him speech because his swollen tongue and mouth made it almost insurmountable. He raised his stock-whip to point.

'Look!' he shouted, 'Look!' And the half-dead Bluey

heard and raised his hanging head. It took a while for him to focus through the slits of his painful lids. But although he could see what Harry had seen, his faith in survival had already died and been buried back along his tracks. He made no attempt to make comment or reply.

Then they saw something else. Away to the left of the line, a thin, sparse, wisp of smoke was rising above it. Every minute of every hour of every day, they had looked for such a thing, Harry in total conviction that if they saw that they were seeing water.

Out of despair, there is nothing like water to resurrect hope in a man dying of thirst and that smoke raised it in Bluey. He dug his heels in to make his horse walk faster and the faint line began to look as green as any field of home.

Only an hour later, a few crested pigeons flew overhead and they sighted a dingo, and a few hours after that, they were not in a condition to assess the sight that lay before them. The water-hole was as wide and long as a river and great flocks of all kinds of birds fled from the branches of the trees in alarm. Harry and Bluey simply threw themselves to the bank and drank until it was heaved back from their stomachs and drank again. But the process of recovery didn't take long and Harry finally sat with his back against the trunk of a tree, looking at the big white bull and the huge mob spread out along quarter of a mile taking their fill, the other horses somewhere amongst them. Never in his life had he felt such a sense of achievement. He had only lost four head in the crossing of that dry, stony country. He looked at Bluey who was still flat on the bank as if unwilling to remove his gaze from the sight in case, by turning his back on it, it might suddenly disappear. Harry grinned.

'I told yer there'd be nothin' to it, mate, didn't I?' he said, but Bluey was still in no mood for lightness.

Unlike Harry, he dwelt on the fact that they would have perished in one more day. Or worse, in two. He didn't have to be told that this water didn't stretch to where they were going. It was not a river but a water-hole and he thought he could see the end of it from where he lay.

'God knows where we are,' he said, not for a moment thinking that Harry had any idea either. But Harry did.

'I reckon it must be Cooper's Creek.'

At that, Bluey rose to turn to him in irritation. He had heard the name Cooper's Creek mentioned from other men but never from Harry. And it was spoken of as if it was some kind of mythical place that was supposed to lie somewhere in the middle of Australia. What he knew for certain was that Harry had never been there or not only he but everybody on Albert Downs would have known it. It was like saying a man had been to the Poles and when he came back just forgot to mention it.

'An' how t'e hell would ye know t'at?' he said.

Harry didn't for sure and was only being guided by his instinct again. He had first heard of it when he was a boy and the news had travelled around that two explorers had died there on an expedition. Better not mention that to his mate. Too superstitious. He wouldn't like it.

'I don't see how's it could be anywhere else,' he said. 'It's the only big Creek around this way. There ain't no other like it, far as I know. It's got ter be the Cooper. I was hopin' we would strike it.'

'Bejasus, did God put a bloody map in yer head when yer mot'er gave birt' to ye t'en?'

Harry was a little embarrassed by that. Although he was sure he was right, there was no further explanation he could make. He had also come to know Bluey well enough to divine that his irritation with him was not because of seeming to know where he was, but having the saving of his life cut so fine. The shadow of death was still hanging over him and Harry understood it. Bluey was somebody who looked back all the time while he himself found it easier to look forward.

'That bit's over, mate,' he said, 'forget it.' Then he looked around. No longer was there any smoke and there was not a single aborigine in sight. 'What we got ter do now is keep an eye open for the blacks. They'll be watchin' us an' we don't want ter frighten 'em. When they sees we's friendly, they'll come ter us. We need 'em.'

Bluey lay down to drink again, then sat looking at the water as if hypnotised by it while Harry gathered wood and lit a fire before going off to find the pack-horse, unload it and get supplies.

Far to the north, there was one aborigine who was not in hiding and as he looked across the stony country where the big white bull and the mob had gone, he knew it would not be easy. He had never been any-where yet where he had been unable to find meat of some sort, even although it often took a long time to find it, but water was another matter. There appeared to be no part of any kind of watershed he could see. That meant he might have to make many big diversions to find it and, in turn, that meant a longer distance. He had no thoughts of any kind on the men with the animals he tracked. Finding the cattle and finding some other white boss man to whom to give the letters were his only aims. But time meant nothing to him in this timeless land. Time was simply the space between one meal and the next, between one drop of water and another. It had nothing to do with ritual, celebration, or the story telling with pigment on stone but all the same, these things were missed. Twice, out of sheer loneliness, he felt tempted to return to his people. Only the thought of all the good tucker his tribe should have been getting from boss McKenzie of Albert Downs made him go on.

He rose from his squatting position in his now dirty tartan trousers. Grasping his stick and spear and with the satchel of letters slung across him, but without any food or water whatsoever, he headed once more after the big white bull and the mob.

As the sun went down over the water-hole at Cooper's Creek, Harry took sweet johnny cakes and a quart-pot of sweet tea to Bluey who was still seated by the water's edge and was pleased to find that he had cheered up a good bit.

'Begod, t'ere's even ducks here, Harry,' he said. 'Not real ducks like on a farm, ye understand, but ducks all t'e same.'

'Yer thinkin' of Ireland again, is yer?'

'I is, I is t'at. An' I t'ink, whatever black deeds did I do for God to bring me to t'is cursed country.'

The shadows were long and cool and the birds were beginning to roost in the tree-tops and the water was calm and shining and turning blood red, and the big white bull and the mob were beginning to lie down.

'Look at it,' Harry said, 'it's a picture. It's beautiful, mate. An' the same God that made yer Ireland, made this too.'

'The question is, did he make it for men, Harry?'

''Course he made it for bloody men. An' I reckon we'll see 'em in the mornin'.'

After dark, with Harry only a few feet away, Bluey curled up and went soundly to sleep. Harry stayed awake keeping guard in case some misguided black was taking them as dangerous, but he kept the rifle hidden. The night life began to emerge. Bats fluttered from under branches and rats scampered over the earth and tiny mouse-like creatures poked their noses out of tiny burrows and somewhere in the distance a dingo howled.

For a few moments, Harry gazed on the sleeping figure with affection and smiled. He didn't know that what he was looking at was shortly to become a one man Irish Rebellion that would threaten to bring all his ambitions to an end.

Seven

Desperation and helplessness her only constant companions, Lilly Boyd sat in the lamplight of her room counting her money again. There was little of it left. It was only to shield her stupidity and keep some pride that she had returned the thirty shillings to Mrs McKenzie. With it she had written in a careful and neat hand, 'Adelaide is a wonderful place and full of sights and there are a lot of people. I want to thank you very much for all you did for me. I have not made up my mind if I will buy the hat shop yet. I hope Mr McKenzie found his white bull. Thank you again. Yours sincerely, Miss Lillian Boyd.'

It was no mistake that she neglected to put her address on it for there was always the chance that some friend of her former mistress coming to Adelaide might be asked to call on her and the truth would be discovered.

For ten days she had tramped the better streets of Adelaide, knocking on doors to ask for work in service, but time and again she was turned away, sometimes without even getting the opportunity to speak to the mistress of the house. On two occasions, the doors didn't open at all, although she could see she was being looked at from behind curtains. And there were few other places left to try.

What she didn't know was that Mrs Googe had cleverly anticipated her efforts. All she had had to do was to mention to one of her Christian ladies, 'I'm not sure I can trust one of the guests staying at my hotel. It's funny for her to be all done up in an expensive green dress when I know she's not that class. She couldn't show me a single reference either.'

It was all she had said and all she needed to. The warning of suspicion and distrust passed from mistress to mistress and servant to servant at a rate Eddie Giraldi in the sparsely populated area of the railhead west of Bari would not have dreamed possible. It was also why two other ladies with their husbands who had come to stay at the hotel for a few days kept avoiding her.

'Why don't you ask her to leave, Mrs Googe?' one of them had asked, but Mrs Googe had the answer to that.

'It wouldn't be Christian, madame, but don't worry. I'm keeping a close eye on her.'

Mrs Googe was doing that all right and her only worry was that Lilly might be doing the same to her. Aware that Lilly sat in her room half the night looking out of the window, she had taken to going out the back at night and returning the same way.

Lilly didn't have to guess who it was when the knock came on her bedroom door. Mrs Googe was the only one in all of Adelaide with whom she had any real human contact and she let her in.

'I don't know if I told you, dearie,' she said, 'about the oil.'

'The oil?'

'For the lamp, dearie. It's extra.'

Lilly had never thought about the oil for her lamp. She had assumed it was part of what she was paying and couldn't remember it having been mentioned. Her assumption had been correct but Mrs Googe had thought it up as she was getting impatient for Lilly's money to run out. She had to make it sound reasonable.

'See, if it wasn't one of the rules, some people would leave their lamps burning all night, wouldn't they? Not that I'm saying you would, dearie, you being a good thoughtful girl, but there's some as isn't, I can tell yer.'

The extra was another blow to Lilly but she reached for her purse. 'I didn't know. I'm sorry. How much is it?'

'Only one an' six up to now, but you can pay me later.'

'No, no, I'll pay you now,' Lilly insisted and gave her the money. Mrs Googe gave her sympathy for a receipt.

'You're a good girl and deserve better, Lilly,' she said. 'I'd liked ter have had a daughter like you, but whatever's going to become of yer?'

Lilly could only shake her head and try to hold herself together from collapsing into self-pity again and Mrs Googe patted her softly with one of her black-clad arms.

'You don't want to worry. Things'll come right for you. I know they will. An' you don't want to starve yourself, you know. How about coming down to the kitchen and havin' a cup of tea with me, eh?'

Lilly was only too pleased by the invitation and even managed to raise a smile through her misery. Night after night she sat alone struggling to think how she could find a way out of her situation, unable to see anything but throwing herself back into some other charitable institution like the one from which she had come. And that brought only tears.

'Thanks very much, Mrs Googe,' she said, and made to follow her through the door.

'Don't forget the lamp, Lilly,' Mrs Googe reminded her and Lilly turned back quickly to blow it out. Mrs Googe's square, red mouth parted in a smile. She had instincts, too, and knew the timing of her invitation was right. It would not be long before she had the girl in her control. The sooner the better. Girls from the country sometimes got their eyes open too soon if they were allowed. And there was the daily danger that she might accidentally chance on some other work and escape. Girls like Lilly were very hard to come by in Adelaide and very valuable because of it. She had to be careful if she wasn't to lose her. What she needed was to have Lilly gain more confidence in her.

'It was wrong of us to think I could er been anythin' else but what I am, Mrs Googe,' she said. 'Childish. But I wouldn't listen, would I? I thought I knew as much as anybody, an' I didn't, did I?'

Mrs Googe took the kettle from the hot stove. The girl was starting to learn already.

'We all have our burdens, dearie,' she said. 'I had mine when my husband disappeared.'

'Disappeared?'

'He was assistant to a Missionary and one day he went out into the bush with bibles and was never seen again. Nobody knows the suffering I had not knowing if he was dead or alive. Speared, they said he must have been.'

Lilly felt sorry for her and said, 'How awful for yer.'

She would have felt a lot more awful if she'd known that Mr Googe had never been speared in his life; a life being served in jail in Sydney for not only trying to murder Mrs Googe but two other women as well. And that Mrs Googe's only burden was the fear of him ever escaping and turning up to try again because it was she who had informed on him in order to get rid of him.

'I don't talk about it any more, Lilly,' Mrs Googe said, 'but I'm pleased I told you. It helps to share. It hasn't been easy making my way. It's hard for a woman. Life doesn't always turn out just as you expected it.'

'I've found that out for myself, Mrs Googe.'

'Of course you have, dearie, of course you have,' Mrs Googe said sympathetically and took out some biscuits covered in sugar.

'The stupidest bit is I was taught you never got anythin' for nothin' an' that only hard work got a reward. Lookin' at meself now, it's only a wonder how they ever managed to teach us how ter read an write.'

'You shouldn't blame yourself, Lilly. Something will happen. You'll see. The thing is to see opportunities when they face you. Even if you think it goes against the grain at first, you should never miss an opportunity when it's offered. A lot of things work out for the best when you don't know it, dearie. Life's full of surprises.'

Mrs Googe dispensed her tea, philosophy and biscuits with generosity, seemingly full of concern for the poor girl. But she knew very well that when Lilly had to go back to her room to sit alone in the dark in order to try and further eke out her dwindling money, she would feel worse if anything. The withdrawal of light and caring would see to that.

Bluey slept long and securely and the sun was peeping up when he woke. He raised himself to find that Harry was not there and looked around, apprehension growing in him. He got to his feet and called.

'Harry! Harry!'

'Over here, mate!' came Harry's voice from somewhere up the creek and he started to walk there. Cattle were grazing all around. Then he stopped as he saw the big white bull standing near a clump of trees near the bank. A rope was leading down from it towards a group of aborigines. They were squatting, completely naked, and holding spears. He couldn't see Harry who was seated out of his vision and thought at first he might have been taken prisoner. He was about to turn and run for his life to find the rifle when Harry's voice came to him again with no anxiety and as if he was reading his thoughts.

'Don't do nothin' ter frighten 'em mate. They're

our friends.'

Bluey hesitated then started to make a cautious approach, and none of the aborigines made a move to threaten him. He found Harry seated casually behind a tree with his hat stuck on the back of his head and the remains of a bag of sugar near his feet. In one hand he was holding the rope which was attached to the ring on the nose of the big white bull which was standing quiet as a mouse.

'Morning,' he said. 'By God yer can sleep. Plant your jack.'

Bluey carefully sat down alongside him. The blacks didn't look at all friendly as far as he was concerned. They looked wild and he gawked at the one who squatted closest to Harry, facing him. He had grey hair and hanging around his neck on bark string like a pendant was a watch. Or at least, it had been a watch, for the glass had long since gone, there were no hands and red earth was imbedded in the cracks of the face. Glancing directly at Bluey, the old man fingered the watch to draw attention to it, just in case Bluey had missed it. He clearly had great pride in it.

Harry held out the sugar sack to him as he had obviously already done several times before, for not only the old man but all the others broke into wide grins. The old man dipped his fingers in, drew them out and sucked them with pleasure and Harry offered the bag around.

'Nothin' like a bit of good tucker ter start off ther day, is there, eh?' he said to them, and although they understood not a word they all grinned back at him. And Bluey, his first fears fading, looked around the scene more relaxed.

'I reckoned the best way of drawin' 'em in was seein' Lord Wallah Wallah Banjo bein' led along,' he said by way of explaining the bull's presence, and he indicated the grey-haired elder with a nod, 'Snowy there couldn't resist it.'

He had certainly been right about that. A huge, powerful, white god of a horned beast with what appeared to be a polished gold ring growing around the nose of its great head being guided by a man it could have crushed in an instant but to whom it seemed as submissive and obedient as any wife was a sight to impress anyone. And the man talked unknown words to it. Presented with such a vision, curiosity had over-whelmed their fears and the elder revealed himself first to show his courage. But when they had first seen the two, scarecrow-like figures approaching on horse-back with what looked like all the animals on earth, they had been terrified, particularly as many of them had never set eyes on cattle before.

It said a lot for Harry's new confidence that in less than a day he had them squatting around him, happily eating out of his sugar bag. But it took a lot longer than that to find out what he wanted to know.

During the following few days as he and Bluey rode to keep the mob from wandering too far, he allowed the trust to develop and the aborigines stayed around watching, their women appearing, too. Then Harry got the elder and others around him again by the side of the big water-hole. The big white bull and the rest of the mob were well recovered and it was important to try and find out what lay ahead to the south-west, the direction he wanted to go. Bluey watched him fill a quart-pot at the water's edge and return to squat facing the elder. He poured some into his own hand and held it.

'Water,' he said, and pointed along towards where he had discovered the Cooper ran to a dry bed. 'Where is water?'

Bluey, already with fresh anxiety rising in him at ever having to leave there, looked on Harry's antics with nothing but cynicism.

'Bejasus, an' ye might as well ask him what time it is,' he said, but Harry kept persevering, pointing at the sun then covering his eyes in an attempt at getting the man he had named Snowy to try and understand the concept of a day. Constantly he poured water and pointed and stretched his arms to try and denote short and long distance and Bluey, losing all interest, got up and walked away.

It was not that Snowy didn't know what Harry was asking. He knew exactly what he wanted but it was impossible to try and tell him. The nearest water to the south-west was a very long way. But neither Harry nor Snowy gave up trying, both feeling the frustration of not being able to communicate and hours later they were still at it. In his own environment, Snowy was a highly intelligent man and had the wisdom of his years.

'Watta,' he said, already having picked up that word and waved to the south-west a long way away with his hand. Then he scooped up a handful of dust and spread it between where Harry had tried to make two small pools. Harry made hills but Snowy flattened them, indicating that the country in between was dry and completely open.

It was late afternoon when Harry returned to Bluey who was sitting in their small camp. What he had clearly gathered was that there were no further waterholes down the Cooper at this time, which, in any case, turned in a great loop to the north-west and more stony desert. The south-west was another dry watercourse and water was a long way. How long, Harry could only make a guess at from all the signs but it was at least a week or ten days at a fast pace. He wouldn't tell Bluey that and did his best not to look worried.

'It's not so bad but we'll have ter dry-stage 'em mate,' he said, as if it was the most natural thing in the world and Bluey got up, anger on his face. Not so bad and dry-staging were a contradiction in terms. Cattle were only dry-staged across waterless country as a last resort and even that was conducted with the knowledge of exactly where the water was. Dry-staging was racing a mob hell for leather through the comparative cool of the hours of darkness to cover as much distance as possible and letting them rest during the heat of the day until the water was reached.

'Ye never dry-staged in yer life,' he said, 'an' neit'er have I', but Harry just casually shrugged.

'We'll just have ter learn.'

'Then ye'll learn on yer bloody own because I'm not goin' into no more waterless country an' t'at's t'at!'

'There is water, I'm tellin' yer. It's only a matter of gettin' to it.'

'T'e savage black heat'en tell ye all t'at, did he? Well, I'll tell ye where t'e water is – it's right here at me bloody feet an' I'm stayin' wit' it until I can find a safe way out of here!'

Bluey's anger risen to a fury, there was no way in which Harry could temper it and appease him. Anything he said simply made Bluey more determined.

'I'm takin' the mob on if I have ter do it on my bloody own,' Harry said but that was to no effect either.

'T'en t'at's what ye'll be doin', ye mad eejit, because I'm finished! I'm not dyin' in anot'er desert!'

Hurt, Harry turned to stand looking at the water-hole and Bluey, nursing his rage, sat down again, gazing at nothing. They stayed like that not moving for a long while. Harry knew he was never going to shift his friend an inch, no matter what he said or did. But if it was close to an impossibility for only two men to dry-stage fifteen hundred head, it was doubly so for only one. At the same time, it was that or nothing. He would have to try and that's all there was to it. He caught his horse and saddled up but Bluey didn't even seem interested in watching him.

The sun was going down when Harry rode up to him

again. His stock-whip was coiled over his arm and he carried a small bundle in a sack that contained no more than a few pounds of flour, tea and sugar in total.

'We's been mates since yer first come ter Albert Downs,' he said. 'I wants yer ter know I never had another mate like yer. Yer took us for a man an' not just a rouseabout. I took you for a man, too, an' I still does, so don't think I think less of yer. An' I'm not blamin' yer. I know we could leave the bull an' the mob here where there's feed an' water, but if I did that there ain't no point in doin' all we done.'

Bluey didn't answer and didn't look up. There was nothing he wanted to say. Harry leaned over towards him and dropped the sacking down gently near his feet, and said, 'That's half the tucker we got left. I's hobbled up half the horses for yer, too.'

He sat for a few moments sadly looking down at his friend, hoping he might say something but he didn't. Prolonging it would only make it worse.

'I gotter get goin', mate. Good luck to yer.'

Choked, Harry turned his horse away. After a while, Bluey heard Harry's horse breaking into a canter and the beginning of his whip cracking and shouts and piercing whistles as he began his lone effort at rounding up the huge, scattered mob to get them on the move.

The sudden feeling of having been deserted to work out his own salvation by a creek in the middle of nowhere had Bluey springing to his feet in yet another burst of anger. He had hoped up until the very last moment that Harry would come to see that their lives were more important and that with the droving of such a large mob, God had given them all the chances they were ever going to get.

'Ye'll never do it, ye mad, bloody yellow bearded eejit!' he yelled after him towards the dying of the light. 'Ye got bloody kangaroos in yer top bloody paddock! Ye's goin' ter die!'

But his farewell went unheard. Harry had gone too far away. It didn't matter. He was deaf to all sense and reason. He was everything they had said about him. Well, he, Bluey McGuirk was going to survive. And the Devil himself was not going to make him shift from the safety of the water-hole until he was ready. He would stay there for months if he had to until he found a way.

Along the banks, cattle lowed noisily. Used for so long to travelling only by day, they were confused by being urged into a drove at such an hour. Even the big white bull was surprised when Harry came up to it to poke it lightly on the rump with the handle of his whip. It had just settled comfortably on the ground to chew its cud.

'Come on, mate,' Harry said to it, 'there's only you an' me left now.'

The big white bull eyed him for a moment as if not too happy with the disturbance, but then it rose.

It was far from simple with the rest. Harry had to ride as hard as he had ever done, voice and whip in constant use as he cantered as fast as he could go from the head of the mob, along the flank to tail and back again, over and over without cease. But there was too much ground to cover, too many head for him to handle. As soon as he got one part of the mob to break into a trot, another lot somewhere else would ease up or spread. As froth poured from his horse's mouth and neck, he tasted the full flavour of his impossible task. But he didn't give up. Quickly changing over to a fresh horse, he drove himself and the mob on. But after the water-hole ended, it was only with the greatest of difficulty that he managed to turn them over the dry river bed to the south side of the Cooper. It was very dark and he prayed that it might become a bit easier when the moon came up later in the night. Although the big white bull, followed by other leaders, was prepared to keep up a good pace, the mob was beginning to stretch out for miles. The ragged figure didn't stop and rode and shouted and whistled and cracked the air with his whip like a man possessed.

Bluey woke in the moonlight, conscious that something had touched him, had lightly run over his body. In some trepidation he opened his eyes and saw two large rats scuttle away from his bag of meagre supplies beside him. In seconds, he was on his feet, clutching at the rifle Harry had left behind in their camp. He looked around and listened. At first, there was nothing to see, and it seemed as silent as the grave. He had slept through every night he had been there in the security of Harry's presence and was experiencing this for the first time. The silence was deceiving and he knew it. Things were there and all about him.

He spun in fright as something splashed in the dark, leaden water and sent broken, shining ripples towards him like a web reaching to entrap him. The sudden black flutter appearing right at his face then darting away at a sharp angle stopped his heart. It was a bat and it had almost touched him. The horror of having a creature of hell tangled in his hair made him dive for his hat and in one move he had it tight down over his ears. He stood again, clutching the rifle hard, looking around him, his imagination growing steadily with his fears. Shadows moved and he was surrounded by black evil. He smelt it in the very air he breathed. 'Holy Mot'er, help us,' he muttered out loud but it didn't help. The tortured branches of the Coolibahs that glowed faintly in the moon became the limbs of long forgotten ghosts waiting patiently for human Christian prey to come within their reach. There were scuffling sounds, scratching sounds, fluttering sounds, and from the distance a low, moaning, vibrating sound.

'Jasus, oh Jasus,' he gasped as the Devil himself appeared in the form of a large snake slithering a little way off along the water's edge and his heart missed more beats as he stepped backwards away from it. Only another noise coming from across the creek swivelled his panic-stricken eyes away long enough to look. And they stuck there. What he saw was a progression of broken skeletons, ghouls risen from unholy graves. And they were coming to get him. He stood transfixed in the complete and absolute terror that comes only to those trapped in a living nightmare and with nowhere to turn.

By then, no man and no Saint could have explained to him that what was moving along the opposite bank through the trees was a group of aborigines who had streaked their faces and bodies with white for a ritual, and that they intended no harm to him.

To the south-west, Harry did not let up. But had it not been for the big white bull, there would have been no chance whatsoever of even keeping the strung out mob going roughly in the same direction. He had been at it solidly for six hours and he neither heard nor saw the rider who came up behind him until the man was almost on his shoulder. He turned his head and with great surprise, saw it was Bluey, his small sack of supplies tied to his saddle and with the spare horses running behind him carrying his loaded water bags. But even in the heavily dusted moonlight, the fury on Bluey's peeling face was clear to see.

'I just wants ye to know t'is, ye mad eejit!' he shouted, 'me mot'er never reared a jib!', meaning that his mother was incapable of bearing and raising any child who would ever back down or back away from even the most awesome of challenges. That he had just had to do so without as much as anybody laying a finger on him was, of course, the reason for both his fury and his words, but he gave Harry no time to say anything at all, quickly swinging his horse around the moment he had spoken to go back towards the tail of the mob, raising his whip and cracking it as he went.

Harry pulled his horse up and sat for a few minutes

listening to him as he worked, and felt utter happiness. It didn't matter that Bluey was still so angry with him. He had come back. He was his mate again. And he was never so badly needed. He wouldn't ask him what had changed his mind. That was his business. There were some things even mates liked to keep to themselves.

He dug in his heels to shoot his horse forward. 'Hi, hi, hi!' he yelled in a whoop of joy. There were still a couple of hours of cool darkness left and, with Bluey back by his side, he set about his task more vigorously than ever.

It was only a few days later when, despite all the diversions he had had to make to survive, a weak and thirsting Wooly approached the big water-hole on Cooper's Creek. And his new tartan trousers had become as dirty and torn as his old ones. But the aborigines did not run and hide from him. There were different procedures to be followed with a black man like themselves who was a stranger than with the foreign white men. Wooly could have represented a kind of trouble they fully understood and for reasons they fully understood. He could have been a messenger of ill-will on tribal affairs. They had no reason to connect him with the white men who had just left.

It was therefore no surprise to Wooly when he saw the grey-haired man and several others come out to challenge him and he stopped and waited for them to come to him. The surprise was all on Snowy's side for, as he got closer, spear ready in hand, he took in the tartan trousers and the leather satchel.

'Wooliallulumba,' Wooly said, introducing himself, and pointed away to the north-east to show where he had come from. Then, finding that they were able to understand each other, he explained that he was tracking the big white bull and the many cattle for a big white boss man who was supplying his tribe with plenty flour and sugar.

'Suga,' said Snowy displaying the knowledge he had gained from Harry, and the challenge on Wooly was all over.

The elder and his men were highly impressed with Wooly. He was clearly a very important man to be tracking the big white bull with the golden nose. And the tartan trousers were obviously a badge of great significance. They all stood happily grinning at each other.

Wooly, delighted by how his new-found friends were regarding him, played his role to the hilt. As they led him to the Creek, he walked upright with pride, all the time fingering his satchel.

As a highly honoured guest, he was stuffed with nardoo cakes and meat until it was coming out of his ears, and he made the very best of it. For two whole days he did nothing but fill himself to the full, sleep it off, get rid of the waste, and start again. But there was to be a lot more hospitality than that for his hosts were proud, too, and they had a lot to show him. After a conference, it was decided that Wooly would see their best sacred paintings that were hidden in a sacred place only a day's journey away. And as the organising for the celebration got under way, men went out to far places where they knew they could gather the right pigments to wear.

In return, Wooly felt obliged to reveal the important contents of the satchel. For many hours, Snowy and his entire tribe squatted around studying the mysterious envelopes with 'To Whom It May Concern' written on them in McKenzie's copperplate hand. They could have been a form of magic. Wooly found it not the slightest bit embarrassing that he couldn't explain the signs although he knew it had to do with the bull and the cattle. They were white men's secrets, he simply told them and left it at that, but by the time they had been returned to the satchel, they had a whole tribe of black men's dirty finger marks on them. Only the women and children hadn't been allowed to touch them.

It was little wonder that Wooly was happy to linger at Cooper's Creek. And perhaps even more of a wonder that he didn't decide to settle there for good and find a new wife, for if it was a dark, evil hole in the middle of a God-forsaken land to Bluey McGuirk, it was being back in the richness of happy civilisation to Wooly. As it was, what it did mean by him staying so long was that if Harry and Bluey did manage to escape perishing from thirst, Wooly would be giving them yet another short reprieve from the gallows.

At the Balmoral Hotel, Mrs Googe made her way up to Lilly's room. For well over a week she had deliberately avoided contact with her. Twice, the girl had come to knock on her door but, both times, she knew who it was and pretended she wasn't there. And to further Lilly's loneliness, she had given her a key to let herself in if she went out. For the past two days, Mrs Googe had noted that Lilly hadn't moved from her room except to go down and empty her po into the large tin drum out the back that was carted away once a week. She knew the time was ripe. Lilly had got to her lowest and was at her most vulnerable. She tapped on the door. 'Are you there, my dear?' she said in her genteel voice and, in a moment, Lilly opened up. Although her face was pale and drawn, Mrs Googe could tell she was pleased.

'Mrs Googe,' she said, and Mrs Googe went in and closed the door behind her, then stood with her hands clasped together at her lap.

'Have you had any luck yet, dearie?' she said, knowing full well she hadn't and Lilly shook her head.

'No, I've tried everywhere.'

'Well, I'm sorry about that. See, I've very special guests coming and they always get this room. It's the best view. You'll have to vacate.'

She watched Lilly's face drop, saw the look of despair return, the struggle to hold back the tears.

'But I've nowhere else to go, Mrs Googe. Nowhere.'

'I wouldn't say that, dearie. There must be a lot of people would want to take in a girl like you.'

'But they don't, they don't. And I don't have the money to go to another hotel, yer know that. People out there don't care. None of them.'

'It's sad to hear such a truth from young lips. I was a lot older than you were before I learned that. But there is people who thinks they do and I should know. I give enough to their charities. Maybe I can get you into one.'

'No! No!' Lilly said, the tears beginning, 'I don't want to. I won't.'

Mrs Googe went to her. The girl looked as if she might faint and she wrapped her black-clad arms around her and comforted her.

'There, there, there's no need for that, Lilly dear. It's not the end of the world. I told yer before nothin's ever that bad, didn't I? You'll find something. I know yer will, a girl like you. There's a lot of opportunities about for them who sore needs them. It's only a case of knowin' them when yer sees them. Even I'm looking for a girl to help out in another little place I've got.'

Mrs Googe continued to hold her, patting her softly with her spidery hand, giving her time to let that bit of news sink in before going on with the rest of it. 'It's only the pity it isn't for somebody like you, even if you is used to the hard life of being a servant girl. See, there's no pay with it, only keep. And you're a cut above. But, see, the right one will be grateful enough when I find 'er, won't she?'

She felt Lilly's head part from her own and released her arms to let her go, seeing the hope rise in Lilly's tear-stained face.

'What's wrong with me? You're wrong, Mrs Googe. I'm not a cut above. I wouldn't care about pay if I had a place. Honest. It would give us time. It could be a start. An' I can work as hard as anybody.'

177

Then Mrs Googe watched the disappointment on her face as she said, 'No, Lilly, no. It's not for you. You can get something a lot better. You wouldn't like it.'

'But I would like it, Mrs Googe. I would,' Lilly said in some desperation, and began to plead for the payless job, willing to work her fingers to the bone. But Mrs Googe kept denying her, at the same time showing motherly concern and sympathy.

'You's made for better, Lilly. An' see, there's other things. I got to be able to trust the girl. I can't run things proper without trust. I won't have gossip. I've got my reputation to think about.'

In other circumstances, Lilly might have stopped to wonder what she could possibly have gossiped about that might be detrimental to Mrs Googe's reputation but she was drowning and the lifeline that was being dangled before her blinded her to all else.

'You can trust me, Mrs Googe. You know you can. I would never say anythin' against yer it wouldn't matter what it was. If you gave us the job I'd be grateful to yer for the rest of me life. Honest I would.'

Mrs Googe made her wait on edge, appearing to waver but still with many doubts.

'I don't know,' she said. 'No, I can't. Well I don't know.'

'Please, Mrs Googe. Please.'

Mrs Googe looked at her as if trying to make up her mind. And finding it very difficult.

'I suppose when I come to think on it,' she said finally, 'there could be other opportunities for you with me but it would be up to you to see them, dearie. An' I wouldn't want to hear any complaints from you mind.'

Lilly's face lit up as it hadn't done in a very long while. 'You mean you'll give it us?'

'All right, I'll try you, Lilly. Just try you.'

Lilly threw her arms around Mrs Googe with relief and delight and Mrs Googe held her tightly, her red lips parting into a smile.

Only an hour later after a welcome cup of tea and a small meal which she badly needed, Lilly, clutching her little bag, got into a cab with Mrs Googe to be taken to her new job. Her head was full of questions about it, but Mrs Googe sat well back and was very quiet. All she had told Lilly was that it wasn't another hotel like the Balmoral, but a house and all that she would be required to do was make beds, clean, do washing and cook for herself. Lilly didn't think it was right to disturb her and didn't want to appear too nosey.

Quiet as she was, Mrs Googe felt well satisfied. The timing of getting a new girl could not have suited her better as the girl Lilly was replacing had finally decided to change her occupation.

The cab went a long way and began to enter an area Lilly hadn't seen before. There were no places there that looked as if they might employ servants and were quite unlike the houses she'd been trying so hard to get into. The dusty streets were narrow with alleys going off. Small verandahs with leaning posts. A forge of some kind. A wool store. Smells, shadows, drunks lying against walls of wood and corrugated iron. She had no idea where she was when they pulled up in front of a house and Mrs Googe said, 'We're here, dearie.'

Lilly got out and stood looking at the house as Mrs Googe paid off the cabbie. The foundations were convict brick up to knee high, the rest weatherboard with peeling paint. The windows were shuttered on both levels of its two stories and the whole place had the appearance of having been deserted long before and left to rot. Only weeds grew around it. A chill gust of wind suddenly sprang up and it brought the first spattering of raindrops with it.

Mrs Googe unlocked the door and Lilly, not knowing what to make of such a broken-down house, followed her in. There was a tiny entrance and another door and

Mrs Googe unlocked that, too.

Lilly stepped inside the house and stopped to stand gawking with her mouth hanging open. She had never seen anything like it in her life. It was luxurious and opulent with colourful carpets, velvet sofa and chairs, silk hangings with fringes and tassels, and crowded with all kinds of expensive looking decorations. Such was the shock of the sight in contrast to the outside, that it wasn't until she got her breath back she became aware of the air being so heavily scented it was almost sickening.

'Up here,' said Mrs Googe, making for the stairs and Lilly, open-eyed in wonderment, followed her up in silence. At the top, Mrs Googe stopped briefly to point along a hall with doorways going off on either side.

'Thems ther bedrooms,' she said, dropping all traces of her genteel accent completely. 'They's very nice an' has ter be kept nice.'

Then she turned to go into a short, narrow passage, at the end of which a few bare, wooden steps twisted around. Lilly followed. The steps led to another short, narrow, dim passage. There, a stained and worn curtain hung. Mrs Googe pulled it aside to reveal a ladder fixed against the wall which went up through an open hatch.

'Up there,' Mrs Googe said, 'them's yer quarters, dearie.'

Still grasping tightly at her little bag, Lilly climbed the rungs awkwardly and stuck her head through the opening. Rain pelted at the unlined roof but had it not been for light getting through a few small holes in it and seeping in from under the eaves at floor level, she would have been unable to see anything at all.

The floor, laid with rough, pit-sawn timber had become badly split and warped and was dirty. On it was an old straw mattress and beside it a lidless box with a hurricane lantern on top and the inevitable po inside.

That was all, nothing else, and Lilly looked on it with a sinking heart. In the country with trees and a creek nearby and with the sun flooding in, it may not have seemed so bad. Here in a town without any money, with the rain starting to leak through in drips and a chill draught running through it, it was soulless and depressing. But there was nothing she could say. Less than two hours before she had made her pleadings and given all her promises for what was starting to look like a form of imprisonment. No matter what kind of people lived below in such silken luxury, for the time being she was stuck with it and there was nothing she could do. There were no alternatives, or so she believed.

'You's can make what yer wants of yerself here, Lilly,' Mrs Googe called up, but it had no meaning to Lilly. She still had no idea that she had come to work as the skivvy in a brothel or that Mrs Googe's intentions went beyond that. Like everyone else in Adelaide, Lilly was not to know that Mrs Googe was once known in Sydney as 'Stella the Bilker'. It was a name that had been given to her by the locals from her habit of picking up sailors fresh off the ships, demanding the money first then, on the pretence of going to open her front door to let them in, would hurry down the side of someone else's house in the dark and take off over their back yards to go and pick up the next gullible customer, leaving the man waiting. This faster method of collecting earned her twice as much as it would have done if she'd had to waste time with copulation every time a ship came in. But many were the innocent doors around her areas of operation hammered on late at night by irate, cursing seamen.

Neither did Lilly realise that the conditions of her job were devised so deliberately or that Mrs Googe had had success with it before. It provided the contrast needed to show a girl that there was an easy way out, right under her feet. Every night she would see the ladies dressed up in the finest Mademoiselle Cooper could provide and with plenty of money in their purses, simply for doing what husbands demanded of their wives for nothing. And they didn't have to do any of the housework, either. In time, a sensible young girl like Lilly would come to see all that.

Weakened beasts lay scattered across the burning, open landscape like litter as a hot moaning wind blew dust and shifting sand against their hides. Although they had been able to graze on patches of dry feed every day since they left Cooper's Creek, they looked as if they might never rise again. But, even if they did, it could have been to no purpose.

Harry stretched an empty sack over the clump of spiky spinifex where a dehydrated Bluey lay, giving shade to his head and ragged shoulders. It was the only comfort left he could think to give him. He knelt on one knee, looking in at him in anguish. This was where he had brought his best friend to. This was what he had given him for helping with the striving for a satisfaction that was rightly all his own.

'It's t'e end, isn't it, Harry,' Bluey said in a hoarse whisper and it was not a question. There was no accusation either in his words or his red-rimmed eyes. Not even anxiety. Simply a sharing of knowledge with someone close to him. It was as if all his angers and fears had been burned up to leave nothing but the ashes of calm. Even the pain of thirst had dulled in resignation. Hell was not, after all, some place of fire and torture underground, but there on the surface of the Australian earth. There was no terror left for him except to be left to perish alone.

Harry could find no more to say to him. He had already said all he could. Anything else would only have been lies.

For six consecutive nights they had cracked their

stock-whips and shouted themselves hoarse through the great cloud of dust, riding as fast and hard as their mounts would carry them as they raced the huge mob through the hours of darkness. And had it not been for the big white bull holding its direction as it ran, head high, out in front, they would never have got so far.

But it was a darkness that had cost them dear in their most precious possession of all, for on the second night, one of the water bags had been torn from the side of the packhorse by a horn without being noticed, to be trampled into the ground by a mass of cloven hooves while another sprang a leak that was only discovered when it had drained to emptiness. Even depriving themselves to the end of their endurance, what water had been left only saw them into the fourth day and Bluey had the last of it.

Harry was well aware that Bluey didn't want to be left alone.

'I's goin' on ahead, mate,' he said with difficulty, 'but I ain't leavin' yer. If I has ter crawl, I's comin' back. I promise yer.'

Then he rose and walked towards one of the horses that stood with its back to the wind, its neck and head hanging low from its withers. He led it back, saddled it up, mounted, then started to walk it through the scattered mob towards the south.

At the head of the others as he rode on, he saw the big white bull lying on its own but as he approached it, intending to pass it, the bull suddenly lifted its head, held it like that for a few moments then started to struggle to its feet.

Harry had not noticed the sudden change in the direction of the wind and as the bull began to trot eagerly towards the east, he thought that it was his own presence that had caused it, the animal believing it was being asked to get on the move again.

'No!' he said to it and rode forward to try and stop it,

but the big white bull refused to be turned or even slowed. There was nothing he could do but watch it go, unable at first to understand its behaviour.

Then, on the part of the horizon towards where the bull was so determinedly heading, he saw it. A dark speck. Several of them. They were green bushes. Suddenly he realised what was happening. The wind had swung to come from there and the big white bull had smelt it. He turned his horse around to go back towards the main section of the mob and Bluey.

'The old bastard's found water!' he shouted with joy from his parched throat, 'he's found water!'

Before he had even reached Bluey, other leaders of the mob were rising to their feet. Quickly, he saddled up another horse and lifted a dazed and confused Bluey up on to it. And in that short time, the landscape had become alive with moving cattle. Only the very weakest were still struggling to get up.

In what seemed no time, Harry and Bluey, their hats still on their heads, were immersed in the middle of an Artesian spring while around them was a solid wall of heads and horns. The air rang with the noises of lowing as beasts pushed and shoved their way in to get their turn. For a full half hour, Harry and Bluey drank and splashed about in the middle of it and all of Bluey's dead emotions were restored.

'Jasus, Mary an' Joseph, Harry!' Bluey splurted, 'we's come ter bloody Paradise!' And he reached out with a rapturous hand at Harry's hat to push him under. Harry came up, grinning all over his face. He laughed, and said, 'There's probably fifteen hundred head er snakes in here as well.'

That was enough for Bluey, for all his fears and superstitions had been revived too and he made a mad scramble for the bank.

'Ye bastard!' he shouted, forcibly pushing his way between the legs of cattle on his hands and knees.

'Come back, Saint Patrick, I need yer!' Harry shouted after him, still laughing.

But the jokes didn't last too long when they discovered what had happened once the beasts had had their fill. A dozen of them had become bogged down in yellow mud up to their bellies and their struggles to get out had only made it worse for them. Using ropes and horses, as well as a good bit of sweating and cursing, it took until dark to haul them out individually. All but one. The last was in almost up to its head and Bluey had an overwhelming desire for sleep. His body was exhausted, his feelings were becoming numb and the lids of his eyes felt heavier than lead.

'Leave it, Harry,' he said, 'one more doesn't matter.' But he might have known better. Harry wasn't leaving it. With ropes secured around its neck and horns, and in mud up to his waist, he dug around with a shovel as Bluey did his best to urge three horses in tandem to haul together. It seemed a futile task, but shortly after midnight, Harry had it free and the beast struggled out. In the faint light of the stars, man and animal both looked as if they had just been freshly and roughly sculpted in wet clay, but Harry was a happy man.

'We done it, mate,' he said, but there was no one to hear him. Looking around for Bluey, he found him fast asleep on the ground near the feet of the horses. And he could afford to smile again.

'No wonder they called yer Bluey,' he said to the unconscious figure with affection. 'Yer spends more time in yer bed than a bloody blanket.'

The one fear that both men had left far behind was the one of ever being discovered. It was no longer a consideration. But in the early morning of that same day they had come on the happy Artesian spring, Wooly had emerged from a bark gunya not far from the big waterhole at Cooper's Creek to continue his tracking. His own survival was never in doubt. He could find water where a white man couldn't, even if it was only a handful six feet down in a dry water course. And there was no need for the bigger game that would have been far too much for one man. If he had to, Wooly could live on insects and grubs, on almost any tiny thing that moved. And on much that didn't. Even on the undigested seed in bird droppings. Delays and diversions or not, there would be no stopping him.

Eight

Ben Deaken was a battler. Taking up the most northerly run in South Australia with so little capital and a sizeable loan, he had to be, but then Ben had never made an easy penny in his life. Struggle was in his blood. In the three years he had been establishing what he had named Gunderindi Station, consideration for his toiling wife and the comforts of his home were what had come last. But it was more from necessity than an eye for opportunity that made him befriend the aborigines who camped only two miles from where he and his wife had built their rough stone hut of a homestead. Badly in need of extra help, Ben Deaken had picked out a few of the most likely blacks, taught them how to ride and handle horses, put them in trousers, shirts and hats, if not boots, and called them his stockriders. For that, once a week, he gave them a hand-out of flour, sugar and tea. And, as his stockriders shared out with everyone else, the whole tribe had become dependent on Ben Deaken and stayed around.

Between such cheap labour and three reasonably good seasons in succession, things were looking up for Ben. The previous lot of steers he had sent down, although poor in quality, had fetched more than he expected. And when he had extra money, it burned holes in his pockets; not for the sake of spending it but of finding a way to invest it and increase it. That most of the schemes he had dreamed up in the past had fallen apart, didn't dull his attraction for new ones.

His situation was a worrying problem for him. He had his yards, and had fenced off a horse paddock, had built a storehouse, but he had no intention of spending a penny more on his house.

He had ridden twelve miles to the north on one of his regular sweeps in order to check that none of his stock had strayed from good feed and water, and was pleased that he had seen no tracks. About to turn around, his eye caught something and he sat in his saddle looking at it, puzzled.

In the far distance to the north, there appeared to be a low cloud of dust. It wasn't a dust storm because it didn't seem to be moving. And it wasn't a willy-willy or it would have been twisting and rising. Curious, he urged his horse into a walk and began to ride out towards it. It couldn't have been created by a lot of people with wagons either as no one could come from there. Beyond was a waterless nowhere.

It was some time before he could discern what it was and he pulled up his horse for a few minutes to look in astonishment. It was a mob of cattle on the move. A big mob. It was utterly mystifying. He pushed his horse forward again.

Harry was the first to notice the lone figure on horseback approach them from ahead, and he rode on past the head of the mob and the big white bull to go and meet him.

Eventually, Ben Deaken and Harry came face to face and Deaken just stared. Harry's clothes were in tatters. The brim of his hat had partly come away from the crown, a mat of yellow hair sticking out from underneath it. His eyes were red and above his yellow beard, bits of white skin hung from almost blackened cheeks, and the backs of his hands looked the same. It was the cracked, swollen lips that brought Ben Deaken to his senses and he quickly reached for his water bag on his saddle and held it out before a single word had been said. Harry took it, drank from it, and handed it back.

'Thanks,' he said, then held out his hand to introduce himself. 'Henry Richards.'

From the very beginning, it had been established that Harry and Bluey would give different names in case they ran into anyone in Queensland, but although that no longer seemed necessary, Harry had liked the name and it rolled off his tongue automatically. Ben Deaken was still almost speechless at the sight.

'Ben Deaken,' he got out, and Harry could see the questions that were written all over his face.

'Come down from Central Queensland,' he said casually.

'Queensland? But there isn't any route down from Queensland.'

'There is now,' Harry said and grinned.

Ben Deaken looked in amazement at the mob coming on with a big white beautiful bull at its head. He could only see one other horseman.

'Where's yer men?'

'There's only ther two of us. I started with more but they didn't like the look of some of ther country an' turned back.'

'Two of yer?'

A stunned Ben Deaken gazed at the big mob. There had to be well over a thousand. Maybe as many as fifteen hundred. Then his eye caught the packhorse. All that was hanging from it were two short-handled shovels, a few tools and an empty rolled-up sack.

'Where's yer supplies?' he said, looking for some other packhorse and not seeing any.

'We's out,' Harry said, 'I reckon we cut it a bit fine.

It'll be easier next time.'

Had Bluey heard him say that, he would probably have fallen right off his horse with the very thought of it. As it was, Bluey was smiling all over on seeing Ben Deaken and rode up. Deaken stared at him too, for his rags and condition were no better than Harry's.

Harry introduced him as his Overseer, Patrick O'Day, and Bluey didn't even blink.

'Is we in Sout' Australia, t'en?' he said, and Deaken was taken aback at that, too.

'You must er been in South Australia for bloody weeks,' he said, and turned to point to the south. There, stretching across the horizon was what could have been a low, blue-hazed cloud. 'That's the Flinders Ranges.'

Harry had heard them mentioned twice in all his years of listening but with little idea of where they actually were while Bluey was only hearing the name for the first time in his life. Yet they both sat in their saddles gazing at the distant hills as if they had just been told that they had reached the promised land.

Ben Deaken glanced from the two ragged figures to the big white bull and the mob and back again, still trying to take it all in. The bull was still strong after such an unbelievable drove and the nose ring gave it away as a good stud animal, and the great herd was not in bad condition either, considering. The incredible accomplishment this Henry Richards had achieved made him a man well worth knowing. He swung down from his horse and quickly opened his saddle bag to take out the damper and cooked beef his wife had packed in it for him that morning. Although he had not yet eaten, generosity sprang with spontaneity and he offered it, saying, 'Here, I've had all I want.'

Harry and Bluey thanked him but had to have another drink of water before they wolfed it down. Although Harry could not have been more grateful, his senses warned him to be cautious with Ben Deaken.

'Will we be able ter get fresh supplies from yer, Ben?' he said.

'After what you've done, Henry, I should give them to yer for nothing and only wish I could. Sad ter say, I just can't afford it. But I'll have my stockriders look after your mob. Lookin' at yer, I'd say you'd want a couple of days ter rest up. Yer can stay at the house.'

It was a paradox with Ben Deaken that, on the one hand, he had a generously spirited nature, and that he was tighter than a pig's jack on a winter's night, as they said about him, on the other.

That was what Harry sensed without knowing what it was and it made him feel uneasy.

'I gotter be honest with yer, Ben,' he said, 'I can't pay yer for supplies with cash.'

Ben Deaken looked a little confused and embarrassed by that but quickly recovered. 'Well, we'll work somethin' out,' he said, 'this is no time ter be arguin' about it.'

Shortly afterwards, Ben Deaken, after shaking both the hands of Harry and Bluey again, took off for home. It was going to be another day before Harry and Bluey brought the huge mob in and it gave Ben Deaken plenty of time to think. It was time he didn't really need for, long before he reached his homestead, he saw exactly what scheme he had been looking for, and it was the chance of a lifetime. With that big white bull, he could improve the quality of his stock so much, he could get twice as much for steers he sent down in a couple of years' time. That was an exaggeration, of course, but Ben was always enthusiastically optimistic when plans were fresh. Without money, Richards would have to sell it to him. Cheap.

It was an excited Deaken who walked into his two tiny-roomed stone house as his wife was lighting the lamp, much too excited to pay any attention to the toddler twin boys who tugged at his clothes for attention.

'Not now, not now,' he said to them and poured out the news of Henry Richards' achievement and of all that had happened.

Nan Deaken's eyes lit up brighter than the lamp with surprise. An intelligent woman, she appreciated every bit as much as her husband what these two men had done. Not only was it extraordinary in itself, it had all kinds of implications for her, including the possibility of further land being taken up, making their own place less remote and more important. She also appreciated company when she could get it and was keen to show that Gunderindi was no different to most other outback homesteads when it came to extending hospitality.

'You'll have to get them to stay, Ben,' she said.

'I've told them that.'

But Nan was also a very efficient woman and when Ben Deaken described the physical condition of Richards and his Overseer O'Day, she made her diagnosis of Mundonna Rot and immediately set about getting ingredients together to boil up an ointment. On Gunderindi, Nan was more than wife, mother and teacher. She was vet, physician, nurse and apothecary. And she was quite happy with her lot. She had faith in Ben succeeding on the run and willingly gave all the help she could to bring it about, including working as another station-hand during mustering and branding and marking. Indeed, when it came to turning a young bull into a steer, she was more skilful with the pocket knife than Ben. And with the railway from Port Augusta pushing up their way, the future looked nothing but bright. She was well aware that two years of bad drought would see them walking off the place penniless, but to have lived with the thought would have negated the purpose of their very existence.

The next day, Harry and Bluey arrived in, leaving the mob on a creek with good feed and water where an eye was to be kept on them by Deaken's barefoot stockriders. It amused Harry to see them and think that Deaken had given such work to men who, only a couple of years before, had been naked nomads, while McKenzie had denied him the same thing on Albert Downs. But he rarely gave thought to Albert Downs any more. It seemed remote and so far behind him. He admired the way the black stockriders handled their horses. They clearly had a rapport with their animals.

'You done well with 'em, Ben,' he said.

'Blacks is blacks, Henry,' Deaken said, reluctant to admit even to himself that they were worth any more than their hand-out. 'You'll know that as much as me. Turn your back for a minute an' the bloody day's their own. Worse than useless most of the time.'

Bluey, who had left it to Harry to do all the talking on their meeting the day before lest he give their game away, began to become voluble. 'Begod, an' is it not a fine place ye got yerself here right enough, Mr Deaken, a fine place. As I was sayin' ter Henry some ways back t'ere, sure t'ere must be some people on God's good earth t'at t'e Saints care for a little more t'an ot'ers, I says, an' I'm t'inkin' t'at your good self is one of t'em. Ye could build yer stock up well here, Mr Deaken, so ye could. Build up well.'

It wasn't often Bluey came out with the Blarney and Harry knew exactly what he was after with all his flattery. Getting Ben Deaken to take the entire mob off their hands at any price and be rid of them while the going was good. He had tried to talk about it the night before but Harry had seemed determined to do what he saw as finishing the job by going on across the Flinders Ranges to the coast and Adelaide. And he was still hoping Harry might change his mind if Deaken made him an offer.

Nan Deaken was delighted to welcome them, but although she had been warned, Ben often exaggerated, and she was still taken aback by their appearance. After she had been introduced, she handed them the pot of ointment to put on their skin, then said humorously, 'Well, we can't have such important gentlemen sitting down at Gunderindi's table looking like that, can we now?' and made Ben Deaken take them over to the storehouse to get new clothes on them. Ben was a little unhappy about having to hand out such supplies before he had come to an agreement on payment but, with Nan pushing him, he was momentarily stuck with the situation.

Harry and Bluey's ragged Alberts were stuck, too, as they hadn't unwound them from their feet since Cooper's Creek and the holed strips of cloth had become almost like a thick, second skin. Deaken was a little surprised that a man owning fifteen hundred head wore Alberts but, on the other hand, appreciated such economy. He had not the slightest suspicion that Henry Richards was other than who he said he was. He knew an upright, honest figure of a man when he saw one. And there was no embarrassment on the upright, honest man's side in being fitted out with new clothes. In cattle, he was perfectly prepared to pay more than double for everything he got, and suspected it would be at least that. So, there was no reason for Harry not to be grinning all over his face as he stood, for the very first time in his life, with a pair of socks on his freshly washed feet. They felt strange but utterly soft and wonderful, especially around his ankles.

'A well supplied store ye keep, Mr Deaken,' Bluey said, 'an' fine built. Can I not see ye in a few years' time ownin' the biggest run in all of Sout' Australia.'

With so little room, a tent was put up for the children and they were banished to it for the night so that they wouldn't make a nuisance of themselves. There was a lot the Deakens wanted to hear from Mr Richards and Mr O'Day about their incredible drove, and it was probably as well that Ben Deaken didn't bring out the bottle of very strong rum until the large meal was well over or they might have heard more of Bluey's past sufferings than was necessary.

With drinks poured, Nan Deaken went off to attend to the children in the tent and Ben, who had been hardly able to wait until this moment said, 'About your supplies, Henry.'

Harry noted that Deaken, although lifting his mug and putting it down again, wasn't actually drinking. He had seen men do that before when they wanted to keep their heads clear for some advantage.

'I'll let yer have as many head as yer reckon's right, Ben,' he said. Never having had to make a deal of any kind before, Harry was at a great disadvantage. He didn't even know how much the cattle might be worth here. At Albert Downs, he had learned from old Charley that the previous year's fats that had been shipped out had averaged just over four pounds a head, but that didn't necessarily give a guide as to what poorer conditioned beasts might be valued at away in the most northerly run in South Australia. In fact, when he had left Central Queensland with his huge mob, the last thing he had been thinking of was their monetary exchange. He was in for a shock.

'Sorry ter say,' Ben Deaken said, 'I can't take 'em. Much as I'd like. Truth is, I got all the stock I can carry.'

And in these few words, Bluey's hopes of avoiding the rest of the long drove were over. But he had another try.

'Bejasus, Mr Deaken,' he got out, 'could ye not take a few more than ye needed an' sell t'em to somebody else an' make yourself a good fine profit?'

'I'm not a gambler, Mr O'Day.'

'I'll give yer twenty head, Ben,' Harry said, making a wild stab, but Deaken still didn't want any and Harry increased it to fifty, then a hundred. It was then that Harry realised what he didn't like about the man. With the advantage he had, he was taking them by the throat. It was impossible to continue without supplies. And for all his lack of education, Harry was able to divide two into a hundred. What it meant was that, even at the lowly price of ten shillings a head, he would be paying more than ten times over for all they needed. And Deaken wasn't even accepting that.

Nan Deaken returned to the doorway, but on seeing the men arguing, went back to the tent. It slightly embarrassed her the way Ben sometimes conducted business, although she knew it had to be like that. Ben Deaken turned down a hundred and twenty head, then it came.

'The only thing I can do for yer, Henry, an' I'd be doin' it only as a favour, is I might take that white bull off yer hands.'

Bluey felt a certain amount of relief in the stalemate being resolved. At least he wasn't going to be stuck on Gunderindi for the rest of his life. And, with his stomach full of good food and a few quick drinks rushing to his head, he was tired.

'T'at's settled, t'en,' he said, draining his mug again, but he might have known.

'No, it ain't,' Harry said, 'the bull ain't for sale.'

Deaken filled up their mugs once more, not realising that if he had poured the entire bottle down Harry's throat it would have made no difference for, if he was soft in other respects, Harry had a very hard head when it came to drink.

'Bejasus, an' would the beast not have a fine place to be roamin' here,' Bluey said, trying to kick his friend surreptitiously on the ankle.

'How much did yer pay for it?' Deaken said, but that didn't embarrass Harry either as he had come to regard the big white bull as his own.

'A lot.'

'Then I tell you what I'll do, Henry. I'm a fair man as

anybody can tell yer. I'm takin' a risk as for all I knows it could be carryin' the pleuro an' I ain't never seen any of its calves. I'm not askin' for a guarantee, but seein' what you've just done, an' not wantin' ter see yer stuck, I'll give yer all the supplies yer need to see yer through and my whole savin's of twenty guineas for the animal.'

'I can't, Ben, it's not for sale.'

Ben Deaken went to his keg of rum to replenish the bottle. Richards was making it tough. All these men with big runs were hard. Richards was typical of them, bringing a huge herd over where there was no route and risking perishing for the sake of trying to get a bit better market in Adelaide.

Bluey retreated behind his stupor but the situation was still the same when they all turned in for the night. But Nan Deaken and the children were the only ones who slept soundly for even Bluey came to again.

'Holy Mot'er of Jasus,' he said in a desperate whisper, the moment he and Harry were alone in their tiny room with one double bed between them, 'what in the hell is yer goin' ter do wit' it if ye don't sell it?'

'I dunno, mate.'

'I knows yer don't know. But ye can't walk around Adelaide wit' it in yer bloody pocket, can ye? Or, begod, maybe ye's t'inkin of gettin' a fine saddle made for it so ye can ride it inter Chapel an' ask the good priest to baptise t'e cursed t'ing. T'e first Christian bull in creation.'

Bluey whisperered on and off half the night with Harry full awake, and despite all the rum he had had, everything he said made sense. And Harry knew full well it did. Yet, even with the realisation that the bull had to go sometime, it didn't make it any easier. He couldn't explain what it meant to him, not even to his friend.

When Harry had first met the big white bull, he had been vaguely conscious that from the animal kingdom, the bull had come as an aristocrat while he, from the human one, had come as a lowly peasant. But the bull had volunteered itself to be his servant and allowed him to become its master. In the relationship, Harry had felt a kinship and it had helped him to grow. The bull had shown him by its behaviour what real spirit and real confidence was. It only appeared to be a servant but wasn't. It was self-contained. It was itself. Afraid of no man. And neither thirst nor hunger nor any other deprivation could rob it of its dignity. It was not a follower but a leader.

It was the most difficult decision Harry had ever had to make and it was daylight before common-sense prevailed. There was no other way out if he was to continue with what he had originally set out to do.

Ben Deaken had tossed and turned all night. The more Harry had refused to part with the bull, the more desirable it had become. He pictured that, with it, people years hence would be heard to say, 'Look, them's Ben Deaken's cattle. Yer can pick 'em without havin' ter look at the brands. It was that first big white stud bull he got that made 'im. Knew what he was doin', did Ben.'

All night, the scheme of getting twice as much for his quality steers looked bigger and bigger, and the big white bull better and better. He couldn't wait for Harry to emerge for breakfast. Nan had already made tea and damper, and had smoked kangaroo leg sizzling in the pan, Ben swearing it was every bit as good as bacon, with the added advantage that it didn't cost anything.

Harry emerged, a bleary-eyed Bluey behind him.

'Mornin', Ben. Mornin', Mrs Deaken,' was all he had time to say and Ben Deaken's words sprang at him fast as Flash Jack.

'All the supplies you need and fifty guineas, Henry. My last offer an' there's no help to it,' he said, and Nan turned with her eyes popping. It was a lot of money for

a battler to be paying for a bull, particularly battler Ben.
Had he waited but a few moments, he could have saved
himself twenty-six pounds and five shillings but he was
none the wiser.

'It's yours, Ben,' Harry said quietly and Deaken's
face shone with victory and success.

'An' begod, is it not the beginnin' of a fine day,' Bluey
said, dragging himself out of his half-dead state. It was
not only because his friend had seen sense but because
the ring of fifty guineas was the ring of wealth. Com-
pared to the five hundred guineas the Drysdale Cattle
Company had paid for the animal in England, it was
very little, but to Bluey right then, it was as much as the
hoard of gold the Little People kept in their pot at the
end of an Irish rainbow.

Harry was far from happy and there was hardly
another word to be got from him while Bluey, on getting Ben Deaken alone, thought it fair to give him a
warning.

'It's a fine bargain ye got yerself, Mr Deaken, but in
some ways it's a strange beast. We didn't mean ter bring
it wit' us, but bejasus it had a mind of its own. If I was
you, I'd keep it yarded for a week or it might t'ink it's
still wit' us an' try to come on after us.'

Two days later when they were ready to leave, the
packhorse loaded up and the horses saddled, Bluey
found that Harry was no longer around. He eventually
found him standing against the rails of Ben Deaken's
yards, looking in at the big white bull that appeared to
be looking back at him.

'Is yer ready, Harry?' he said but there was no reply
and he went closer, 'Harry.'

Then he realised that Harry was weeping like a child,
tears running down over the ointment on his cheeks and
trickling through and over his big yellow beard. There
was nothing Bluey could say. In embarrassment, he
walked away, and had to wait quite a while with the

saddled horses before Harry reappeared. His tears were wiped away but they still ran inside and he didn't speak.

They had already said all their thanks and the Deakens stood to watch them go, the toddlers clinging to Nan Deaken's skirts and being made to wave. The aborigine stockriders helped to bring the great mob together, then Harry and Bluey headed the river of cattle towards the Flinders Ranges.

From the information Deaken had given them, Harry had the alternative of taking them a hundred and fifty miles to the south-west and arranging to ship them down by rail, but on learning that there were stock routes with reasonably good feed on them, he opted for that. He wanted to reach Adelaide with his mob brought up to the best condition possible.

For the first few days out from Gunderindi, that hardly seemed to matter. There were no grins or laughter to come from Harry's face as he rode back and forth along the mob, keeping them on the move but allowing them to graze as they went. Wisely, Bluey left him alone, simply watching him. He was a strange man, but they had made a total misjudgment of him at Albert Downs simply because he could cry like a baby. And he had changed since they had started out. There was a nobility about him now. He was a bigger man than he had been and at Gunderindi had stood out as superior to Ben Deaken, despite the battler's hard striving for the bull. What was absolutely certain was that Harry was no longer anyone's rouseabout. He was a real boss, and a good one.

It wasn't until the fourth night as they sat at their fire that Bluey made an attempt at getting a response from his friend.

'I's finished wit' t'is cursed country,' he said, and Harry looked at his firelit face and asked, 'What d'yer mean?'

'I mean t'at when we get rid of t'e mob, I's goin' back home to Ireland. I'd like ye to come wit' me, Harry.'

'What the hell would I do in Ireland?' Harry said, 'this is my country.'

'Oh, bejasus, Harry, t'ere's no better turf God's made in all t'e earth. I swear on t'e Holy Mot'er's Son it rains gentle down on every single day of it an' t'e grass is so soft and green, it could strike a man blind if he's never set eyes on it.'

And he saw Harry's face break into a grin.

'Yer want ter bloody blind me, do yer?'

Bluey went on with the exaggerations of his home that the crossing of the Wild Heart had brought him to, with all memories of the barefoot poverty in which he had been raised obliterated.

'Would you not at least like ter see where your mot'er an' fat'er was born in England?' he said, and Harry was much more attracted by that.

'I would, mate,' he said, 'I reckon I might like that. But I'd come back here after.'

Bluey was delighted.

'T'en t'ere we are, Harry. We'll catch a ship to England t'e two of us an' to t'e Devil wit' all the rest.'

They celebrated the decision with another quart-pot of Deaken's cheap Jack the Painter tea, so called because it was nearly as green as Bluey's Irish grass and had a whiff of turpentine about it. But it was with a false security they later lay down to sleep thinking about their great sea voyage to the other side of the world together.

The following evening as a blood-red sun began to lower itself down through hazy light cloud to the west, Wooly arrived at Gunderindi and, at first unnoticed by anyone, squatted himself down outside the rails of the yards to gaze in on the big white bull. Grinning from ear to ear with pleasure and satisfaction, he stayed like that without moving for an entire hour. This was the quarry he had tracked and it was there in front of him, appearing a little restless but nevertheless lying chewing its cud.

'Big pella go 'im longa way,' he said to it and the bull turned a watchful eye on him, its nose ring glinting like red gold.

Although he had come to know its hoofmarks almost like a friend, he was setting his eyes on the animal for the very first time and was savouring every moment of it. Never had he tracked anything so far before and it seemed highly unlikely he would ever do so again.

The last tip of sun was about to dip swiftly down when Ben Deaken spied the figure with the spear, and hurried there in fear that his treasured possession might come to harm. Even from some distance, he could tell that the black wasn't one of his own.

'Get off yer bastard!' he shouted as he went. 'Get to buggery or I'll have yer bloody hide!'

Wooly rose and faced the angry white boss coming towards him but held his ground.

'Him pella call 'im Wooly, boss,' he said when Deaken reached him, and Deaken took him in, surprised by the sight of both the tartan trousers and the heavily scratched leather satchel. There was the possibility that the black might have murdered somebody for those, but if he had he would be running for his life, not standing facing him. It was curious.

'What d'yer want here?' Deaken said.

'Pella Wooly track 'im big pella bull, boss,' Wooly said and started to undo the satchel to dip into it for a letter, Deaken watching him in puzzlement. Wooly handed over a filthy envelope but the writing of 'To Whom It May Concern' was legible enough and Deaken tore it open, his face becoming ashen as he read, then turning dark with fury after he finished.

'You stay here! Don't you bloody move, you understand? You stay here!'

'Yes, boss,' Wooly said, not knowing what all the man's anger was about. And as Deaken ran to his house roaring curses, Wooly turned to squat down again to continue looking in on the big pella bull. He had not expected any strange white boss to thank him for the great distance he had travelled in his tracking, so there was no disappointment in Deaken's treatment of him.

Nan Deaken jumped with fright as her husband rushed into the house and the toddlers looked terrified in case it was something they had done and were in for a belting.

'Gully rakers! Thieves! Poddy dodgers! The robbin' bloody bastards!' he shouted, throwing the letter at his wife. 'They've bloody ruined me! They forced me into buying that bloody bull and knew exactly what they were doin'! I'm goin' after them an' gettin' my money back!'

And he ran back out again, not knowing what to do first, hardly able to think through his blind anger.

With the children clutching tightly at her skirts and burying their faces in them in hope of safety, Nan Deaken read the letter with anxiety. It told her about the great cattle theft with the big white bull that had taken place on a run called Albert Downs in Central Queensland, about the man Walford with a yellow beard and the Irishman, McGuirk. There could be no mistake, no confusion. The men who had given their names as Richards and O'Day were clearly the same; the same Ben had not stopped praising for their importance and achievement ever since they'd left. It was yet another of Ben's ideas that had gone wrong and cost them dear but she didn't blame him. She had been just as fooled herself. Walford, particularly, had appeared to be a man of stature and honesty. But unlike Ben, she was not out-raged and felt no despair. They had overcome much worse disasters before and would no doubt do so again. She crouched and held the twin toddlers in a hugging embrace.

'It's all right,' she said comfortingly, 'it's all right. It's nothing you've done. Nobody's angry with you.'

It was almost dark at the yards where Ben Deaken had been joined by two of his aborigine stockriders as he confronted Wooly further. Over his initial, blind fury, he had started to see again. Going after the two men was not the best thing to do. They could have taken a different route to the one he advised and, for all he knew, could have hidden his money. And with such bold criminals, there was also the danger of getting shot.

For over half an hour he had done his best to get Wooly to hand over the other letters but every time the black had just said, 'No, boss. Kenzie boss tell 'im Wooly, boss,' and the black stockriders, although they knew nothing of what was happening and were only impressed by Wooly, backed him up. 'Kenzie tell 'im Wooly,' they kept saying without the slightest notion of who Kenzie was, whether he was black, white or brindle, or what he might have said. And Ben Deaken, feeling he might be alienating his stockriders to the point of rebellion over their desire to protect the blacktracker in the tartan trousers, stopped pressing. If they went walkabout on him, he would be unable to carry out the plan that had developed in his mind.

What had really swung him against going after Harry was the sudden realisation that if the bull had been imported from England as the letter had indicated, it was much more valuable than he imagined. In turn, that swelled his desire to use it while it was still in his possession and get much more than his money back. But cows didn't simply come into season when you asked them and to take full advantage of the bull would mean a lot of looking, a lot of mustering and most of all, time. And the only way he could obtain the time he would need was to hold up the news of the two gully rakers from getting out. Hence his desire to get his hands on the other letters. With that possibility gone, he had to turn to other ways.

'You go with my fellas to their camp,' he said to Wooly, 'I give you plenty tucker to fill your binjee. You stay with my fellas until I say. You understand ?'

'Yes, boss.'

Deaken had faith in the principle that the best way of keeping a black rooted to the spot was by keeping his black belly bloated.

Wooly was led off by his new friends to their camp of Mia Mia made of twisted branches and bits of bark two miles away while Deaken went back to the house. He was not a man of vengeance. Nobody could ever say that about Ben Deaken.

Nan, worried that he might indeed chase after the two men instead of leaving it to the police, was relieved to hear that he wasn't, but looked shocked when he said he was going to put off sending McKenzie's letter down the line of other properties to the nearest police station.

'You can't do that, Ben,' she said.

Yes, I can. They're going to get caught anyway, there's nothin' surer. Why should it be me who has to dog on 'em? All I'm doing is given' them an extra couple of weeks. They deserve that after all they done an' been through, gully rakers or no gully rakers. An' I'll be doin' no harm to the bull usin' it in the meantime.'

It was Ben Deaken's way of justifying what he was doing, although it was more like several months than a couple of weeks he needed and was out to get. Nan Deaken didn't have to be told that and looked at him with concern.

'People'll say you're obstructing the law, Ben,' she said.

'As long as I keep the blacktracker here, people aren't going to bloody know, are they?'

After a while, Nan could see that there was going to be no possibility of changing his mind, and although she was unhappy about it, felt it was her duty to give him help.

The following morning she walked to the aborigine camp to fetch the woman she occasionally got to take care of the children and later mounted up. From then on, Gunderindi became the busiest run in South Australia as the frantic search for cows coming into season began, while Wooly was kept so stuffed with food that he looked permanently pregnant. And it was not too long before Lord Wallah Wallah Banjo was presented with the first herd of eager ladies.

Totally unaware of what was going on behind him, Harry sat on his horse on a high vantage point amidst the Flinders Ranges looking across its timbered hills with deep defiles and gorges for as far as the eye could see. It was a sight of magnificence to him and it made him a happy man. Somewhere ahead over more of that spectacular, rugged country to the south lay the slopes that would lead down to the coastal land and to their destination. Once, it had only been a childish, impossible, and unattainable dream to conduct such a gigantic drove. A madness that several times over had driven him to ask the best friend he had ever had to be prepared to perish for him. Now, the madness had become a sanity, the dream a reality, and the end within his grasp. Yet, in a way, he half wished it was an end that would never come.

Some way below, Bluey stopped to look up at him, the great mob of cattle wending its way through trees towards a pass floored with grass, the spare mounts and the pack-horse coming up behind. Bluey was a happy man, too. Every step took him closer and closer to home. Harry seated on his horse was silhouetted against the sky. Bejasus, did he not look like a bloody general inspectin' out over his troops an' field of battle?

'What's ye lookin' for?' he shouted up.

'Heaven, mate!' Harry shouted back.

'Well ye's not takin' me wit' yer! I'm gettin' off this bloody horse at Adelaide!'

And their shouts and Harry's laughter echoed back around the hills.

Wooly woke and looked up through the sticks of the Mia Mia at the night sky. Tired of eating and sleeping, he felt restless. He had eaten nothing of what had been given to him the morning before and had not even drunk water. It was not so much McKenzie's instructions but an instinctive desire to simply move that drew him. After a few minutes of wakefulness, he quietly picked up his satchel, made his way out to where his spear and throwing stick rested against the outside and, after picking these up too, stood for a few moments longer. The eyes of others lying crowded in the tiny Mia Mia opened at the slight disturbance, saw him there and closed again.

Wooly began to walk towards the south through the night, aimlessly but more contented. It was not until after dawn that he began to look for the marks of Harry's herd, and he zig-zagged across east and west, seeing many other cloven hoof marks on the way. It could have been much more difficult for him had it not been for the sheer volume of the big mob and, when he found what he was looking for, even although they had been crossed and mixed by the tracks of many of Gunderindi cattle since, the big mob from Albert Downs was as clear to him as the morning light. And he began to follow towards the Flinders Ranges.

The following evening, Ben Deaken returned with one of his stockriders and a couple of dozen likely cows after two days away. After yarding them and checking to see how Nan had fared, he rode to the aborigine camp to check on Wooly.

'Where is fella call Wooly?' he said, and knew immediately by the blank, black faces, that he wasn't there.

'Where is he?' he said again angrily and the women

looked nervous.

'Pella call 'im Wooly go, boss,' a voice volunteered and Deaken turned to see it was one of his stockriders who was bold enough to tell him.

'When did he go? Where did he go?'

'Dark time, boss.'

'Where?'

The stockrider pointed to the north, 'Tink 'im Wooly home, boss.'

In fact, neither the stockrider nor anyone else knew where Wooly had gone. It was simply natural for them to think that a man who had come so far from his own territory would want to go back to it. It wasn't the way Ben Deaken saw it. They were lying to him. They were always lying to him. And bloody grinning in innocence while they did it.

'You useless mob of black bastards!' he shouted at them and swung his horse around to go back. There was nothing for it. If he wasn't to be accused, he would have to sit down and write a letter to add to the one from McKenzie and pass it on to the neighbouring run to the south-west. To cover himself, he would backdate it by several weeks and blame a black for going walkabout with it on the delivering.

It was the big white bull that, this time, had given Harry an extra reprieve, but Harry knew none of it.

'They're dead, aren't they?' Dora McKenzie said, and Don looked up at her from the breakfast she had cooked and served herself. He had been trying to tell her that for some time, but she had not wanted to listen so he had stopped saying it. Now she was coming to her senses and believing for herself. He wanted to say, 'Of course they're damned well dead and the more dead they are the better!' but he still had to be careful.

'There's no other conclusion can be drawn, Dora,' he said.

Certainly, there was not. Even the police as far down as the Colony of Victoria had made extensive enquiries and searches on behalf of their Queensland colleagues without success.

From outside, the sound of wood being chopped for the stove reached in as the rouseabout worked. A surly youth of seventeen, Dora had hardly spoken to him since he arrived. So, it was not his fault that the vegetable garden lay dead, a piece of dry, barren ground, or that the fresh meat went off so quickly or crawled with maggots, for the youth had to be constantly told and did nothing if he wasn't. And she still refused to have a servant in the house to replace Lilly. Her hands were coarse with housework and washing but it was the only way in which she had been able to keep herself busy enough to give some rest to her tortured mind. Even old Charley had been sent back to his book-hole for good. Day after day she had hoped it would end and that Harry would be found, fully able to give an explanation of himself and prove that, whatever else, they had all been mistaken about him. But none of it happened, and so much time had passed, she knew in her heart that now it never would. Painful as it was, it would have been more than dishonest not to have admitted it.

'We'll never know the truth, then, will we?' she said.

'No.'

It was the first time, too, that McKenzie had made such an admission for previously he had always been so adamant about knowing exactly what the truth was. But nothing had been easy for him either and the many nights alone with his worries had brought about a few cracks in his hard, blustering exterior. He exploded less, no longer swore at her, and was prepared to listen a little more carefully, even although the number of his problems had by no means lessened. He still lived in dread of hearing back from London on his incompetence in losing their valuable bull and so many head of stock by theft and, the more overdue their reply became, the more his dread increased. And following that, he had had to write to tell them that the shipments of fats he had sent down fetched only four pounds a head.

'What will they do with Purdy and Spence?' Dora said.

'I don't know.'

Dora said no more about the subject that had dominated their lives so completely for so long and neither did McKenzie. And Dora behaved no differently than he expected during the day. It came as a complete surprise to him that same night when he went to turn in late. The lamp was alight and Dora, in her best nightdress, lay in their bed, appearing to be asleep, her long red hair spilled and shining on the white pillow. At first he stood confused by the sight and the unpredictability of it. He had said or done nothing to bring this surrender about. Absolutely nothing. For the first time since it had all begun, he noticed that his wife's face looked thinner than it had been. He began to feel moved and wished there was something he could say, but he could think of nothing. As if nothing had ever happened, he undressed, blew out the lamp and, careful not to shake the bed, slid quietly in beside her. But he made no attempt to touch her, sensing that it might be a fragile peace and happiness for a while. All the same, as he began to fall off to sleep, it was with a comfort and contentedness he had not felt in a very long while.

But both he and Dora were wrong in their belief that the matter of Harry with the stolen fifteen hundred head and the big white bull was over. And McKenzie was quite mistaken in his belief that Dora had made any surrender of her long-held faith in the gentle, obliging rouseabout she felt she had come to know so well in his six years on Albert Downs.

They slept soundly in their innocence.

Nine

A strong, cold wind with spots of rain in it heralding winter swept through the streets of Adelaide. But not far out of town, Harry and Bluey were hardly aware of it in their excitement. They stood aside looking on and trying to listen amidst the noise of lowing cattle as cattlemen, butchers, provision merchants, beef salters, dealers and tallow merchants crowded the top rails putting in their bids for lots by shouts, nods and lifted fingers as Bob Campbell's voice rose and fell in the non-stop staccato rattle of his trade. Albert Downs cattle were going under the hammer, or in this case, Bob Campbell's big fist hard into the palm of his other hand.

Bob Campbell, a big, heavy cheerful man with a round stomach and ruddy cheeks, was delighted with Henry Richards for arriving in with fifteen hundred head when he did. As auctioneer at the Adelaide Stock Yards, he had been about to cancel the sale day for the lack of stock and postpone it for another week.

'Mr Richards,' he had said, grasping Harry warmly by the hand, 'it's a good lookin' lot you've brought in an' I'll get you top prices.'

Campbell had been impressed with Harry, both as a man and as a boss drover. It was rare for stock to be driven down from a run north of the Flinders Ranges and arrive in such prime condition. And that was from where Harry had said he had come. It was after Ben Deaken's reaction to his crossing all the way from Central Queensland he decided to mention it no more. It was obviously going to attract far too much attention. So, everyone he ran across in the Flinders from travellers to copper miners were not told either.

Unused to auctions, Harry and Bluey had difficulty following what was going on.

'What's t'ey gettin', Harry, what's t'ey gettin?' Bluey said.

'I dunno. But if he said top prices, I believe 'im, mate.'

'What's a top price, t'en, what's a top price?'

'I dunno that either.'

Bluey peed happily against a post. Whatever it was, he was sure it was going to take him home and that was the best of it.

It wasn't until the last lot was sold and the buyers had settled up that big Bob Campbell approached them smiling, papers in hand.

'I told yer, Mr Richards, didn't I?' he said, 'you done well. Congratulations.' And he shook both Harry's and Bluey's hands. Harry liked the man and noted that he didn't give any of the credit to himself. Campbell glanced at his papers to check.

'Averaged nearly six pounds a head. A total of eight thousand, eight hundred and twenty pounds less commission. If you'll come over ter the office, we can settle up.'

Bluey stood with his mouth agape and came close to falling over but Harry just grinned. He also reckoned that anybody worth that much was entitled to call even the Queen by her Christian name.

'Thanks, Bob,' he said, 'you done well for us.'

'My pleasure, Henry,' Campbell smiled and headed

for the hut that served as the office. Harry had to give Bluey a bit of help to get his feet moving, for Bluey stood there still looking stunned.

'Congratulations ter you, mate,' he said quietly to him, 'you should be able ter buy half er bloody Ireland fer half er that.'

'Holy Mot'er of Jasus,' Bluey just managed to get out.

Forgetting the eight hundred entirely, eight thousand was such a vast sum that Bluey just couldn't take it in at first. There was nothing he could measure it against. It would have helped if he had known the cost of a castle or a ship but he didn't. It was simply unbelievable wealth to which there was no end. It was a shock. Not once in all the way from Central Queensland had he stopped to try and put a value to the mob. That hadn't been of any importance. Only water had had any value or meaning. And Harry had never raised the subject either. He badly needed the drinks big Bob Campbell poured out as the business was concluded in the office and other drovers began to take away their big mob which was now split up into many smaller ones.

Although Harry was unable to make head nor tail of the figures on paper, he studied them as if he did and was fully satisfied. And on discovering that Campbell had his own property twenty miles out and was obviously the kind of man who looked after his animals, he said, 'As I got no need for 'em, but too much care to want ter sell 'em, I'd like yer ter take me horses in the way of thanks, Bob. I'll give yer their names.'

It was a very good day for Bob Campbell and only the first of the gestures Adelaide was to remember of the generous Henry Richards, even although it was all to take place over such a brief period of time.

Soon afterwards, Mr Henry Richards and Mr Patrick O'Day walked out of an astonished bank with two large leather bags containing well over four thousand pounds in each. From there, they went straight to a barber who also had a bath in a room and, after that, walked into A. Costello & Son, finest gentlemen's outfitters, where Mr Costello was only too pleased to advise them on what the finest gentlemen in not only Adelaide but in Europe were wearing.

'Three suits did you say, sir?' said Costello, doing his best to hide his amazement from the yellow bearded gentleman.

'Three,' Harry said, and Bluey was not to be outdone.

'An' begod, will it not be t'ree for me, too.'

Costello beamed and began to flute on about the unsurpassable quality of his goods, throwing wide his arms in uninhibited admiration of the way his customers looked as he dressed them. Never before had he sold six suits with all the accessories in so short a time, and never had he had two gentlemen so easy to please for they bowed to his every suggestion.

When Harry and Bluey emerged on to the windswept street loaded with bags and baggage, few would have recognised them as the same two men who had gone in. Neither were they bothered by the uncomfortable restrictions of their new outfits for they stood at least four feet taller in their pride. They stood for a moment, simply gazing at each other, and a little overawed by the sight. Harry was dressed in a grey frock-coat, complete with pinned cravat and grey topper while Bluey stuck out of a brown suit with brocaded vest and had a curled, brown bowler on his head. It mattered not at all that Harry's trousers were a little at half-mast and Bluey's too long. They were not accustomed to such refinements to notice.

'Cab, sir?' a cabbie said, pulling up his horse, and Harry and Bluey piled in, the first time they had been in a cab in their lives.

'Where to, gentlemen?' said the cabbie through his hatch.

'A hotel, mate.'

'A good one,' Bluey added.

The side-whiskered cabbie was an honest man. He drove them just around the corner and pulled up at the Flinders Hotel. Harry and Bluey who'd hardly had time to start enjoying the novelty of it, felt they had been cheated and were disappointed. Bejasus, t'ey hadn't gone t'e lent' of a dacent man's spit. And Harry made no attempt to get out either, but they were still far too shy of their surroundings in such a large town to complain.

'Could yer take us a bit further, mate?' Harry said up to the cabbie.

'Where to, sir?'

'Anywhere, it don't matter. Up an' down a bit.'

'It's your money, sir,' the cabbie said and moved off again to their delight. Harry grinned happily out of one side and Bluey out of the other, enjoying every minute of it as they were driven around the streets going nowhere.

'Look,' Bluey said, pointing, and Harry moved across to look.

'What is it?'

'It says Agents for the P & O Shipping Line.'

'Over there a minute, mate,' Harry directed the cabbie who pulled up his horse for a moment to let a wagon-load of wool bales pass then swung around.

Once, old Charley had made the strange remark to Harry that although money didn't make a man, it could talk a lot louder, and Harry was beginning to understand exactly what he meant.

'Certainly, sir,' the shipping clerk said and obligingly opened up the office he was in the process of locking up for the evening.

Harry and Bluey stood surrounded by notices of sailings.

'We wants two tickets for t'e boat to England, mister,' Bluey said.

The clerk was not at all surprised by the hard working hands and underlying roughness of Mr Henry Richards and Mr Patrick O'Day. Often, men made quick fortunes in the Colonies, one way or another, and he was as polite and accommodating as he would have been to anyone. That was company policy. It was also his duty to point out the different prices for the different classes – First, Second and Steerage.

'First,' Harry said.

'We never travel any ot'er way,' Bluey said. As a youth he had travelled steerage overnight on a boat from Ireland to England and had had a choice of bedding down either with the pigs or the cattle.

'Then I can offer you berths on a fast packet sailing direct in three days' time, sirs,' the clerk said, and, in no time, they had their tickets, had paid their money, were given all the details they needed, and were on their way back out to the waiting cab with their bags of money.

'It's a fine town, so it is,' Bluey said cheerfully, 'a fine town.'

For a very long time it had been Bluey's intention that if he ever got to Adelaide, the first thing he would do would be to seek out the good priest and make his confession. But now that he was there, when he thought more about it, in consideration of the fact that it had been English owned cattle and an English bull involved, it made much more sense to wait until he got home. T'ere, t'e Fat'er would have much more understanding of his weakness.

Harry's confidence amongst the crow-eaters, as the South Australians were called, quickly grew. They were only people.

Outside the Flinders Hotel, he handed a large white five pound note up to the cabbie who just stared at it.

'I can't give yer the change for that much, sir,' he said.

'Then buy yerself a new horse with it, mate,' he

grinned and strode into the hotel with his baggage, a smiling Bluey behind him, leaving the cabbie astonished.

At first, Harry thought he was being robbed when a man inside tried to take his bags away from him, then felt foolish when the surprised porter explained he was only doing his job.

'Sorry, mate, I thought yer was somebody else,' he said, and gave him a large white note, too. There was a lot Harry had to learn about a way of life he had never experienced but in his generosity to all around him, he got all the assistance he needed and learned quickly.

The night was a spree of drinking and spending but when Bluey went to Harry's room in the morning, he wasn't there. He was about to go and look for him elsewhere when he noticed the foot sticking out from under the bed. He lifted the covers and shook him awake.

'What's ye doin' under t'ere?'

'I couldn't sleep in the bloody thing. It was too soft. An' it wasn't that bloody good under here, either. I couldn't dig a hip-hole.'

'Did ye know ye hired an open carriage to come for us t'is mornin'?'

'What for?'

'For t'e children, ye said.'

'Oh, yeah,' Harry muttered, remembering.

'Ye shouted half t'e town last night. Begod, t'ere won't be a man sober for an honest day's work in t'e whole of Adelaide.'

Heads turned when the yellow bearded gentleman in the grey frock-coat and half-mast trousers walked through into the dining-room.

'Good morning, Mr Richards,' they greeted him, and Mr Richards was well advised what to have with his breakfast. The champagne did wonders for how both he and Bluey felt.

With more of it to hand a little later, they boarded the open carriage with both that and an enormous bag of sixpences that Harry had arranged for; no less than two hundred pounds worth. The coachman drove them with two black horses in shining harness to the poorer area where, on sighting his first group of grubby children, King Henry of Adelaide dipped into the heavy bag for a fistful of the silver coins and scattered them to the air behind him while Bluey opened another bottle. In no time, every urchin in town, as well as many men and women, followed in their wake, scrambling for the money and cheering.

'I t'ink I'll buy meself t'e finest farm in all Ireland, Harry,' Bluey said, dead marines rolling around at his feet. 'I'll keep pigs an' cows an' ducks an' geese an' fine fields for growin' of t'e crops as well. Bejasus, I might even keep meself a good wife. An' I'll have fine fast-footed horses t'at can show t'eir tails to t'e Devil an' t'e wind.'

'If yer do,' Harry said, 'would yer do somethin' for us?'

'Anyt'in', Harry, anyt'in'.'

'Get yourself a big white bull, call it Lord Wallah Wallah Banjo and never sell it.'

'Begod, I'll do better t'an t'at. I'll call it Lord Harry Harry an' keep it in the finest, green field I has 'till t'e day t'e good God is short of meat.'

And the coachman drove on as King Henry studded sky and earth with another shower of silver.

There was no one there just outside of town to see a blacktracker in torn and dirty tartan trousers carrying a leather satchel arrive at the Adelaide Stock Yards. Wooly stood looking in at the many empty pens. There was not a single beast or man to be seen. But there was absolutely no doubt that this was where the big mob had come.

It had been an uneventful journey for Wooly across

the Flinders Ranges. Several times he had tried to make approaches to white men but on each occasion had been chased away. And once, a man had shot at him and he had had to run many miles away to hide. But, later, he had returned to find the tracks he had left and kept doggedly on.

He could not tell how far he had come in following them since he had left Albert Downs, but it was further than the known world and it was natural for him to think he might have reached the boundaries of Egland to where black men went when they died.

The big mob had come to there, then gone away again in several different directions. He looked across the silent, empty yards in a confusion of satisfaction and fear. Where he was he didn't know, but he knew it was all over. This was where it all ended. After all the great distance he had come, he had to imagine what the great mob had looked like in the flesh and what colours they might have been for there was nothing left to see. For a whole hour he stood there perfectly still, looking. There was nothing more he could do.

All that remained was to find a friendly white boss man to whom to give a letter. Then he could go back to Boss McKenzie of Albert Downs, try to tell him of where the big white bull and the mob had gone and return further to the north and his family. Whether that would be as he was or jumped up a white fella with plenty sixpence was still not clear.

He moved to the edge of town and completely overawed by the enormity of its size and all the people, squatted on his haunches gazing at it, afraid to go any closer. He had already learned that blacks were not welcome in any town, but this was not even a town. It was a whole land that had been built upon and inhabited, and he didn't know what to make of it. All day he squatted there wondering if it might be Egland and if he would have to die before he was allowed in.

It wasn't until evening that his curiosity drove him to try and he rose to walk cautiously towards it.

On the outskirts of town, Harry and Bluey emerged from a hostelry of wine, beer and spirits, Harry looking dishevelled and annoyed, his grey topper dented.

'If yer does that again,' Harry said, 'I'll bloody kill yer.'

'T'was only a joke, Harry, only a joke. But begod ye can fight.'

The joke was that Bluey in his cups had begun to boast to all and sundry that his friend could fight any two men at the one time. And even although it was Harry who had been generously paying for all their drinks, the challenge was far too much to resist.

Harry calmed, forgave him, then grinned.

'All right, mate, but don't do it again.'

'I will not, Harry, I will not.'

They stood for a moment looking around, wondering where to go and what to do next. Sailing the following day, they wanted to make the best of it.

'What we need now,' Bluey said, 'is a good woman. Two of 'em.'

'How?'

'Ah, t'at's t'e worst of it. I don't know.'

But Harry was very much attracted by the idea and thought about it. He had heard men say that in big towns a cab driver could get you anything and that they knew more than anybody. There was no better time to find out if it was true and he began to feel excited at the prospect. Although the street there was empty of traffic, he raised his topper to the air, let out a piercing whistle and yelled 'Cab!'

Bluey whistled and shouted, too, and so intent were they on getting any cabbie within a radius of a mile to hear them, they hardly noticed the black in the tartan trousers approaching them in the dusk.

Wooly looked at them as he got closer and, never

having seen them before in his life, could at least see they were very happy men who were not trying to chase him away but clearly in celebration of some kind and it crossed his mind that they might have been relatives who had just jumped up white pella with plenty sixpence. Whether or not, they were very obviously big white boss men now, just the men to whom he could give a letter.

It all happened quickly. A cab came trotting around the corner as Wooly dipped into his satchel. And as the cab pulled up alongside Harry and Bluey, he moved forward and held out a stained envelope to Harry. But Harry was far too consumed by other things and was not interested in buying whatever it was supposed to be. He just stopped long enough to quickly dip into his pocket for a handful of sixpences and put them in Wooly's other hand.

'Here, mate,' he said, and dived into the cab after Bluey.

The cab drove away with Wooly still holding out the letter in more confusion than ever. He looked at all the shining sixpences in his hand. It was the first time he had ever touched money and at first didn't know if he was dead or still alive. He looked at his skin. It was still black.

In the cab, Harry spoke up to the cabbie.

'We want ter find a couple er donahs, mate,' he said, donah being the term for sweetheart, and the cabbie pulled his horse to a stop before talking back down, somewhat annoyed.

'I don't know what yer mean, sir. I can't find yer any girls. What d'yer think I am?'

'Ah, t'is t'e worst of it right enough,' said Bluey, crestfallen. But Harry got out a five pound note, stuck it up through the hatch and waved it in the driver's face.

'That an' another one the same if yer can find 'em for us,' he said. The cabbie stared at the note for a moment in disbelief then grabbed it before it had a chance to disappear.

'I'll see what I can do for yer, sir.'

He drove on, Harry and Bluey inside happily grinning at each other.

It was Constable Harris of the South Australian Police who noticed the black lurking on the outskirts of town and as he walked towards him, waved him away. 'Off with you. Go on, off with you!'

If the uniform was a little different to others he had seen, Wooly, although still very much confused, knew what it was and didn't like it. But as he started to walk away to get out of town, Harris noticed the satchel he was carrying. That was unusual enough to raise suspicion of theft. He ran after Wooly and caught him.

'What've you got there?' he said, taking the satchel from him and opening it, but Wooly was too frightened to say anything. It was a fear that sprang not from any desire to escape any physical pain, but from being confined. He needed the earth beneath his feet, the sky above him and the free spaces around him every bit as much as the air he breathed.

Harris was surprised to find letters, all reading 'To Whom It May Concern' being carried by a black and tore one open. And although it was almost dark, he was able to read what it said.. It was mystifying being addressed from Central Queensland and telling of stolen cattle. The black couldn't have come from there. What cattle?

'Where did you come from?' he said, and Wooly pointed simply to the north. That told Constable Harris nothing. None of it made sense. The mystery needed clarification.

'You come with us,' he said and began to push a reluctant Wooly ahead of him back in the direction of the Police Station for questioning. Despite all the sixpences in his pocket, Wooly came to the swift conclusion that he was not dead, that the man was not a relative, that he was still black, and that this was not Egland.

Miles away, the cab with Harry and Bluey in it pulled up at a shuttered house that appeared to be empty of light and life.

'Wait there,' the cabbie said and got down to go to the door on his own and knock on it. It was several minutes before it opened and Harry could just make out that he was talking to somebody. Like Bluey, he had begun to feel nervous. After all their self-built excitement, they were very unsure about how to behave in such a place. Images of naked thighs, soft flesh and breasts swept over them like fire, thrilling them and terrifying them all at the one time. It wasn't that they didn't know what to do, it was the whole idea of some strange woman submitting herself so easily and without question.

The cabbie returned. 'All right, sir, they'll take yer,' he said, and Harry and Bluey tumbled out.

Harry paid the cabbie the rest of the money and said, 'I don't want yer ter leave us here. Could yer wait for us?'

'How long is yer goin' ter be, sir?'

'I dunno, but if yer hangs around for us I'll pay yer for it.'

That was good enough for the cabbie who had already got a small fortune out of these two men whom he took to be diggers who had struck it lucky and couldn't wait until they didn't have enough left to buy a pick-axe.

'I'll hang around, sir.'

Harry and Bluey, more nervously aroused by the moment, couldn't make out the figure who let them in until they were through the second door into the dimly lit fantasy of satins and velvets smelling heavily of scent. And then both their faces fell on the sight of the smiling Mrs Googe, and they both thought that this was what they were going to get and she looked bloody horrible. For a brief moment, all desires sank to their boots, but Mrs Googe held out her spidery hand to ask for three times the normal price.

'Ten pounds each an' I'll see what girls is ready for yer.'

Thank God for that. It wasn't her after all and their desires sprang up again as they paid her. Mrs Googe tucked the notes away in her dress. These two were easier marks than she had ever encountered. She held out her hand again.

'If yer wants 'em to take everythin' off, it'll be another two pounds each extra,' she said.

It wasn't parting with more money that held them both inactive and dumb. It was shock and embarrassment. There was no possibility of either of them revealing to somebody's grandmother that they preferred women stripped entirely naked. To have handed over the other two pounds would have been like letting the entire world know the depths of their depravity. They just pretended they hadn't heard and Mrs Googe looked at them a little sourly. They were stupid as well.

'Take a seat over there, then,' she said, and made for the stairs. Harry and Bluey sat on the edge of the velvet sofa twiddling their hats in silence. Another well dressed gentleman sat buried in the shadows of a corner.

'G'day, mate,' Harry said across to him, hoping to strike up a conversation and learn more of what to expect, but the man didn't answer.

After a few minutes, Mrs Googe came down with another well dressed gentleman and let him out before nodding to the man in the corner. He got up and, careful to keep his face turned away from the two strangers on the sofa as he went, followed Mrs Googe upstairs.

'How long does ye t'ink we has ter wait, Harry?' Bluey whispered.

'I dunno, mate,' Harry whispered back.

The parlour was conducive to whispering. There were no sounds of girlish giggles to be heard resounding through the rooms, no screams of ecstasy, no happy shouts or the clinking of bottles. Only the creak of floorboards above their heads when someone moved. It was a very orderly house that Mrs Googe kept for her protection. And all strictly businesslike. As far as Mrs Googe was concerned, gentlemen could come here for their fornication and go and have their fun somewhere else.

But Harry and Bluey didn't have to wait long and shortly afterwards Mrs Googe reappeared and led them up. Businesslike or not, their hearts raced and their legs weakened in fresh excitement and expectancy.

On the upper landing, Mrs Googe pointed to two, closed doors.

'That one an' that one,' she said and while Harry and Bluey shyly hesitated now that their great moment had arrived, Mrs Googe moved to a further door and rapped hard and impatiently on it.

'Hurry up in there, there's other people waitin'!'

Nothing infuriated Mrs Googe more than a man trying to get more than his money's worth.

Bluey hurried in through his door but Harry hesitated a little longer. He was a man, not a boy. He gathered his courage, pride and dignity, walked in as if he had been doing this all his life and said to the bored-looking, rose satin and black lace figure lying on the bed, 'Yer don't have ter worry about me, lady. I won't be keepin' yer long.'

Neither he nor Bluey were to know that while they enjoyed the doubtful pleasures of Mrs Googe's skirt-lifting ladies, the innocent harbinger of their deaths sat on a bench only a few miles away in the Police Station.

Sergeant Liddle was a big burly man who had made few errors either in his life or in his career with the South Australian Police. Hard as he could be at times, he was a likeable man. And having spent years of his duty in the bush, he was used to dealing with blacks. This one was different. Over and over as he questioned this one, the dark eyes looked directly back into his own with a boldness that could easily have been taken for impudence. It was only the incredibility of his story that raised any suspicion of lying. And if his English was very limited, there seemed little doubt that he understood it when it was spoken.

'You're telling me,' he said to Wooly for about the fourth time, 'that two men drove this big plenty mob and a white bull all the way from Central Queensland through where there's no known route and you tracked them all the way to here?'

'Big pella bull Gunderindi place, boss. Plurry plenty big mob dis place, boss.'

'Tell me again who gave you the letters?'

'Kenzie, big pella boss, boss.'

It was hard to know what to make of it. No one in their right mind would have sent a blacktracker after stolen cattle without supervision. If you sent a black to a creek for a bucket of water only fifty yards away, you had to watch him to make sure he came back.

Constable Harris came out of an inner office with a list.

'There is a Gunderindi, Sergeant, and it's as far north as you can get. Name of Deaken.'

That was puzzling, too.

'If this is all true and not some hatter's idea of a hoax, why hasn't he sent a message through?'

Had they but known it, the explanation was simple. After creating his own long delay, Deaken had not taken the letters to the new railway line that lay only a hundred and fifty miles to the south-west. Instead, he had disposed of his responsibility by passing them on to his nearest neighbour to the south. And the neighbour, amazed at the boldness of such gully rakers who could find a way through from Queensland, quickly became terrified that they might have added to their enormous mob with another of his own. He immediately set about trying to make a bang-tail muster for a count with no hand to spare for carrying messages. It was a further three weeks before he began to feel satisfied that he hadn't been robbed. And the letters were only just then reaching the nearest Police Station which consisted of three tents.

Sergeant Liddle wasn't a man to bother his superiors with unconfirmed fairy tales, but the more he looked at Wooly, the more the blacktracker impressed him. The first avenue of enquiry was obviously with the Stock Yards.

'Get out to Bob Campbell's' he said to Harris. 'Tell him we want him to bring in all the records of recent sales with the brands.'

Although Harris had been on duty since early morning, he made no complaint of having to do a twenty mile ride there and back through the night. He felt excited at the prospect of it all being true. To be involved in such a big and important case would be a feather in his cap. He hurried out to the yard to saddle up a horse and Liddle turned to look at Wooly again. There could be more the black could tell them. He had to be detained in case he was needed.

'Fella Wooly sleep this place tonight,' he said, and Wooly got slowly to his feet. Liddle had seen that look of fear in black men's eyes before and knew what it was but he had no alternative. To have let him out would mean never setting eyes on him again. He led Wooly to a cell and put him inside, doing his best to explain to him that he was not a prisoner but had to be kept.

'Fella Wooly not bad fella,' he said, but good or bad, it made no difference to Wooly. And, as he stood there he felt the stone walls closing in and crushing at the instinctive freedom of his spirit, the rising and the setting of the sun and the turning of the stars dying through each moment of captivity.

Harry wasn't quite sure how he felt as he emerged from the room in Mrs Googe's house but his self-satisfied grin turned to an expression of wonderment and puzzlement as he caught sight of a figure in a crumpled green dress hurriedly put down a large enamel jug and scuttle into a narrow passage way. Harry just stood there for a moment, wondering if he had imagined it. But he had seen her face clearly and although it looked drawn and far from well, she had looked for all the world like Lilly Boyd who had worked at Albert Downs. That was impossible. Yet, he was so filled with curiosity that he went into the narrow passage to try and get another look. Carefully mounting the few steps, he saw a lit hurricane lantern on the floor of the other small section of passage, and the opened curtain, and caught the smallest glimpse of a woman's boot disappearing from the top of the ladder at the hatchway above. He stood there looking up. Maybe the strange experience with the bart had cracked his cobra. It couldn't have been her. Even if it was, not here. It was all the drink. He'd drunk himself sober.

But the image of the face he had seen and his curiosity wouldn't go away and he felt drawn to find out. Who was going to bloody kill him for it? He picked up the lantern and cautiously made his way up the ladder. His head through the hatch, he held the lantern high. The girl was backing away looking terrified.

'Go away, go on,' she said, and the voice was the same, too.

'I ain't goin' ter harm yer,' Harry said, 'it's just you look the exact same as somebody from up Queensland.'

Lilly stopped backing away and stared at the lit head with the mop of yellow hair and yellow beard. It sounded just like him. For a full minute they just looked at each other, unable to believe it.

'Harry?' Lilly said, 'Harry Walford?'

'Yer. An' you is Lilly Boyd, ain't yer?'

Harry went right up and they stood face to face, still trying to take each other in. The rouseabout dressed like a wealthy gentleman in frock-coat was a sight Lilly could never have imagined if she had been asked to. And the picture of the housemaid, Miss Boyd, whom Harry had always taken to be beyond him in terms of even close friendship, standing there in a fashionable lady's dress, even if it was in a bit of a state, was something he had never imagined seeing either, particularly in a brothel. But Harry's surprise was soon overtaken by concern. Before the questions as to how each had come to be there began to flow, he noted the rash that was just beginning on Lilly's cheeks and the illness in her eyes.

'You's not well, is yer?' he said.

Bluey emerged from his room and was already wondering if he might not have another ten pounds' worth and not seeing Harry, went to Harry's door to put an ear to it. If he could hear something, it would be a fine thing to be able to put up to his friend later.

'What's yer doin' there?' Mrs Googe said, appearing at the top of the stairs, and Bluey stepped back.

'I's waitin' for me friend,' he said, and Mrs Googe wasted no time in rapping on the door.

'There ain't nobody here,' a girl's voice came from inside. 'E's gone.'

'Downstairs,' Mrs Googe directed Bluey and he went, Mrs Googe following to make sure he was not going to cause any trouble. But Harry wasn't there either and Bluey started to argue, wanting to know what had happened to him. Harry would never have left him there. Never. He started to hurry back up, Mrs Googe after him. They had just reached the top of the stairs when Harry emerged from the narrow passage with Lilly, carrying her little bag. Both Bluey and Mrs Googe gaped for different reasons for a moment before Mrs Googe sprang in anger.

'You take yer bloody hands off her!'

Harry struggled to hold her off as he started to get Lilly down the stairs.

'Get off yer bloody raddled up old poler!' Harry said.

'She's my Lilly, yer hear us! Take yer bloody hands off or I'll bloody kill yer!'

Bluey was still stunned by the totally unexpected sight of his friend suddenly appearing like magic in the company of Lilly Boyd, for she could have been no one else. More than once after a hard day's work on Albert Downs she had walked into his dreams. He could have been dreaming again had it not been for Harry waking him up.

'Don't bloody stand there, give us a hand, mate,' Harry said back up to him as Mrs Googe cursed and tore at him.

Bluey ran down and tried to grab Mrs Googe from behind but Mrs Googe got a sharp elbow into his face. In the parlour, two gentlemen who were waiting stood on their feet looking horrified and Mrs Googe, still fighting for all she was worth, appealed to them.

'They's stealin' my Lilly! Help us, for God's sake! She's mine!'

'I'm not hers!' Lilly shouted at them fiercely in denial.

'Get ther doors open, mate!' Harry said, doing his best to shield Lilly from Mrs Googe's furious attack as she clawed, struck and kicked for the possession she had so carefully nurtured and whom she had brought to the verge of surrender. It was as well, perhaps, that the two gentlemen chose not to enter into the violent dispute. Not only were they not of the fighting kind but they began to feel terror, for both their lives and those of their families could not have withstood the scandal if they were exposed as ever having been in such a place. And the noise, not to mention the foul language, only had to reach the ears of a constable.

'I'll have yer bloody hangers off, yer bastards!' Mrs Googe screamed at Harry, 'an' yer bloody cock as well! Let 'er go!'

The moment Bluey had the doors open, the two gentlemen fled so fast through them that they almost knocked Bluey off his feet. On the upper landing, half dressed men and women were hurrying out of other doors in the belief that police had already arrived and they ran looking for escape. Bluey dragged Mrs Googe's cursing figure from Harry's scratched neck and, with all his strength, hurled her across the parlour. The last he saw of her was landing on her back on the sofa, her black-clad legs flailing the air as she let out a fresh scream of oaths, for there was no more time to stop and look as he dashed after Harry and Lilly out into the dark street. They ran to their cab which had been circling around waiting and dived in, the bewildered cabbie having enough presence of mind to take off. Harry stuck his head out to look back. Figures were pouring out of Mrs Googe's house to tear in all directions into dark alleys, but no one was coming after them.

'Is yer all right, Lilly?' Harry said with anxiety.

'Yes, I'm all right. Thanks, Harry.'

But although Lilly could not have been more grateful for finding herself with people she knew for the first time since leaving Albert Downs, she was dazed by all that had happened so unexpectedly and so quickly. Her mind was a whirlpool that stirred illusion and reality, for the moment making them difficult to separate. All at the one time, there was a closeness and a distance about it. It was Harry and it wasn't. She was aware of the beads of sweat rising on her forehead but she was cold. And she felt that at any moment she was going to retch and was forced to fight it.

'In t'e name of God,' Bluey said, finding his breath, 'apart from fightin' off unholy witches, would somebody mind tellin' us what's goin' on?'

'It's Lilly,' Harry said, 'an' she ain't well.'

'I can see it's Lilly an' I can see she's not well, but how t'e devil she get in t'ere from Albert Downs?'

'You can tell him how stupid I've been,' Lilly said.

'You wasn't stupid,' Harry said comfortingly, 'yer just run inter a bit of bad luck, that's all.' And he turned to Bluey, 'Now just leave 'er alone, mate.'

Bluey just looked from one to the other as they looked at each other. It was perfectly clear he was going to have to wait for an explanation. Bejasus, it was a quare an' cronky world right enough when it came to a big town t'e size of Adelaide. Anyt'in could happen in a place like t'is. T'e sooner t'ey set foot on t'e boat t'e better. If ye could run into one just like t'at all t'e way down from Queensland, begod, could ye not run into two?

It was far from accepted practice for men to walk into the Flinders or any other hotel at night with a girl and expect to book a room for her. Suspicion ran deep. Lilly was rejected with suitable, polite apology, but it only made Harry more determined and unusually angry. He pulled the man aside.

'Miss Boyd is more respectable than any of your ladies in Adelaide,' he said, 'an' if yer thinks anythin' else, I'll pull down this place bit by bloody bit ter prove yer wrong. An' you with it, mate.'

Between that and the sum of twenty pounds, all moral scruple, if not suspicion, was quickly swept away and a room was found for Miss Lillian Boyd.

'You rest,' Harry told her when they got her into it. 'Yer need it. We'll come an' see how yer is in the mornin'.'

Lilly did her best to smile her gratitude, desperately wishing she could say all she wanted to. Then, the moment she was left alone, she dived for the po and allowed herself to vomit into it.

'I's glad we's clearin' out er here termorrer, mate,' Harry said over more drink, 'I don't reckon I like big towns. Too many cuffs an' collars an' too many bloody hummers. It's no life for a man.'

'An' don't I know it about yer. I's t'inkin' ye was never happier t'an when ye was perishin' in t'e middle of t'is God-forsaken, sunburnt land.'

And Harry laughed.

But it was with unease that Bluey eventually laid his head down to sleep that night and he knew very well why. The sudden appearance of Lilly was an omen to him, a warning of approaching bad luck. The hour for boarding the ship couldn't come soon enough.

The bad luck came at first light in the shape of big Bob Campbell. Accompanied by Constable Harris, he walked into the Police Station with his records. Sergeant Liddle who had slept there to wait, was already up and another Constable had come on duty, while Wooly squatted in misery in the middle of his cell, having already served several years in the space of that one night, his food untouched before him, his mug of tea long since gone cold.

'I can't believe it,' Campbell said. 'What kind of damned gully raker could find a way through from Queensland? An' with a mob that big in top condition?'

What Campbell couldn't believe either was that his judgment of a man's character could have been so wrong. Nobody had ever been able to fool him before.

But the evidence was there before all their eyes. The brands on the cattle Campbell had auctioned for Harry Walford and the Irishman, McGuirk, alias Richards and O'Day, were the same that the Manager of Albert Downs in Queensland, Mr Donald McKenzie, had clearly indicated in his letters. And if there were any doubts left, an excited messenger from the Overland Telegraph Office arrived with a message to dispel them. Deaken's communication had reached its right destination at last.

'I'd like you to stay here and help us with identification, Mr Campbell,' Liddle said, but if Harris, despite his tiredness, looked delighted, the Sergeant did not. He knew that men who had done what Walford and McGuirk had would not be taken easily. What he didn't know was how little time he had left to take them at all. Shipping out didn't even enter his head because gully rakers and bushrangers didn't ever do that and always made back to the bush.

At the Flinders Hotel, Harry and Bluey packed up their bags then went to Lilly's room.

'Holy Mot'er of God,' Bluey said at the sight of her.

Lilly lay in her bed in fever, a red rash spreading all over her, and near her head was the po into which she had been vomiting and dry retching.

'You stay here,' Harry said to Bluey, 'I'm going ter find a doctor.' And Bluey was immediately anxious.

'What about t'e boat, Harry? What about t'e boat?'

'I'll be all right, Harry,' Lilly said weakly, but Harry went.

Bluey sat uncomfortably on a chair well back from the bed.

'I's sorry you's like t'is, Lilly, but when Harry gets t'e doctor, we has to go. Ye understand?'

Lilly nodded and tried to smile.

It took a little longer than Harry thought trying to find help before he was directed to Dr Duval's and Dr Duval had just that moment returned from being out. But he made no objection when the yellow bearded man, clearly very worried, asked him to come and see a friend who was very ill. He simply picked up his bag and followed. It wasn't until they were starting to cross the street towards the hotel that Dr Duval said, 'I hear there's some excitement about this morning. Something about men having brought stolen cattle all the way through from Queensland. Quite extraordinary, if it isn't only a rumour.'

Harry could have stopped dead in his tracks but somehow managed to force himself on after only a split second, appearing not to have missed a step, and he knew the Doctor would expect him to make a comment on such news. He had to say something. Anything.

'I reckon rumours is rife,' he said, remembering old Charley having said something similiar at one time, although in an entirely different context, but Duval accepted it.

In Lilly's hotel room, while Dr Duval made a brief examination of Lilly, for that was all that was necessary for his diagnosis, Harry pulled Bluey aside.

'They's on to us, mate,' he whispered, and had he not held Bluey with the tightest of grips by the back of his coat to keep him firmly in place, Bluey would have fled faster than the two gentlemen from Mrs Googe's, right there and then.

Duval turned to them. He had never seen a more anxious expression than the one on Bluey's face. The girl clearly meant very much to him, too, but there was no help for it.

'It's scarlet fever, I fear,' he said, and his words were followed by silence. Although Harry had never known anyone with the disease which was common enough, he did know that people could die of it, and he did not want Lilly to die.

'It doesn't help that she is undernourished,' Duval said, 'but I'll do what I can. Is there anywhere she can be taken?'

'No,' Harry said, and Bluey, held speechless, said nothing.

'Then she will have to be kept in isolation here,' Duval said. 'I'll go and make arrangements. I don't suppose the hotel will like it but they'll have no alternative.'

Harry quickly took out a bundle of notes and gave

them to him.

'I want ter thank yer, an' I want yer ter do everythin' yer can for 'er. We has ter go north on business.'

Duval looked at all the money he had been given. It was much much more than was required but he didn't say so. It was as well when people were overgenerous as it helped to balance up for the ones who didn't pay him at all.

'Thank you,' he said, and went.

'Holy Jasus,' Bluey said in a gasp the moment Duval was out of the door, and wanted to know what was happening and how they could have been discovered, but Harry knew no more than what Duval had told him. And he seemed more concerned about Lilly than anything else. He sat by her bed, looked at her and tried to raise a grin.

'You's not ter worry. You's goin' ter be all right. God and Dr Duval's goin' ter see ter it. A couple of mates of mine had that an' now they's both stronger'n a team of bloody bullocks.'

Lilly smiled. Bluey didn't.

'In t'e name of all t'e Saints, Harry, what's ye doin'? We gotter get on t'e boat! T'ere's not'in' more ye can do for t'e poor soul. Not'in'.'

Harry knew that but he continued to sit, trying to give comfort.

'Jasus, Mary an' Joseph!' Bluey said and shook him hard. Harry rose, then reached for Lilly's little bag and stuffed it with notes. Even then, the frantic Bluey had to drag him away.

They reached the front of the hotel with their bags but they could see no police and took off into a side street. If Harry wasn't thinking well, Bluey's mind was racing. It was getting to be too dangerous to get a cab. The police might question the cabbies. Bluey stopped a carter whose cart was almost bare but for empty sacks and he held out twenty pounds to the astonished man.

It was almost as much as he earned in six months of hard toiling.

'T'is for gettin' us to t'e docks an' never havin' seen us,' he said, 'for we has two sore witches of wives after us.'

The carter could hardly believe his luck, and as he turned his horse around, Harry and Bluey hopped on to the cart and covered themselves over with empty wheat bags.

At the port, they dusted themselves down and looked around carefully before approaching their vessel. Most had already boarded and were crowding the rails, waving to friends and relatives who had come to see them off. Not a single policeman was in sight.

They boarded nervously but without difficulty. No one tried to question them after they had handed over their passage papers to the officer at the top of the gangway. Still hanging on to their bags they made their way forward along the deck to get to a part of the rail where they could get a view of the dockside and make sure no one was coming after them. For half an hour they stood there in silence, but without seeing a uniform. Then the gangways were hauled away, the rail closed, and men stood by the mooring lines.

'T'at was t'e skin of our bloody teet' t'at was, Harry,' Bluey said with enormous relief but Harry didn't reply. Bluey didn't have to look at him to know of his friend's unhappiness, and he hoped it was for only one reason.

'I know how it feels when you's leavin' yer own country, Harry, but t'ink on it. Ye's goin' ter see the turf yer people was raised and worked on. T'e very place. An' can ye not come back the very minute ye's feels safe? Begod, yer country won't be missin' you.'

The spring lines on the dock were let go, then the bow and stern lines, seamen winching them to the decks as a fresh burst of waving and shouting passed between rail and dockside, and the ship began to inch away from the heavy, hardwood timbers.

Suddenly, Harry lifted his bag at his feet and, without a word, started to push his way desperately through people towards amidships, Bluey after him in anxiety.

'What's t'e matter? What's yer doin'? Where's yer goin'?'

Harry turned his head back to him for only an instant and if there were no tears in his eyes, there might as well have been, for they were certainly in his voice.

'I can't leave her like that, mate,' he said without stopping, and Bluey couldn't get close enough to him to grab him as his friend reached the maximum beam of the vessel where the gap of water was still only about eight feet. In an instant, Harry threw his bag to the dockside, sprang on to the rail between passengers and jumped into flight. It was as well he landed on a coil of rope that helped break his fall, because getting off being the one single thing in his mind at that moment, he hadn't aimed for it. People staring at him, he got up unhurt, picked up his top hat to put it back on, retrieved his bag, and stood only for a moment to wave to the shock-faced Bluey clutching at the rail as the ship moved further away.

'Good luck to yer, mate,' he muttered quietly, 'yer deserve it.'

Then he turned away to make his way through the curious crowd of people before he attracted any more attention.

Shattered, Bluey clung to the rail as the ship taking him to safety moved further and further away, his Irish heart more emotionally rent than it had ever been. What had so suddenly left him was not simply Harry but a part of himself. Part of his happiness and of his doubts and agonies that had taken him to the very jaws of hell and back again. And it was highly unlikely that he would ever know where that part of him had gone or what was to become of it. He should have known. It had been the same with the big white bull and the mob and the beast that had become bogged to the neck at the spring. But he had been unprepared.

Even as rain stung at his face and the ship heaved into a rising sea as it headed to round Cape Jervis, Bluey stood alone on deck, still clinging to the rail.

When Harry returned to Lilly's room, fear struck at him. A large white sheet hung over the door. Not knowing it was a sign of quarantine, it could have been a sign of something worse. But when he went in, Lilly was the same as he'd left her and despite her condition, looked surprised.

'Harry,' she said, pleased to see him again, 'Harry.'

That she was still alive brought a grin to his face.

'Yeah,' he said, 'an' I's stayin' with yer till yer right. I's just goin' back out ter get yer things I reckon yer'll need an' get meself a razor ter shave off me beard. An' I'll probably have ter get meself another place ter bunk down, but I'll find a way of seein' yer. Just know I ain't leavin' yer on yer own.' And he went back out.

It was foolish of him to believe he could ever do it, even in a big town like Adelaide, but he was unable to help himself. Sooner or later the outcome was inevitable. And it came sooner. He was never to return to the room again.

It was reasonable for Sergeant Liddle to start his enquiries at the best hotels, considering the fortune Walford and McGuirk had made from the sale of the mob. The Flinders Hotel was the third to be tried.

As Harry reached the bottom of the stairs, Liddle, together with three other Constables including the tired-eyed Harris, and big Bob Campbell, were just entering the hotel. Harry saw them and the group saw Harry but, on first glance, Bob Campbell was not sure it was him. He had only seen Harry in his droving clothes and with his beard untrimmed and wild, not as a gentleman in frock-coat and top hat. But Campbell was trying to measure him up and Harry knew it. There was only one thing for him to do and that was to try and brazen it out. Without hesitation and without any sign of recognition that he had ever met Campbell before, he made towards them, heading for the door. Within a second, Campbell became absolutely sure Harry was the man but because he had liked him and secretly admired his achievement, half of him wanted to keep his mouth shut. Then he heard his other half say, 'It could be him', and immediately wished he hadn't.

Liddle stepped in front of the passing Harry to block him.

'Excuse me, sir,' he said, 'could I have your name?' But even before he had finished speaking, he knew from the flash of anger in Harry's eyes that he had his man, and Harry, too, knew that it was all up. And Liddle was right in believing that the men he sought would not be taken easily. Suddenly, Harry struck out, a signal for Harris and the other two Constables to immediately spring at him in flying tackles to knock him down. But it was far from over as Harry bounced back to his feet and fought the four policemen together with all the strength and ferocity of a maddened bull. Bodies flew, ornaments crashed, and batons struck out wildly and with force to connect with Harry's face, skull and body. But they still couldn't subdue him or bring him down again.

What Harry fought for was not his bag of money, nor even for escape, but for dignity and spirit, for the safety of the best friend he had ever known and whom he'd lost, and most of all, for a girl who had just turned eighteen and who needed help.

It wasn't until Sergeant Liddle demanded of big Bob Campbell and others that they help and the spectator-ringed reception parlour of the Flinders Hotel had become a total wreck, that the battered Harry was overwhelmed and eventually struck to the floor. But there was little need to hold him as the torn and panting

Constables got manacles on him. Blood flowed freely from Harry's face and head and all he had left to fight was unconsciousness. Liddle knew he would never have Walford in better condition for questioning than he had right then and, his own face beginning to swell from blows, knelt by him on one knee and shook him.

'Where's McGuirk?'

Even in his half-darkness, Harry was aware of the opportunity being presented to him.

'Goin' ter New South Wales,' he mumbled through bleeding lips.

'Where in New South Wales?'

'Ter buy a sheep run.'

It was the first real error Liddle was ever to make in his career, for he took it to be the truth and no enquiries were ever to be made with shipping agents, and the carter who had been so well paid to take two obvious fugitives to the docks didn't ever come foward. And Harry was never to say anything else about where Bluey had gone.

'Somebody's got ter look after Lilly,' he muttered before he could fight no longer, and the darkness became complete and he was still.

Liddle wasn't interested in the gully raker's girl friends and the money that was stuffed into Lilly's little bag in her isolated sick room lay there intact.

A crowd of curious, silent onlookers both inside and outside the hotel watched as the unconscious figure of a manacled gentleman with blood trickling from his head, face and yellow beard, was carried out into the rain-swept street, thrown into a black horse van and carted to the Police Station where he was placed in the cell next to Wooly.

And, in no time, the telegraph wires between the Colonies of South Australia and Victoria and New South Wales and Queensland were running hot with the news.

Ten

Had Eddie Giraldi told them in his excited drawl that far from being bleached bones and a handful of yellow hair, their ex-rouseabout, Harry Walford, very much living flesh and blood, had taken the stolen fifteen hundred head to the planet Mercury and sold off the big white bull at Venus on the way, the effect could not have been more electrifying.

Like everyone else on Albert Downs, Don McKenzie was at first stunned to silence. There was much to take in, not least that Walford had got nearly twice as much for the cattle in Adelaide than he, the Manager of Albert Downs, could have got for them in Queensland. That was a spade of embarrassment that was going to dig up other embarrassments he had hoped might have been buried for good. Was there no God-damned end to the troubles this man had caused him?

Only the week before, McKenzie had received the dreaded reply from his employers in London on all that had happened. 'It is beyond our comprehension,' it ran in part, 'how you came to take such criminals into our employ.' The words 'outrage', 'dissatisfaction' and 'inefficiency' ran throughout like sticks down a creek in full flood. The entire tone of it had been that of senior school masters to a pupil who had been caught trying to burn down the premises and his eyes had raced on lines ahead looking for what he had feared most. But he was not expelled. It had ended, 'It is fortunate indeed that our Underwriters hold us personally in such high esteem, for they have agreed to make full settlement on the loss of the bull. It will be with considerable inconvenience and difficulty that we will find another of similar breeding. In the meantime, it is fully expected of you to make up these present, unaccountable losses within a period of two years.'

There had been considerable relief for him when, after a second reading, he could still find no suggestion of him being replaced. He couldn't blame them for their anger with him. Under the circumstances, their reaction was excusable. If you looked hard enough, you might even be able to read between the lines some understanding of both his problems and his managerial ability. The most important aspect was that the entire business could be put behind him. Normality could return and he could get on with the job properly. Even Dora had been gradually recovering. Not even she, with all her energy, could go on wanting to prove the same point forever. And although he knew perfectly well that the gesture was probably more of a memorial for Harry than the blacktracker, he felt no qualms and even voiced his approval when she had suddenly said, 'I think, Don, that a Christian Mission is badly needed to the north. I'll write to the Bishop in Brisbane about it.'

And Eddie Giraldi had brought it all back. God Almighty! Damn it to hell! Curse the rouseabout for coming back from the dead! Now he would have to be tried and hanged! Dora would be upset all over again! She would blame him for the hanging of the man and her beliefs, not the damned authorities! And he would have to write to the Drysdale Cattle Company in London and tell them they would have to give their Underwriters their money back! As if that wouldn't make him look foolish enough, they would demand an explanation as to how this criminal he had described to them as simple-minded managed to get so much more money for the stolen stock than he could! They wouldn't understand, no matter what he told them!

Dora's mind was thrown into turmoil at the news, and she, too, had been unable to utter a word. But unlike Don who had hurried to his tiny office to avoid everyone and to try and sort himself out, Dora had to do something with her hands. Anything. She went to the kitchen to make tea. As she filled the kettle to put it on the stove, she struggled for some clarity in her confusion. She had been cheated. How had Don and everyone else, even old Charley, managed to convince her that Harry had long since died when, in her heart, she knew differently? They hadn't. She had convinced herself for the sake of marital appeasement. She had been weak. It had been wrong of her. She had been right. And if she was right about that, she could be right about everything else. What good was that going to do Harry? They were going to see him hang. All of them. There was no doubt about it. But if it was inevitable, he would not go in the belief that no one cared.

The tea made, she walked into Don's office with the tray, but Don was afraid to glance up. Conversation with Dora on the resurrected subject was the last thing he wanted on earth. He would be unable to contain himself. He was therefore taken completely by surprise by the tone of Dora's voice.

'You mustn't worry, Don, I'm sure it will all be sorted out. I'd say the Company will be only too pleased at getting the bull back, as well as a considerable amount of money. They can only praise you.' And she sat to pour, Don raising his staring eyes to the rest of her words. 'I've been thinking more about the Mission. If you have to go to Brisbane, I'd like to come with you and see the Bishop personally.'

No anger, no accusations nor anything else he had expected. Not a single mention of Walford. Not a mention of trials and hangings. Not even anxiety in her eyes. For a few moments, he was completely speechless. Good God. Was there no end to the unpredictability of women? It was beyond man's ken to calculate how their minds worked. Reason was no part of them. God had left it out. Until she had returned to his bed, she had made him suffer intolerably over her belief in the goodness of her rouseabout. And now that the man had been caught and was headed for the gallows, she wasn't showing the slightest sign of being upset. Instead, she was being supportive to him and talking about her mission as if none of it had ever happened. Happiness found his voice.

'I will have to go to Brisbane,' he said, 'and of course you'll come with me. Knowing you, you'll get your Mission. You're a good woman, Dora. I'm pleased I married you.' And with no one else there to see, he took her hand.

He simply had no idea that the mission which was to sustain his wife was of a different kind, and concerned the Bishop not at all. But, in the following days as argument on Harry Walford and his deeds raged outside and, for the first time ever, old Charley went around offering drinks to all and sundry and Jim Hill was hardly to be seen at all, there was nothing but accord in the house at Albert Downs. The name of Harry did not pass Dora's lips and McKenzie threatened to sack anyone who brought any mention of him through his door.

Two weeks later in Brisbane, Dora was ushered into the office of Samuel Merritt by a clerk and Merritt stood to greet her. Middle-aged, plump, balding and with greying side whiskers, he did not extend his hand, but simply gave a little nod of his head, gestured to a chair, waited for Dora to settle in it, then resumed his seat behind his desk. It was unusual for a woman to come to see him alone, and unique for one to make an appointment while refusing to divulge even a hint of her purpose. He was intrigued, but with the caution of his profession, he never gave anything away. He simply sat back, fingering his watch-chain, and waited for the woman to state her business. From the moment Dora had come through the door, she had tried to measure him up, but too much was hidden. He had been recommended to her as one of the best barristers in the Colony. Well, she just had to trust him. There was nothing else for it, and there was no point in delaying it.

'I want you to defend the man, Harry Walford, who's being brought back to Bari for trial,' she said, and although Merritt only moved a little, it was as if he had suddenly sat bolt-upright. He didn't have to be told who Walford was. The incredible story was all over the newspapers. But it was hard to see any kind of connection there could possibly be between that man and the well-dressed, well-spoken woman before him. Then the name McKenzie struck him. It was the same as that of the Manager of Albert Downs from where the cattle had been stolen.

'It could not be, madam, that you are in any way related to Mr Donald McKenzie?'

'He's my husband. Actually, he would be paying you, but he must never know. No one must ever know.'

It was not often that Samuel Merritt, Barrister at Law, was stuck for words, but he was then. The boldness and temerity of the woman astounded him. He pulled himself together and sat over his desk with his hands clasped.

'Mrs McKenzie, before you place any more unwarranted burdens on me with your secrets, let me be frank. I know of the case and there appears to be absolutely nothing that anyone could use to help defend this man. You would be wasting your time.'

But Dora was not to give up so easily.

'Don't you believe in fair trials, Mr Merritt?'

That stung Samuel Merritt. He was proud of his profession and considered himself an honourable man. He also knew perfectly well what the trial of Walford was to be since the authorities were determined to make an example of him, particularly to those who were sympathetic to the 'Australia for Australians' cry. It was to that end they had appointed Mr Justice Collins to sit on the bench, or 'Trapdoor' Collins as he had become known amongst the less savoury sections of society.

'Are you suggesting, madam,' he said, 'that I would participate in any trial I considered unfair?'

'No, I should hope you'd condemn it. And condemn this one, because it seems to me that the outcome is already prearranged.'

'I know nothing of that, but if what you say is true, then what good could I be to you?'

'Simply that if I see someone trying, I'll feel better about facing it. I know I'm only a woman and not expected to behave like this or talk like this but I believe unless someone makes an effort, it's your profession that'll be the poorer for it. Please, Mr Merritt.'

Merritt looked at her. She was a very unusual woman. Temerity or not, she was clearly deeply sincere and intelligent. What she had said was true and he knew it, but he knew also that her reason for being there was not because of her anxiety about his profession. He questioned her on her true motives and Dora was quite straightforward with her answers. He sat back again, wondering just what kind of man McKenzie was to have taken on such a strong-willed woman for a wife. With everything else, she could be naive, too, as she very clearly was in regard to the criminal Walford. Almost touching.

In the long silence that followed, Merritt had already

made his decision, but there was much of the actor in him and he held his intense audience in suspense for as long as he could.

'Very well, Mrs McKenzie,' he said at long last. 'It seems that we are to make fools of ourselves together. I'm not sure about yourself but I think my own reputation can survive it.'

And all the tension lifted from Dora's face and she glowed.

'Thank you, Mr Merritt. Thank you,' she said.

And it was as a much happier woman that she stepped out into the warm sunshine of a Brisbane winter.

The delays in Adelaide were not simply because of the necessary legal procedures that had to be followed, but because of the many statements that had to be gathered, and witnesses and evidence brought together. It wasn't until a complaining Ben Deaken arrived by rail with the big white bull and Sergeant Willis had come all the way down from Bari that all was ready. And it was to be the most tormenting and frustrating period of Willis's entire years with the Queensland Police.

'All I want to do is to be allowed to question the prisoner on my own,' he said, but Sergeant Liddle quickly picked his bananalander colleague and gave him no opportunity.

Harry had already been questioned for weeks but they hadn't been able to get anything out of him. His only concern was for Lilly Boyd and although he agonised over wanting to know what might be happening to her, he didn't mention her name again. If he did, they might find her and take away her money. If she lived, she would need it. And Dr Duval, in protecting his patient's confidence, did not go to the police with either his knowledge of the two men or the large amount of cash in the girl's bag.

'I done what I done, an' that's ther end to it,' was all Harry said at every interrogation, but without any hint of arrogance or defiance, yet when they prepared a confession and read it to him, he refused to put his mark to it.

It was early morning, gloomy and drizzling when Harry, in leg-irons as well as manacles, was transported to the railway station to begin the long journey on different trains and rail gauges through South Australia, Victoria and New South Wales that would return him to Queensland.

'I'm demanding compensation for all me time off me run,' Ben Deaken said angrily as he had to board a carriage with big Bob Campbell. 'I'm goin' ter write ter the Governor.'

Bob Campbell, trying to be cheerful enough, wasn't very happy about going to Bari either. It was only with the greatest reluctance he was going to have to give evidence against Walford but there was nothing else he could do.

Sergeant Liddle felt pity for the black. His dark eyes had become vacant, his body skeletal. Knowing that Wooly would only feel further confined in a closed van, he led him to an open goods wagon with covered sacks in it.

'You hop up there if you want, fella,' he said, pointing, and Wooly climbed up to squat in a corner in his ragged, tartan trousers, droplets of rain clinging to his wild hair and dripping down the dull, dark skin of his bare torso. The first time he had been taken near one of these great fire-breathing monsters, he had been terrified, and when it had suddenly hissed, he had run three clear miles before slowing. But he was in no condition to remember it. It was going to take a lot longer than that before he was to sense the space of earth and sky around him again.

The big white bull moved with dignity as it was led

up a ramp into a van of its own where it was tied but able to feed while Harry was secured in the corner of another. With him was his official escort, the frustrated Sergeant Willis, accompanied by Sergeant Liddle and Constable Harris who were also required as witnesses. But all of them held armed guard and only one of them would be sleeping at a time.

With the departure kept a tight secret in order to avoid curious crowds and any attempt by the still missing McGuirk returning to try and make a mad rescue attempt, very few people were there to see the train with Harry Walford pull itself out of Adelaide in belchings of black smoke and steam.

For two whole days, Harry sat with his legs pulled up before him and didn't sleep, but all Willis could do was kick over his water or bowl of food when he got the opportunity, making it look like an accident each time. Then the bush telegraph began to run far ahead of the tracks, and at every stop that had to be made, sightseers gathered to try and get a glimpse of the infamous cattle duffer. Apart from the times when the transfer of trains was being made, all most of them saw was the black squatted on top of goods in some open wagon and they weren't interested in the black.

But with all the indications that had already been given on that lengthy journey, none of them was pre-pared for the sight that met their eyes when the train from Brisbane eventually pulled into Bari.

'What the bloody hell!' Sergeant Willis said, looking out.

It was not the quiet town he had left. The railway station was surrounded by a sea of people that seemed to go on forever. And without enough room to accom-modate them, tents had sprung up all around and were everywhere. They had come on horseback, in sulkies and on anything that would carry them. Station-hands, labourers, cattlemen, businessmen, drovers, greasies, railway workers, people of all kinds. And, amidst them, newspapermen scribbled in their pads.

Inspector Duncan appeared at the van door with a small troop of men from the Native Mounted. He had wanted none of this great influx of people but the men most interested in Brisbane had encouraged it in order to get as much publicity on the punishment of Walford as possible.

'Bring him out, Sergeant,' Duncan said, and Harry, still dressed in the remains of his frock-coat, was led out and flanked by his new guard. At the sight of him, the great crowd fell to a hushed silence, gazing on in awe. This was what they had all been waiting for. In turn, Harry was in awe, too. He couldn't understand why so many people might be interested in seeing him sentenced to death, for Willis had made it perfectly clear to him that the gallows was to be his end. But, keeping his head up and walking as well as the restrictions of his leg-chains would allow, he looked anything but a sorry figure.

'Harry! Harry!' a familiar voice rang out and Harry turned his eyes to it. It was old Charley and he was waving. Never had he seen the book-keeper do such a thing before. Unable to wave back, he managed to raise a grin for him, but he was beginning to feel strangely detached from himself. As if this was not him but somebody else they were all staring at. Dreamlike. As he went, he caught brief glimpses of other images in the crowd. The Head Overseer, Jim Hill, chewing behind his big, bushy moustache. Frank Murray with his baby-faced mouth hanging partly open. And the peering, piggy eyes of the blacksmith, Jimmy Case.

'I knew 'im,' Eddie Giraldi drawled from under the shade of his big, black hat to those around him, 'met 'im often when he come ter ther railhead. I can tell yer all about 'im.'

No one paid any attention to big Bob Campbell or

Ben Deaken as they emerged from their carriage and few saw Wooly clamber down at the direction of Constable Hackett to be taken to the rear of the Court House where he was to be kept in the open yard. But there was a fresh surge of interest when the big white bull was led out. After a brief examination by Don McKenzie to make a positive identification, it, too, was led to the yard behind the Court.

The only two, free people in the entire swollen town who were not there to see the arrival of Harry Walford were Mr Justice Collins who sat in the ante-room of the Court House studying legal documents and Dora McKenzie who sat alone in her hotel room, not even taking a single glance out of the window as she stitched determinedly at a small, fine piece of needle-work she had brought with her.

Sergeant Willis burned with further frustration to find that the Inspector had turned his Station into a police camp rather than go to the expense of getting bloody tents for them. He had been nursing the hope ever since he left Adelaide that once he got back he would be able to get his longing hands on the prisoner but there was no chance of it. All his pleasure would have to be satisfied with the hanging. At least it seemed he was not going to have to wait long for that.

'Notices for jury service went out yesterday,' Inspector Duncan said. 'The trial is tomorrow. It's not expected to take more than a day, two at the most.'

The unseemly haste was justified. The concerned men in Brisbane were not fools. They had seen how a lowly, misguided section of the public had tried to raise sympathies for murdering bushrangers in the other Colonies. It was almost to be expected of the sons of the worst convicts. The same kind of warped, criminal minds that began the 'Australia for Australians' cry. The authorities were allowing no opportunity for any sympathy being given time to grow for Walford.

In the evening at the hotel, Don and Dora McKenzie were sitting in the parlour when the talk amongst the ladies and gentlemen around them turned to the mystery of who could have engaged Samuel Merritt. Dora, who had to fight to stop herself blushing and who had hardly uttered a word all day, said suddenly, 'I think I know.'

Every head in the parlour turned to her, and waited. Even Don.

'I should have thought it was perfectly clear. It was all those people out there wanting to see a little justice done in their town. They probably all threw into a hat in order to engage this . . . whatever his name is.'

It sounded utterly plausible and the rumour spread quickly to the streets. Before the last head had lain down that night, half the people in Bari claimed they had thrown into Dora's mythical hat, while the other, more honest half, wished they had done. Dora had no idea the effect her words of desperation would have but she was to be very pleased that she'd spoken.

It was a very early morning for everyone as all the preparations were made, and Inspector Duncan saw to it that Purdy and Spence were closely shaved and made to look as respectable as possible in their new clothing. And it was still early morning when the first of those called for jury service turned up to present himself to Mr Brind, Clerk of the Court. His name was Francis Fuller, short, dark-haired, and with a pasty face.

'Yer know I's related ter Harry Walford on me mother's side,' he said. Brind didn't know and was surprised. He knew Fuller who worked as a baker and had never heard anyone mention the relationship before. It was a nuisance, as it meant he would have to find a replacement.

'That will make you ineligible, Mr Fuller.'

'Will it?' Fuller said, wide-eyed.

Fuller knew bloody well it did. It was why he had

said it. And he knew that even if he was suspected of lying, it would take a lot of people a lot of time delving into records all over the Colonies and even back in England to find out.

But it wasn't until the second potential jury member turned up and claimed family relationship to Walford on his father's side that Brind started to wake up to the fact that the court had trouble on its hands. And he could not have been more right. Every single one of the twelve men called claimed to be a relative of Harry's. All men of trade, none of them wanted the stigma of sending a man who had opened up a stock route through the Wild Heart all the way to South Australia to the gallows. In consideration of local feeling, it could have been ruinous for business.

Mr Justice Collins fumed with anger when he was told.

'It's a conspiracy between them!' he said, stating the obvious, 'and if I can find them out, I'll see they get twenty years for it!' But he knew as well as anyone that a full enquiry would also take years. He had been looking forward to this trial and this attempt at obstruction of justice was outrageous and abhorrent to him. Collins believed in justice. He believed in the law carved in stone that Moses had brought down from the mountain. And it was his belief in God that made him believe in maximum punishment. Good had to be protected against evil. If the punishment did not fit the crime, there was no justice at all. The Devil in men's souls could only be cast out finally with death and returned to Hell where it belonged. And society could only prosper if men were given a permanent reminder of it.

'Choose your men more carefully, Mr Brind,' he said severely, 'I'll tolerate no such occurrence again. I want good men. Honest men. Find them. And quickly. There will be no more delays.'

The trial had to be postponed as Brind sat down once

more to go over his list and make selections. There was no reason whatsoever to suspect the local office clerk, Barratt, who had been taken on temporarily for the trial to help out with all the extra work. Brind had used him many times before when he needed him. He was an efficient and reliable man.

By midday, all the new notices were ready and were given to the police to serve.

A Constable of the Native Mounted knocked on the door of Mr J.F. Fernhill and it was opened by a nervous-looking woman with children of various ages gathered anxiously behind her.

'Mr Fernhill,' he said.

'He's not here.'

'Where is he?'

'He left to go to Bordman's Creek on business.'

Bordman's Creek was a property a hundred miles away, although at that very moment, Mr Fernhill had only just cleared town, riding hell for leather in another direction to get as far away from Bari as he could. And so were all the others who knew notices for jury service were on their way to them. Barratt knew all of these men personally, and he had to live there, too. Afraid that they'd blame him for not warning them, he had slipped the list of names out the back door past the squatted Wooly and the big white bull. And the list had travelled round faster than a straw in a full force willy-willy.

Only Jackshay Jack was having a field day as yet more farthings dropped into the pot around his neck, and without being arrested once. Already he had enough to keep him blind drunk for six months, if the terrors of the hundred snakes that sometimes shared his ragged blanket didn't get him first.

In the lamplit ante-room of the Court House that served as the Judge's chamber, the hanging black gown and the wig on a wooden head practically shook as

Collins raged at the gathering. Present were Inspector Duncan, Sergeant Willis, Brind, and William Gibson, a barrister who had been especially appointed as Prosecutor the moment Samuel Merritt had announced himself. Merritt, as welcome as a fox in a chicken run, had not been invited to the discussion.

'What kind of irresponsible community do you have here?' Collins shouted at Brind, Duncan and Willis. 'Is this an entire town of criminals? I want a jury!'

But, despite Brind dismissing his temporary assistant and getting another, it made no difference. A week later they still had no jury and half the male residents of Bari were either in bed with severe Beliander spew, had gone bush, or into hiding under houses.

'It's intolerable!' Collins said, suffering from unbearable frustration and wishing that God might send bolts of lightning to strike all these people down.

'The only way is to get them from Brisbane, sir,' Inspector Duncan said. Although that was going to take at least another week, Collins was still sane enough to see there was no other solution.

'Then get them, please.'

At the rear of the Court House, Don McKenzie visited the big white bull to see how it was faring, and he carried a parcel in his hand. Wooly, squatting patiently by the step at the back door, watched him. He didn't blame McKenzie for all that had happened to him, but at the same time, he knew that he would never work for the white man again. There was too much he couldn't understand about their ways and he had started to wonder if jumping up white fella with plenty sixpence was worth it.

After McKenzie made an inspection of the animal, he went to the blacktracker and handed him the parcel then, without a word, turned and walked away. He worried about Dora. She hardly spoke and just sat in the hotel concentrating on her needle-work. But she didn't have to tell him that all the time she was thinking of Harry sitting chained in his cell. He'd been mistaken in believing she no longer cared.

Wooly opened the parcel. It was a brand new pair of tartan trousers and he grinned widely at them. Then he stood up and pulled them on over his old ones.

'Lookim pella call 'im Wooly, big pella,' he said to the big white bull and it looked at him.

For nine long days, the town hung suspended in the still, fresh mornings and the hot noons and the red sun swiftly dying. Then, it ended.

There were more people than ever surrounding the railway station when the train carrying the jury from Brisbane pulled slowly in and jerked to a stop. Amongst the waiting crowd were all the deserters who, notified by bush telegraph, had returned to their homes.

Inspector Duncan, Sergeant Willis and the troop of Native Mounted waited on the platform to escort the jury members safely to their arranged accommodation where they were also to be guarded. It hardly seemed necessary. As the men were identified and began to alight, there were only murmurs of interest. No voices or shaken fists were raised against them. They were all stern, unsmiling men who had been carefully chosen. Men of honour and integrity in down-to-earth suits and hats with watch-chains hanging from their vests. No one paid any attention to the other passengers amongst them, including the girl who emerged behind the last of the jury. They saw only the man, a tall gaunt, impassive figure by the name of Borthwick who was to be chosen as Foreman. But before he was escorted away with his companions, he half turned and politely but briefly raised his hat to Miss Lilly Boyd as a gesture of farewell.

Lilly, in long, black skirt, plain white blouse and black, silk bonnet, stood for a few moments anxiously watching him go. Not only had she recovered but she had filled out on Dr Duval's good food and had become more of an attractive woman rather than the young, thin girl she had been.

'Do yer mind, sir?' she had said when choosing her seat beside Borthwick, for she had become much more knowledgeable about men and knew she would be safe with him. But she didn't know who he was. It wasn't until she broke fifty miles of silence and started to tell the stranger how the man they wanted to hang was the kindest in the world and Borthwick stopped her with, 'That's enough, miss. You're speaking to a member of the jury,' that she knew. For a while, as Borthwick looked stonily out of the window, she didn't know whether to find another seat or stay but, in tearless sorrow and in silence, stayed.

The trial began the following morning. The Court House was packed tightly to the closed doors with as many as could squeeze in, the rest of the town and its great influx having to be satisfied with crowding the wide, dusty street outside, and with faces peering in through every available window-pane.

There was a hush as Harry was brought in, manacled and leg-ironed, to stand in his crumpled frock-coat in the dock. And it was at Collins's suggestion that he was surrounded by so many armed police. It helped to highlight the dangerous man they were dealing with. Although every pair of eyes was on him, Harry saw no one, standing erect, looking neither to right nor left. He'd had enough of waiting, enough of Willis's surreptitious sharp prods and kicks and tripping and foul insults. The sooner they got it over and made their end of him the better. He would not complain. All that mattered were Bluey and Lilly Boyd, but he didn't know the fate of either. He only had to turn his head to see that Lilly was still very much alive and had fought hard for a place at the back in the hope of giving him some comfort, but he didn't know.

Neither was he aware of McKenzie's gaze. But although McKenzie looked at him long and hard, he could see no sign of the rouseabout who had pleaded so ineffectively in his tiny office at Albert Downs for a better job. The yellow bearded man standing there was a man of stature, a self-assured man, a man of spirit and of dignity. The fool had gone and it made him very uneasy to look on him further.

Harry's eyes didn't move as the assembly stood and Mr Justice Collins entered in wig and gown, taking his time with carefully measured slow steps as he always did in order to impress on everyone the gravity of the occasion. Then he finally sat and delivered his usual warning.

'I would remind all those present,' he said, 'that this is a court of law. If any disrespect is shown or there is the slightest disturbance of any kind whatsoever, I shall have the public gallery cleared immediately.'

The initial proceedings over and all the charges read, Collins gestured Samuel Merritt to come to him, then leaned over to speak in tones low enough for no one else to hear.

'I still fail to understand what your true purpose in this case is, Mr Merritt, but I wish to direct you to keep any words you have as short as possible and not waste the Court's time.'

'Yes, your honour,' Merritt said quietly and returned to his place, inwardly angry at the direction. If Collins had his way, he would not only have dispensed with the defence but with the jury, too. Not that Merritt had found any defence he could make. His role was but a gesture and little else.

Gibson called Don McKenzie as his first witness. Aware of Dora rather than the jury hanging on his every word, McKenzie was unusually hesitant and Gibson found himself having to probe. But the evidence was clear enough and Gibson finished with him. He was surprised when Merritt took his right to question his witness.

'Tell me, Mr McKenzie,' Merritt said, 'were you surprised when you discovered that the accused was one of the men suspected of being involved?'

'Yes.'

'Why was that?'

'I didn't think he was capable.'

'Why didn't you?'

'It was my judgment of him.'

'And what exactly was that judgment?'

Damn the man and damn his wig! It was embarrassing. But McKenzie needn't have worried. In an instant, Gibson was on his feet making his objection on the grounds that the question was irrelevant and not directed to produce evidence. Both he and Collins knew perfectly well that if Merritt had been allowed to go on along that line he would end by forcing McKenzie to admit that Walford had done something he himself could not. And that would only be demonstrating to the jury that McKenzie's judgment of men was badly impaired while, at the same time, giving the accused a character reference.

'Objection sustained,' Collins said quickly, and Merritt knew he would not be able to continue with Don McKenzie. He only wondered what the man might have said had he known he was paying for him.

'That is all,' he said, and as he returned to his place, a low discontented whispering started to break out amongst the public.

'Silence!' Collins shouted, banging down his gavel, and immediately silence returned. But it was a silence that could be felt.

If McKenzie had to be pushed, Jim Hill had to be almost struck over the head for his replies, and they were laconic ones at that. No man ever felt so relieved to be released from a witness box and his jaws ached with longing for the plug of tobacco in his pocket.

With no witnesses of his own, the best Merritt could hope for was an admission by one of these men of Walford's achievement. Not that he expected the impassive jury to be influenced by it, simply that he believed it should have been publicly noted and recorded. But not for a moment was he ever allowed to get close. Every time the danger was sighted, Gibson, on occasion prompted by Collins, sprang to his feet and, every time, Collins was quick to uphold the objection. And, three times, Collins called Merritt to the Bench to warn him.

After each failure, Merritt threw a brief glance towards Dora who had been joined by McKenzie as if to indicate the hopelessness of his situation.

'What does he keep looking at me for?' McKenzie whispered.

'I don't know,' Dora whispered back. She kept her eyes only on Merritt, Gibson, Collins and the witnesses, for she couldn't bear to look directly either at Harry or the men who were going to pronounce his guilt.

But for the first time, Harry turned his own head and McKenzie looked at him. In the crowded court their eyes met. There was no accusation in Harry, no anger, no condemnation or even recognition. Yet Harry held his glance and it was McKenzie who was first to look away. All the same, no silent damning or cursing of the man would make him go. He felt rather than saw the eyes being lifted from him, and was relieved.

What had removed Harry's gaze was catching sight of an anxious face under a black, silk bonnet right at the back. For a moment, it was a figure of wonder and surprise that was guarded in the dock, then the entire court heard the rattle of his chains as he moved and grinned. Heads turned to see the object of attention and Dora's followed them.

'It's Lilly!' she said to McKenzie in an involuntary

gasp of surprise.

'Order!' shouted Collins at the slight shuffling and movement, 'or I'll clear the court!'

Outside, the big white bull, restless, butted with its big head and horns at a loose rail and, in the ensuing silence, the noise reached in like that of hammering. For all intents and purposes it might have been maintenance being carried out to the gallows in Brisbane gaol. To the ears of both Lilly Boyd and Dora McKenzie, it was the drums of Harry's death. But it was only Lilly who could bring herself to look at him, for her own memories were that of a man, while Dora's were that of the child she had never borne.

'I took 'im for an honest overlander,' Ben Deaken said from the stand, 'an' put my little boys outside to make my house his own.'

With the steadying hand of his wife, Nan, so far away, Deaken attempted to walk the dangerous edge between pride and begging. Seeing Walford as a condemned man and a lost cause, he was at pains to point out the great losses he had suffered as a result of his kindness. His hope was that someone might see fit to take pity on a poor battler and offer him much more than simply compensation for his lost time. The Drysdale Cattle Company with a run the size of Albert Downs was obviously a big outfit who could afford it. He was out to see what he could get. He told how the bull had been pressed on him and how he had been talked into parting with his years of savings. He had been tricked. Robbed of his last penny. And him a man with a family to raise, struggling against all odds in the backblocks.

Nan Deaken would have squirmed in the depths of shame if she had been there to look at him. He had teetered over the side to emerge as a crow-eating whinger and a hum.

He simply failed to mention that the big white bull

had successfully covered no fewer than a hundred of his best cows in all the time he had had it, and that out of the drop he could hope to have at least a dozen well-bred bulls that would improve the quality of his stock for many years to come.

Gibson, aware that his witness was coming over as less honest than Jackshay Jack, finished with him as quickly as possible. And Collins was red with anger when Merritt insisted in taking him over.

'Mr Deaken,' Merritt said, 'what did the accused say to you when you first met?'

Deaken was confused.

'I think he said "G'day". Something like that.'

The main body of the court laughed and Merritt immediately took advantage of it.

'How illuminating, sir!' he said and they laughed at Deaken more. Collins looked furious and restored order in seconds.

'And where did he say he came from?' Merritt asked of Deaken.

Deaken, already briefed by Gibson to make no mention of his astonishment at seeing Harry and the Irishman come out of the empty north with the huge mob to Gunderindi, glanced quickly to Gibson for guidance but got none.

'Queensland, he said.'

'He made no attempt to hide the fact?'

'No.'

It was the cue to bring Gibson to his feet on the objection that Merritt was leading the witness and, again, Collins supported him, cutting Merritt off. But when Ben Deaken stepped down, the battler was only too aware that every public face was smiling at him and that he had become their fool. He headed straight back out of the side door from where he had come, dragging his tattered dignity and pride behind him.

But it made little difference. Borthwick and the rest

of the jury remained stony-faced throughout. They were not men to allow laughter to lessen the weight of their responsibility. However, in a pause, Borthwick did allow himself to wonder about the girl who had sat beside him on the train. He could see her out of the corner of his eye and could still feel her sorrow. It seemed strange that such an obviously respectable girl would have had anything to do with the kind of man the prosecution was trying to project. Clearly, she had quite an opposite view and he looked to Walford to see if he could divine it. Harry was smiling at her.

Mystery of relationship or not, the evidence against Walford was already enough for his conviction, even before Purdy was brought in, unmanacled to show he was not a dangerous man, and looking neat and tidy.

'He said he'd kill us if we didn't go in with 'im, sir. I wanted ter tell Mr McKenzie what he was up ter, but it would er been me life I would er paid fer it. He took us out at night ter muster inter ther gully at gunpoint an' promised ter let us go once he got away. Either him or the Irishman kept a watch on us all ther time, day an' night, sir. An' we did all we could ter try an' stop 'im takin' the bull knowin' it was fer breedin' good beasts there, but 'e just told us if we didn't shut up he'd put holes in us right then.'

Merritt didn't have to be told that since Purdy and Spence were both Queen's Evidence their stories would be the same, and judging Spence to be the weaker of the two, he declined to question Purdy. Apart from that, the element of disbelief in that two such men could have been so easily cowed might be magnified on the second time of hearing. He wasn't wrong. As Spence began to relate his own account, it was almost word for word.

Even Don McKenzie started to feel sorry for Harry although Harry himself didn't even appear to be listening. Any other man might have been excused for shouting out denials of such lies, even if he was carted off out of hearing for it. Damn him for so readily accepting his fate! Shout out! They can't damn well hang you twice!

'At night he kept us tied up,' Spence said, 'but with only him an' McGuirk havin' ter do all ther riding round in the dark they was gettin' tired goin' without sleep. If it wasn't for that, we wouldn't be alive ter tell of it. It was on the edge of the desert when they both needed sleep so bad they was out to it. Me and Purdy got ourselves free an' escaped on our horses while they was still lyin' there by ther fire. An' that's ther truth of it, sir.'

A satisfied Gibson thanked him and Merritt took over.

'What did they tie you up with?' he asked, and Spence immediately looked uncomfortable.

'What d'yer mean, sir?'

'Well, was it rope, stirrup leather or what?'

Spence could only see some sort of trap and although he didn't know what, knew he had to avoid it. In doing so, he fell right into it.

'I don't remember, sir,' he said, and Merritt said no more of it.

'Tell me. When you got back out of there, why didn't you go directly to the police?'

'We was frightened.'

'Frightened of what?'

'That they wouldn't believe us.'

Merritt looked at him with delight and threw his theatrical arms wide.

'My dear fellow, and who could blame you!'

The laughter was immediate and Collins, dark with rage, banged his gavel as both he and Brind shouted for silence. But it was too late for that. In the eyes of the public at least, Purdy and Spence had been discredited. And Merritt, anticipating that Collins was going to call him to the bench yet again, got in first.

'No further questions,' he said quickly.

Big Bob Campbell told his tale with reluctance and Gibson was unable to stop him when he said, 'Henry Richards or Harry Walford, I took him for a good boss drover and still do because the mob he brought in were in prime condition.'

Sergeant Liddle was another matter. Whatever his private thoughts, his duty was clear and he read from his report how Harry had fought like a madman in resisting arrest, injuring several of his men and causing extensive damage to the property of the Flinders Hotel. It made Harry sound like an extremely violent man. But to many men there, that only served to heighten Harry's stature, for toughness of that kind was as essential as food and water for survival in the hard lives they led in the bush. Had they been told he was a man who also wept, they would not have been of the same opinion, but no one had made any mention of it.

For all that, there was nothing in the way of evidence to save Harry when the summing up stage had been reached. There was not the slightest shadow of a doubt in any of the jury's minds that the man standing in the dock in his crumpled frock-coat was other than who he was or that he had been the leader of the great cattle robbery. Not even Harry himself was making any attempt to deny it.

'There is nothing that can be said for this man,' Gibson said, facing Borthwick and his colleagues, 'nothing. Not a hundred head did he steal, gentlemen, not two hundred, but one thousand five hundred and an extremely valuable stud bull that had been brought all the way from home for the purpose of improving the stock of our Colony. In all, a fortune few honest men could ever dream of. And in doing so, this blackguard was prepared to take the lives of innocent men for his outrageous gain. He was prepared to kill. He deceived. He cheated. He robbed. He defrauded. And had he not been caught, no man's property might ever have been safe again. This is the man who was given every assistance by a struggling family it was possible to give. He ate their bread and their meat and slept in the comfort of their bed. And they loaded him with the very best of their supplies. And, in return, without thought or the slightest care for their welfare, he cruelly brought them close to ruin.' He threw out an arm to stab a finger at Harry, a trick he always used. 'Look at him, gentlemen! Look at him!' And the jury looked. 'Do you even see any remorse in him for all his villainy? No, you don't. Not a single sign of it. You may have even, like I have, seen him smile on occasion. But he is very much mistaken if he believes we are all fools, for you are not, and neither am I. Your duty could never have been clearer, gentlemen.'

Outside, Wooly squatted in his two pairs of trousers, gazing at the restless bull while at the front of the Court House the great crowd filling the street stood in silence, not knowing what was happening. And the late afternoon sun struggled to shine through heavy banks of cloud.

'Gentlemen,' Merritt said, addressing the jury, 'I know it would be foolish of me to deny my client's involvement.' And he paused. 'I have never condoned theft of any kind and never shall. But perhaps that is because my own personal view is a shallow one.'

Collins and Gibson exchanged anxious glances, wondering what deviousness he might be getting up to.

'So, let me consider a man who due to my own greed and lack of concern for another fellow human being is deprived and starves.' Merritt went on, 'At the first opportunity he steals bread and meat from me. The law demands that he is punished for it and punished he will be. But where lies the guilt? Where is the justice?'

Collins was unable to restrain himself.

'The accused is not such a man, Mr Merritt!' he said, and Merritt turned to him and gave a bow of apology.

'No, M'lud, he is not,' he said, then turned to the jury again. 'He is certainly not. Lowly paid as he might have been, he had meat and bread aplenty. His stomach was full.' And again, he paused, 'But I have to ask myself: is there another kind of starvation? Another hunger of a more obscure kind? Is there such a thing as hunger of the heart? A desire for love. A hunger of the mind? A desire for knowledge and identity. A hunger of the soul? A desire to communicate with Christ our Saviour. Do they exist?'

Collins felt desperate to stop these dangerous words but was afraid that the newspapermen who were furiously trying to scribble it all down would accuse him of being sacrilegious when he was the most God-fearing man there.

'If so,' Merritt continued, 'what kind of hunger did the accused have? That is what we must ask ourselves. Was it simply pure greed? He had been there six years and must have had plenty of opportunities of satisfying it before. And no evidence has been presented to indicate he was an avaricious man. Far from it. The money he got he threw around like a sower in a wheat field, giving to anyone who asked and to many who didn't. Irresponsible, perhaps, after all the privations he must have suffered, but never avaricious.'

'You will remind the jury, Mr Merritt, that it wasn't *his* money!' Collins said in a frustrated burst that was close to a shout, and Merritt turned to him again with a bow.

'Yes, certainly, M'lud,' he said before facing the jury once more, 'it was not his money, gentlemen. It belonged to the Drysdale Cattle Company of London, not one member of whom has seemingly taken sufficient interest to be here.'

'The jury will ignore that remark!' Collins said, almost scarlet. 'It is no part of evidence or anything else. And either you must close, Mr Merritt or I must call an adjournment until tomorrow.'

An adjournment was the last thing Merritt wanted. To have divided his speech could have amounted to destroying it. He could feel the warmth of the public if not the granite-faced jury.

'I will close, M'lud,' he said, and made his final short address. 'I end only by pleading with you to look at the accused again, a man who can neither read nor write, and ask yourself this: what kind of hunger did he suffer from that drove him to such a remarkable achievement?'

Short or not, Collins was half to his feet with anger. Merritt had got in the word he had been most anxious to avoid. Come to that, the godless man had said everything he had wanted to avoid. He had to make corrections to that.

In his direction to the jury, he pointed out the overwhelming weight of evidence against the accused, a criminal on a scale the Colony had never seen before. A vicious and violent man who was without mercy. There were no mitigating circumstances that could be taken into consideration. None. And they were to cast all of Merritt's remarks from their minds. Not only were they inadmissible in terms of evidence but sophistic in the extreme and unworthy of a member of the Bar. In view of all that, there was only one verdict to be considered and he warned that he would not accept any recommendation of mercy in conjunction with that verdict.

The jury retired to consider, Borthwick intimating that they would take no longer than five minutes.

Lilly looked at the dock, knowing that at any moment she was going to break down. And Dora McKenzie, her head bowed, looking at her lap, knew she was going to do the same.

In the tiny ante-room Gibson and Merritt shared, both stood clutching at their files. Gibson could afford to be patronising and held out his hand.

'Brilliant little speech, Sam,' he said. 'Pity in a way it was wasted.'

'Perhaps I could do better if I took up politics,' Merritt said, 'got into Parliament and accused the Government of the crime of collusion in conspiring to deny one poor devil the due process of law.'

Gibson resented the reprimand from his colleague but was thick skinned.

'Never mind,' he said, 'you'll have plenty of other cases.'

In his own small chamber, Mr Justice Collins practised putting the black cloth over his wig in front of a mirror he always carried with him for the purpose on such occasions. It was always a worry in case he should fumble it or not have it on exactly straight. Even slightly askew would detract from the solemnity of the moment. The most important moment of all. And, as was his habit when about to pronounce the death sentence, he muttered a brief prayer for the evil-doer's soul.

Borthwick was as good as his word and ten minutes later the Court reassembled. With the slow, carefully measured steps, the slightly hunched, sharp faced figure of Collins re-entered, the black cloth folded neatly in his hand. And the silence of the court was so complete when everyone was reseated that the buzz of a single fly could be heard clearly from one end to the other. And only the fly moved.

Then they heard the rustle of the gown as Collins turned towards the jury and requested of them their verdict. There was no expression on any of their faces. Borthwick stood up, and hesitated, but there was no doubt in anyone's mind what he was about to say.

Harry stood looking dazed. Although he had been long prepared, he felt strangely moved and vaguely lost now that the time had come. There had been so much ritual, so much droning of words that he had not heard but simply drowned in them. And all the words had ended. All but one.

Lilly could bear to look at him no longer and Dora's head was bowed as she struggled to try and hold herself together. Even Don McKenzie's eyes were down. Jim Hill had stopped chewing and old Charley wished he hadn't come.

Although Borthwick's hesitation was but seconds, it seemed interminable before he spoke and when he did, it was quietly.

'Not guilty,' he said, and there was only the buzzing of the fly. Like everyone else, Collins thought he must have misheard. It was impossible to think otherwise.

'Would you speak up, please,' Collins said in the complete and utter silence that remained. Borthwick hesitated again, as impassive faced as he had been throughout the entire trial. Then he spoke loudly and clearly.

'Not guilty,' he said, and lowered himself on to his seat.

There were those who had hoped this body of righteous men might disregard Collins's direction against clemency and force a lesser sentence, but only Lilly Boyd and Dora McKenzie had actually dared to hope for more. It was not surprising that the verdict took time to reach the senses. Even Samuel Merritt was confused.

Collins sat staring at Borthwick in total disbelief. Then, suddenly, the truth struck the public all at the one time and they were springing to their feet in an uproar of joy. And, at the same time, Collins jumped up, shaking with rage.

'You can't do that!' he tried to yell at the jury above the noise, 'You can't! It's anarchy!'

But they had, and they all sat there looking as stern as ever. They had made their decision and hadn't made it lightly, and they were annoyed at Mr Collins trying to tell them it was the wrong one.

In moments, the doors were thrown open and as the crowd surged forward to get at Harry and release him, the entire town tried to force its way in through every door and it became pandemonium.

Brind felt obliged to rescue the still raging Collins, and had to be helped by the Native Mounted whom he restrained from opening fire on the charging mob.

Sergeant Willis lost his balance as a dozen men tore his keys from him to unlock Harry's manacles and padlocked leg-irons. But such was the density of people trying to surround the dock that the sergeant was unable to struggle up. Boot after boot trampled heedlessly on his body and face until, blinded by his own blood, he became unconscious and felt no more.

At first, Harry hardly knew what was happening as men he didn't know released him from his chains and lifted him shoulder high. He had only heard the word 'guilty' which was all his dazed mind had expected. It wasn't until he was being carried through towards the front door amidst a completely solid mass of cheering bodies that he began to realise he had been freed.

'Lilly!' he began to shout above the roar and tried to look for her amongst the sea of heads beneath him, but he couldn't see her.

In a corner, Don McKenzie fought to shield Dora with his body and save her from being crushed to death, but Dora, not knowing whether to laugh or cry couldn't have cared right then if her own life had been squeezed out of her.

Harry was carried outside into the main body of the crowd and Lilly appeared, forcing her way through it to reach him.

'Harry!' she shouted, and Harry turned and held out his hand towards her, grinning, then grasped her own hand and held on to it.

'I's glad ter see yer better,' he said, and tears of

happiness misted her eyes.

Don McKenzie got Dora outside and they stood watching the huge procession start to make its way down the main street, Harry held high.

'I hope now you're bloody satisfied,' McKenzie said.

'Yes, I am. But I told you all along he was innocent, didn't I?'

McKenzie could find no answer to that.

'Look out, Harry, yer got a blacktracker after yer!' a man's voice warned, and Harry managed to turn his head far enough to be able to see him.

Behind came Wooly, grinning from ear to ear, the sixpences Harry had given him in Adelaide and which Liddle had allowed him to keep, jingling in his pocket. If he didn't know exactly what had happened or was now happening, at least he recognised a celebration when he saw one and was intent on joining in. It wasn't often he saw the white men joyous, and he, too, felt freed. He was going home to his family and he would have a lot to tell them.

Half the men from Albert Downs stood watching from outside the Court House.

'He conducted himself well did Sam Merritt,' Dora heard old Charley say to someone behind her. Sam?

'Yer know 'im?' she heard Eddie Giraldi drawl with interest.

'Once, I did. We went to Cambridge together, but he wouldn't know me now.'

Eddie Giraldi couldn't resist that.

'Come an' I'll buy yer a drink.'

'That would be most welcome, sir.'

It was all Dora was ever to find out about old Charley. Or Eddie Giraldi either, for old Charley continued to keep the rest of his past hidden. Harry's past, on the other hand, had suddenly become a valuable asset.

A well-dressed man pushed through to him and spoke

loudly up to him to overcome the din.

'My name is Dyson, Mr Walford,' he said, 'I'm one of the owners just formed a new cattle company here. We're looking for someone to find fresh land, set up a new run and manage it. We'd be prepared to give him five thousand head to start it off. I'd like to offer you the job, Mr Walford.'

For a few moments, Harry was speechless. He'd hardly had time to absorb the turn around in his fortunes as it was, but he managed to gather his wits about him, and turned to grin at Lilly.

'What d'yer say?'

'Yes,' Lilly said, 'Yes.'

And Harry turned back to the man, reaching down his other hand as best he could to seal the agreement.

'You're on, Mr Dyson,' he said, 'I'll find yer fresh country.'

And Dyson looked delighted.

Less than three months later, Harry set off with the great collection of cattle. The sight of five thousand head in one mob was one that few men had ever seen. And the twenty hands he had personally selected to go with him rode hard and willingly for their yellow bearded boss drover as their whips cracked through the great cloud of dust that almost blotted out the sun. With them went pack horses and spare mounts with mares and stallions while a team of other horses driven by a fair-haired youth pulled a wagon loaded with supplies and tools. And behind them came the young Mrs Walford at the reins of a sulky, carrying her own personal possessions, amongst which was some pretty material for curtains.

Harry drove the enormous mob north-west and, on the way, passed through an Albert Downs that had returned to normal. For a while, Don McKenzie needlessly worried that some Albert Downs stock might be picked up on the way and he felt relieved when Harry had cleared the run. But it was a worry he was extremely careful to conceal from Dora who, happily busy running the house with a new rouseabout and a new housemaid, and with her libido fully restored, had never mentioned her Mission again.

It took a long time going right through Queensland, but eventually Harry pushed on into the Northern Territory. There he found what he was looking for. A vast tract of land that would clearly see good feed up to their waists in a good season and with some permanent water-holes. Amidst it also was a large area of slightly undulating low hills which, despite the intense heat and the flies the cattle had brought, was pleasing to Harry's eye.

'Look at it, boys,' he said, 'you ever seen anythin' so good? This is it.'

There Harry stayed to build up one of the biggest cattle properties in Australia while his young wife taught him to read and write. And he called the run 'Lilly Downs'.

A cool westerly off the Atlantic swept over County Clare in Ireland as Mr Michael McGuirk pulled up in his pony and trap to inspect a field of his farm. Well-dressed in brown with yellow vest and leggings, he opened the tiny back door of the trap and stepped down with a spade. Then he straddled himself over a stone dyke into a green field of grass. There had only been geese grazing in it when he had bought the farm and he wanted to test the ground to see if it could take a crop of potatoes. There could have been a lot of rock just under the surface that would make ploughing impossible.

He walked to the middle of the field first, stopped and dug in the spade with his boot. It looked all right and he dug down further and looked into the hole he had made. But as he continued to gaze at the rich, dark earth, all thoughts of potatoes drifted away on the wind and he spoke quietly into the hole.

'Is ye still alive down t'ere, Harry?' he said, 'for I've prayed often enough for ye an' t'ere isn't a Saint t'at doesn't know ye. Well, I'd like ye to know I'll never be forgettin' ye. Begod, is ye not the best mate a man ever had?'

And it began to rain.